PARASITE

Insatiable Series

Book 4

Patrick Logan

Books by Patrick Logan

Insatiable Series

Book 1: Skin
Book 2: Crackers
Book 3: Flesh
Book 4: Parasite
Book 5: Stitches (Spring 2017)

The Haunted Series

Book 1: Shallow Graves
Book 2: The Seventh Ward
Book 3: Seaforth Prison
Book 4: Scarsdale Crematorium
Book 5: Sacred Heard Orphanage

Family Values Trilogy

Mother
Father
Daughter (Spring 2017)

Short Stories

System Update

ISBN-13: 978-1534951952
ISBN-10: 1534951954
Fourth Edition: February 2018

PROLOGUE

"FORGIVE ME, FATHER, FOR I have sinned."

"Yes, my son. When was your last confession?"

Carter Duke paused and tilted his head to the side.

He had to think about that one.

"Never," he replied with a shrug.

Now it was the priest's turn to pause.

"Never? And why is that, my son? Have you not sinned before now? Or have you just recently found the Lord?"

Carter's lips twisted into a wry smile as he turned toward the dark lattice that separated him from the priest on the other side.

Look at me, you putz. I want you to look at me.

But the priest's head was predictably pointed downward, staring at some supernatural oracle embedded in the floor.

Okay, don't look. But you will; you will soon. I promise.

His smile grew.

"Oh, Father, I have sinned," he answered with a chuckle. "I have *sinned*. But, alas, this is the first time that I have come to confess my sins. And as for finding the Lord? Well shit, I'm still lookin'."

He saw the priest's head turn slightly at the curse, but his gaze remained down.

"Well, son, there is no time like—"

"I have *fucking* sinned, Father."

This time the priest turned his head, and Carter smiled at the man's silhouette. He couldn't quite make out the man's expression in the dim light and through the lattice, but he was fairly certain what it was.

Shock.

And fear. Oh yeah, he bet there was a lot of fear in the priest's face.

"Son, this is the house of the Lord. I am grateful that you have come to this house to share your sins, but please be respectful—"

"Well, that's the thing, *Peter*. I didn't come to the house to repent; I came to this house *to see you*."

Carter thought he heard the father on the other side of the partition swallow hard. When the man spoke again, his voice had lost the soothing, monotone flavor. Now it was dry and tight.

"What is this?"

Carter chuckled again, and he idly scratched at his short, dark beard.

"Oh, I think you know, Peter. I think you know."

"S-s-son, I don't know what you think—"

Carter laughed, and he crossed his hands over his lap. Then, to mock the other man, he held his head low, as the priest had done when Carter had first entered the confessional.

Fine, play it this way.

"Alright, then, let me tell you my sins, Father. I hope you brought a cushion and some rations, though. This is gonna take a while."

He cleared his throat dramatically.

"When I was nine, I had this friend—"

"Who are you? What do you want?"

"Ah, right to the point. I figured as much. You're a straightforward man, aren't you, Peter Stevens? So let me spell it to you straight. I have these—how should I say it?—*proclivities* toward younger men."

Carter took a deep breath and let out a dramatic sigh.

"Ah, hell, why shroud the truth? There is confidentiality here, right? Okay, it's not younger men, it's boys… there, I said it. I like little boys, usually around eight or nine years old. Sometimes even as old as eleven, but these are more rare. And, let me tell you, I have sinned with these boys—"

"What is this? I will not stand for this—for this *blasphemy* in the house of the Lord. I will not listen to this filth."

The priest stood and moved to the door of his confessional, his eyes remaining focused on Carter. Carter, gaze still low, just shook his head side to side.

"Oh, I think you want to hear this, Father. Or should I call you Daddy? After all, isn't that what you make them call you?"

The priest visibly recoiled.

"I don't—I don't know what you are talking about. But I won't stand here and listen to it. You need to leave. *I* am leaving."

Then he left his confessional, leaving Carter alone, shaking his head.

Oh, this is gonna be fun.

"Wha—?" he heard the priest say. "What do *you* want? Are you going to hit me? I am a man of the Lord, I do not fight. You wouldn't hurt a priest. I have done—"

Ah, the good ol' guilty ramble. Could have predicted that one.

With that, Carter stood and left his confessional.

"I see you've met my friend Pike," he said with a nod toward the neatly dressed man to his left, who was blocking the priest's path.

Carter was surprised by how thin Father Peter Stevens was; the man was all gray skin and sinew. He had thick lines on his face, and his eyes were so pale that if it weren't for the way he kept glancing nervously at Pike and his double-breasted suit and pale yellow tie, Carter might have thought him completely blind with cataracts. But no, Father Peter Stevens could see just fine.

"You have no proof," the man stammered.

Carter wagged a finger.

"Ah, wrong again, Father. For someone instilled with the powers of the Almighty, you seem to be wrong about a great many things. For one, it's not okay to molest little boys, which—"

"I don't have to listen to this!" the priest shouted. He took a giant step to his left, but Pike shadowed his movements and any inclinations of fleeing left him.

This part always amused Carter, this nearly visceral reaction to as little as a single step from his friend and partner. After all, Pike wasn't a particularly large man; in fact, he was pretty much average by every measure. About six feet in height, a few pounds shy of two hundred, with neatly parted black hair and a clean-shaven face. Maybe it was the fact that he was always dressed so impeccably, in full, double-breasted suits, irrespective of the weather, indoor or out.

But Carter knew that it wasn't any of these things that gave near everyone pause when they encountered Pike.

No, there was just something about the man's face, so very ordinary, yet so unflinching, that was unnerving.

Unnerving, yeah, that's a good word for it.

"—and you're also wrong about the proof, Father."

A look of sheer horror crossed the priest's face.

"Oh yes, Father, we have proof."

Carter reached into his pocket and pulled out a digital camera. After a contemplative pause, if for no other reason than to build tension, to make the man even more uncomfortable, he held it out to the priest.

"You wanna see? I have some just beautiful photographs of the church's basement that you might want to take a look at. The architecture—" Carter held his head high and whistled. "Well, it will just blow your mind, if you catch my drift."

The priest's face, which had been ashen to begin with, turned almost completely translucent. Ironically, at the same time, his oversized ears were turning a deep crimson.

"What do you want?" he whispered, swallowing hard.

A smile crept onto Carter's handsome face, and again he scratched at his thick black beard.

"The safe?" He nodded. "Yeah, the safe will do nicely, for starters."

The man's eyes darkened for a second, just long enough for both Carter and Pike to take notice. Then a fairly candid look of confusion crossed over him.

Nice try.

"I don't know what you are talking about."

It was Pike who answered.

"You're lying."

Father swallowed hard again.

"No, no, I don't know what you are talking about. Really, I don't—" He tried to put on an angry voice, but it was thin and watery despite his efforts. He settled for obstinate, petulant even. "I don't know about anything you're talking about."

"You're lying," Pike repeated.

Carter shushed him gently and then started whistling quietly. He turned his attention to the camera, and with the two other men watching on, he began cycling through the images that illuminated the digital screen.

"You need to leave," the priest said hoarsely.

"We'll leave after you empty the safe," Carter replied, his eyes fixed on the camera.

"You need to leave *now*," he hissed. His pale hand suddenly shot out, a lame attempt to snatch the camera away. His arm fell way short.

Carter laughed and Pike spoke up again. As usual, his voice was calm and even.

"After you open the safe."

"Ah, here it is," Carter said, turning the viewfinder of the digital camera to the priest. The priest looked at the image and then quickly averted his eyes. "More? Want to see more? 'Cuz I've got more… many more."

Carter pulled the camera back and scrolled to the next image. He was about to show the priest when the lights suddenly flickered above them and all three sets of eyes angled upward.

"Ha, looks like your God doesn't even want to look. But here is another, just in case you thought the first was taken out of context."

Context.

That almost made Carter laugh.

The priest took another glance and, like before, immediately looked away.

"I'll open the safe if you give me the camera," he mumbled.

"What's that? I'm not sure I can hear you," Pike said.

Eyes trained on the floor, the priest repeated his previous sentence.

"I thought you might." Carter turned off the camera and tucked it back into his pocket. "Go on now, lead the way."

*   *   *

There was more money in the safe than either Pike or Carter would have ever guessed. It looked more like the daily earnings of a successful accountant than a church.

Carter whistled loudly.

"Whoo-eee! Where'd you get all this from? Were you in charge of the Askergan coffers or what?"

The pale-faced priest bit his lip, but curbed a response.

"Put it in the bag, Pike," Carter instructed. He was nearly giddy. "Put it all in the bag."

Pike scooped stacks of cash into the bag, and when he cleared the frontmost row, to both of their delights there was another stack behind it. But there was something else there, too, something completely unexpected in this supposed place of worship.

Pike picked up a small white baggie, one of several hundred, and held it for Carter to see.

"Carts?"

Even Carter, who had seen so much in his thirty-odd years on this planet, couldn't keep the surprise from befalling him.

Didn't see that coming.

"Please, don't take the drugs. They're not mine, they're—"

Carter hushed the man by pulling the camera out of his pocket and waggling it back and forth.

"This just keeps getting better and better! Put the drugs in the bag with the money, Pike."

"It's not mine…" the old man whispered. "You can't take it. You don't know what he'll do to me."

"Ahhh, I don't know about that. I've got me a *preeetty* vivid imagination. Besides, you're a man of God—the big man will protect you, won't he?"

The priest looked up, his eyes blazing.

"No? Why not? Have you sinned, Father? When was your last confession?"

"Sabra is not a man of God."

Carter shrugged as if to say, 'not my problem'.

"Put it all in the bag, Pike," he reiterated.

Pike began to scoop the baggies into his satchel, but paused when they heard a bang against the front door. It wasn't the first that they had heard since entering and locking the large church doors, but it was definitely the loudest.

Pike and Carter exchanged a look.

"Please, you have the money, the drugs—can I have the camera back now?"

The priest was nearly in tears, and for the briefest of moments, Carter almost felt bad for the old man.

But then he remembered the tears in the young boy's eyes in the photographs.

Fat chance of that.

"When we get outside," he lied.

It was obvious that the priest was dubious, but what choice did the man have? He was too old and frail to think of trying to pry it from Carter's hands, and even if he somehow managed... well, he had Pike.

And Pike was enough.

"Get up," Carter instructed, and the old man slowly brought himself to his feet. It was as if the man had aged a decade or more since he had angrily burst from the confessional. Pike stood next, and he slid protectively between Carter and the priest.

"Move," the man in the suit ordered. Shoulders hunched, the priest led the way out of the small office and toward the altar. For a second, Carter thought that the man was going to cross himself as he passed by the old, wooden bench and the even older-looking candleholders on top.

Carter glanced behind the altar, his eyes focusing about ten feet above their heads on the plaster of Paris Jesus affixed to what looked like a plastic cross. But Father Stevens didn't cross himself; instead, he made an abrupt turn and staggered down the aisle between the pews.

Such shitty props in a place with so much cash.

There was another series of bangs at the door, and the lights in the ancient church flickered again.

"Sabra," the priest nearly moaned, but Carter paid this comment no heed.

He had heard of Sabra, of course, and the particularly brutal way that the drug dealer punished those who failed to pay. But this didn't concern Carter; he didn't plan on sticking around in this Podunk county for any significant period of time.

Nevertheless, they had to get out of the church, and there *was* something out there. Carter pulled a small pistol out of the back of his jeans and clutched it in his right hand. Pike noticed this motion and glanced over at him.

They exchanged nods.

The gun probably wasn't necessary; after all, he had Pike, and that was almost always enough.

Still…

Carter squeezed the butt of the gun.

When they made it to the door, the priest hesitated, and Carter slowly slid off to one side. Pike moved to the other side of the door.

"Open it," Carter said. "Open it slowly."

The priest's hand was shaking as he brought it out to the slide lock. When he hesitated, Carter repeated his previous request.

Sabra is a just a mid-level drug dealer with a penchant for dramatic ways of torturing those that don't pay up. He isn't a clairvoyant... he couldn't be here already. Could he?

Father Peter Stevens moved the slide bolt back slowly with his narrow fingers and opened the door a few inches. The man took a deep breath and hung his head. It was clear that he'd expected Sabra to reach his fat hand through the two-inch gap and grab him by the throat.

But this didn't happen.

Nothing happened.

Now that imminent death had been avoided, the man seemed imbued with something akin to courage, and he pushed the door a little wider. When still nothing happened, the priest threw it all the way open.

Carter leaned out and chanced a peek.

The sky was a strange orange color, an odd dusk-like glow that seemed wholly out of place during this early dawn hour, but other than that, he could see nothing else out of the ordinary. Just the same dirt expanse that he had rolled in on.

When the priest turned to face him, Carter could see that the old man had been crying, his tears following the deep grooves in his face like water drying in ravines.

"The camera," he said, his voice hoarse.

Carter's expression turned smug.

"I don't think so."

The priest's face contorted.

"But you said—"

Carter looked skyward.

"Oh, I said a lot of things—I *say* a lot of things. Problem is, Father, that you *did* a lot of things. And these are things that even your holy God can't forgive. And if He can't forgive, how would you expect a thief, a conman, an imposter such as myself to forgive?"

He turned to Pike.

"And Pike? Do you forgive?"

Pike remained stone-faced.

Carter shrugged and pouted his lower lip.

"Nope, sorry padre, he doesn't forgive either. Maybe you should—"

Before Carter could finish his sentence, something struck the priest in the back of the head and he stumbled a few feet back into the church. As he did, he passed Carter, who was still off to the side, and he glimpsed something round and flattened stuck to the back of the man's head.

To Carter, it looked like some sort of crab.

Pike quickly stepped in front of the priest and held his arms out, ready to intercede should the man continue into the church.

The priest moaned, and his hands went to the back of his head. He started pulling at the creature, trying desperately to tear it off, but it seemed almost glued there. And with each one of these yanks, his balance became more and more unsteady, and when he stumbled forward again, Pike shoved him backward.

The push was strong enough that the man's direction completely changed, and he receded several feet onto the gravel walk that led to the church's entrance, backtracking so quickly and stirring up so much dust that he almost seemed cartoonish with whirlwind legs.

Carter squinted into the dawn light, his eyes darting from Father Stevens' head to the dirt walk. He spied a few more of the crab-like creatures, all perched high on knobby legs and scrabbling toward the priest. When it looked like the man was about to fall on his ass, Pike quickly took two aggressive forward and grabbed for him. While his hand missed Father's body, his fingers managed to wrap around his collar.

Gripping that white collar, the only thing keeping Father from falling to the ground, Pike turned to face Carter.

Carter, still trying to grasp what was going on, could only manage a confused expression.

"Please," the old priest managed to croak, his eyes rolling back. "Help me."

To Carter, it was an oddly inappropriate plea that did nothing to sway his reaction. After all, the boys' expressions in the photos on the camera in his pocket were equally as horrified.

And they had probably uttered those same fateful words.

Help me.

But no one had helped them, had they? No one had helped them escape from Father Peter Stevens, so why should he help the disgraceful man before him?

Instead, he shook his head, and Pike's lips pressed together tightly.

The man in the suit raised his right foot—adorned with polished oxblood wingtips—and kicked the priest square in the chest. Carter didn't know if Pike had intended to keep his hand on the man's clerical collar, or if he had simply forgotten to let go, but it didn't matter; the white fabric that signified the man's priesthood came away in his hand.

Father Peter Stevens fell backward and he landed hard enough that the air was forced out of him and he made an *oomph* sound. Before the man could draw a breath, three more of the creatures flung themselves at him, landing on his face and hands, anywhere he had exposed flesh. Carter spied more of the things now, many more, maybe even dozens of them, all scrambling through the dirt, seeming to come out of nowhere. As the priest screeched in agony and tried to pull them off of him, the other crab-like creatures turned toward the open door.

Carter never hesitated.

He stepped around Pike and slammed the door closed, moments before the crab-like things smashed into it. With the hand not holding the white piece of cloth, Pike slid the lock into place.

Sweating, both men took a step back from the door and stared at it as several more of the things flung their bodies ineffectually at the warped wood.

Thonk, thonk, thonk.

Somewhere deep in his mind, Carter wished that it had been Sabra knocking at the door, and not these strange crustaceans. But he said nothing for a few moments, and neither did Pike.

There was another heavy hit to the door, and then both men instinctively cowered as an explosion somewhere nearby rocked the church.

"What the fuck!"

Carter turned in time to see Jesus fall to the ground, smashing into the altar and showering it with pieces of plaster of Paris and plastic.

The bangs against the door suddenly ceased and an odd silence fell over the church and its two inhabitants.

Pike eventually turned toward Carter, an expectant look on his face. There was no need for him to formulate the question — the look was that obvious.

What now?

Indeed, what the fuck now?

Carter thought about that for a moment.

What should we do now?

His initial inclination had been to leave Askergan after they had relieved the pedophile priest of his cash. But now that the man had gotten his just desserts, maybe they didn't need to leave so soon.

A smile slowly crept across Carter's face. He reached out and took the white clerical collar from Pike.

"I don't know what the fuck is going on out there," he said, pointing toward the back door. "But what I do know is that the people of Askergan will be looking for a scapegoat and a savior after whatever is going on out there passes."

Carter brought the small piece of white fabric to his throat and flipped the collar of his shirt over top of it. "And, Pike, my good man, I think we just found both."

PART I - WALTER

1.

"STUPID, STUPID COPS," **WALTER** Wandry said with a laugh as he pealed onto Main Street.

The man's pupils were wide and unfocused, which blurred the dark landscape before him. It didn't matter; nobody was on the road on this night—nobody still alive, that is. He didn't even feel the cuts on his arms and legs, the pieces of glass embedded in his skin from when he had squeezed his way through the tiny window in the big sheriff's office. He didn't feel the bruises on his narrow hips from the window frame, or both of his twisted ankles as a result of the fall from the window.

The tires of his dilapidated Chevy crunched over several of the crab-like creatures—the crackers, as the son of a bitch sheriff and his deputies called them—sending shell shrapnel flying. But, like the pains in his arms, legs, hips, and ankles, he didn't notice this, either.

Walter aggressively rolled down the window, sending the pane of glass awkwardly tumbling into the door.

"Fuck you all!" he shouted out into the warm air. Then he stomped on the gas again. "Fuck you all!"

The stupid cops had been so eager to throw him in the cell, to get him to shut up, that they hadn't even searched him. Good thing, too, as he had had three ounces of heroin and all the beautiful accouterment necessary to get the drugs in him tucked into... well, tucked away in a dark place.

Walter's eyes flicked from the road to the passenger seat, and the smile, which had faded somewhat at the thought of the black cop and his anorexic deputies, returned, revealing two rows of yellow and black teeth.

The black drug case *had* been tucked away, but he had since extricated it, and now it lay on the center of the passenger seat in all of its fake leather glory.

It was a beautiful thing.

The world around Walter confused him—confused him even more now that he had seen the crackers, and had witnessed how they somehow embedded themselves into the flesh of the few people that weren't safely locked away when they had started to... well, *invade* from wherever the fuck they had come from.

The crackers had oddly left him pretty much alone, however, which was both confusing and a blessing. A blessing, because this had given him the time he'd needed to get high. And confusing because, well, what the fuck? All they seemed interested in was eating people... just not him, evidently.

And then there was the sheriff. Fucking big black Sheriff Paul White, who for some ungodly reason had actually let him out. And that was a mistake that the man would live to regret.

No one fucked with Walter Wandry. No one stole his shit, and no one locked him away in a fucking cell.

His father had tried that once, and, well, that had ended badly for one of them.

Walter turned to the open window and took a deep breath of the sour-smelling air. It was still warm outside, despite the fact that it was only leaking into the wee hours of the morning. The air that rushed in through the window caused his beard to flap, and he closed his eyes for a moment, pushing his head further out of the window like some sort of deranged puppy.

The image of Sheriff Paul White's face popped into his mind after a few moments of mere bliss, and his eyes snapped open.

Walter yanked the steering wheel to the right just in time to avoid a car parked sideways across both lanes. There was a satisfying crunch of another half-dozen or so crackers that were all suddenly heading in the same direction as he—fleeing the station. For whatever reason, this seemed to invigorate him, to enhance his high, to further blur the already fuzzy line between fantasy and reality.

"Join me!" he shouted out the window.

His words mingled with the hot air and seemed to swirl about his head like some sort of verbal smoke or fumes.

"Join me!" he screamed again as the car tires crushed untold numbers of the strange white creatures and sent spurts of equally white liquid flying. "Join me!"

Walter didn't bother slowing when he hit the intersection, turning left onto Highway 2 from Main Street, trying to put the shithole that was Askergan County behind him as quickly as possible.

Just as he pulled his head back inside the vehicle, he caught sight of a police cruiser parked on the other side of the road, only several blocks from the gas station on the corner... that he only now realized was ablaze, large tendrils of fire reaching high into the air like organic spires. He also spotted several silhouettes, police officers maybe, cowering from the blaze, nearly hidden out of sight.

Walter's eyes remained trained on the yellow flames as his car whipped by, his eyes locked on the sight like a moth transfixed by a lamp.

"What the fuck?"

An explosion tore the words from his mouth, and his beaten Chevy was sent flying, the entire left side of the car lifting off the ground with the concussive force.

2.

GLASS.

That was the first thing that popped into Walter's mind: *glass.*

Even before he opened his eyes to see it, he could feel it everywhere: in his long gray beard, in his neatly parted and slicked black hair. He could feel it biting into the backs of his arms and the base of his neck. It was embedded in his cheeks; it had sliced his upper lip.

Walter gasped, his narrow chest drawing in a huge breath for what seemed like the first time in ages. And then he started to cough, a thick, throaty cough that was accompanied by the familiar coppery taste of blood in his mouth. Eyes still closed, he spat, not caring where the thick wad landed.

The ringing in his ears droned onward, but now he recognized another sound, one that was just as persistent.

The ocean? Is that water I hear?

But that couldn't be; he had been driving, hadn't he? He had been driving down the cracker-covered street when…

Everything came flooding back to him and his eyes snapped open, his pupils so wide that his dark irises were all but invisible.

It wasn't the roaring of seawater that he was hearing, but the sound of fire, the eager sound of flames consuming everything in its path.

Walter Wandry was lying on his back in the center of the road, his head angled to the left. His eyes slowly began to focus on what remained of the gas station that cornered Highway 2 and Main Street, the same gas station that he had passed less than a day ago when he had come racing into town, looking for his lost son.

For Tyler.

He cracked his jaw and closed his eyes for a moment before quickly opening them again.

The cop car. Where is the cop car?

Keeping his head still, his eyes scanned the fiery blaze, looking for the cop car or the dark figures.

He didn't see anyone. There was nothing, only smoke, fire, and crispy shells.

I hope they burned. I hope those fuckers burned.

Images of the final few seconds before the explosion started coming back to him, and his heart began to race.

My drugs.

"No," Walter grumbled, the sound rolling around in his mouth, making friends with blood and saliva. He spat again, this time making sure that the offending substance landed on the tarmac instead of on himself.

"No."

With a groan, he rolled onto his stomach, and then pushed himself onto his knees, trying his best to brush as much of the glass off of him as he could. It was an impossible task, as he quickly realized that the Chevy's windows must have blown inward, and all of the tiny cubes of shatterproof glass had collected on his person as if he were some sort of magnet for superheated sand.

So Walter gave up and went back to searching the road for the cop car or the Chevy... *his* Chevy, the one with his drugs on the passenger seat.

His eyes widened when he saw three crackers begin to make their way toward him, their fluid movements somehow erotic, enticing. Six legs, all of them moving and bending in such coordination over the road littered with burning debris. It appeared as if they were floating.

"Out of the way!" he roared, shooing them with his left hand as he crawled in their direction.

The crackers paid him no mind and continued past, all still heading in the same direction like a school of chitinous fish.

Another explosion ripped through the air, and Walter turned his gaze toward the east. A giant fireball licked the skyline, bathing the tops of the trees in a dirty orange glow.

What the fuck is going on?

But the thought was fleeting—only one thing mattered to Walter now.

He squinted as he scanned the asphalt, and his eyes eventually fell on something familiar. A smile graced his thin face.

His black pouch was lying on the road between the white hash marks roughly ten feet from him.

Walter crawled forward again, ignoring the fact that it seemed every muscle in his body was crying out for him to stop, to just lie there and wait for help. It occurred to him that he couldn't see his car anywhere, that he must have been thrown from the vehicle with the explosion, but his goals and motivations, as they had so many times in his life, became singular. And creeping forward literally one inch at a time, the fact that his left leg was nearly numb and his jeans were sticking to his skin from his thigh down to his ankle barely registered.

He had nearly made it to his black case when he saw the first cracker die. It wasn't something he would have noticed— truthfully, when he got like this, even the most basic of needs, be it eating, sleeping, or shitting, went ignored—but this happened but a few inches from his face and would have been impossible not to see.

At first, the cracker's movements seemed to slow, the rhythmic bursts of air exiting the top of the shell becoming hastened, irregular. Then with the next few steps, the many joints of the frontmost leg refused to lock and then became limp, and the other five legs resorted to dragging it along like a numb, arthritic finger. When another leg stopped working, and then another, its forward progress was significantly inhibited. It was only when the fourth leg was paralyzed that it fell to the asphalt. One of its legs, one of two that still seemed to be clicking and clacking, tried to drive itself into the road and force the shell up again, but it failed. After a few more desperate, grasping attempts, it too fell limp. The final leg soon followed suit.

Dead; the air stopped pulsing through its white shell.

It was finally dead.

And Walter couldn't have cared less. He crawled another foot forward and watched—only because it was still in front of him—as the thing began to turn translucent. A moment later, the legs curled upward, articulating those many joints not in the smooth, fluid movements as it had made its way over the uneven terrain, but like jerky drying in the sun. And there they remained, all six of the roughly eight-inch protuberances pointed into the air until the cracker resembled something of the exoskeleton of an overturned crab.

Turning his head to the side, Walter spat again. And then he reached out with his left hand, trying to grasp the case without having to pull his body forward another inch. Like the dead cracker before him, his left leg had become nearly completely useless, and dragging it was becoming more and more difficult.

He wheezed as he stretched out, grunting as the muscles in his chest and shoulder screamed at him.

Nothing; his fingernails only came back with grit buried beneath.

Walter, eyes closed tightly, head to one side, crawled forward another foot and then a second before collapsing onto the road again. This time when he reached out blindly, his hand closed on the familiar shape and texture of his black faux-leather case.

A sigh escaped his lips, vibrating the blood and saliva that clung to his bottom lip.

His relief was short-lived, however. A second later, he felt something graze the back of his hand. It only brushed against him at first, but then, as if gaining courage, he felt six distinct pressure points in his skin. Then he felt those points lazily make their way onto his wrist, then up his forearm in an awkward, drunken gait. Walter was so tired and sore that he couldn't even be bothered to turn his head to look at what was crawling on him.

But one thing was certain: it was much different from the itching that happened under his skin when he went more than a day without a hit.

Hit; drugs. I have my drugs.

As if to affirm this thought, he squeezed the leather case with his hand, and a smile again crossed his thin, pale lips.

He closed his eyes when the crawling reached his shoulder. For a moment, he thought he had fallen asleep; that the only reason the thing had stopped moving was that he had passed out again. But then the cracker nestled the soft underside of its shell against his skin. It felt oddly comforting—*drugs; I have my drugs*—but this sensation only lasted a short moment.

The cracker's conveyor-like teeth suddenly clamped down on Walter's shoulder and then began cutting their way into his flesh, slowly, carefully, *meticulously* dissecting his skin, before the entire cracker forced itself *beneath*.

High or not, in possession of his drugs or not, Walter couldn't help the scream that bubbled from deep within him.

Despite the power of the cry that rocked his frail body, when the sound finally escaped his thin and chapped lips, it was more a whimper than a wail.

Then Walter's mind started spinning, and he tumbled into a pit of unconsciousness.

3.

THE SUN SHONE BRIGHTLY down on Askergan County that morning, illuminating the dark embers from the multiple fires that floated in the air like disinterested pixies.

Thousands of the crackers had either died or had been destroyed in those early morning hours, their corpses with their upturned legs drying in the sun like forgotten fruit. There would be much cleaning and restitution after this day was done, but Walter Wandry had no interest in participating in this effort.

In fact, he had no interest in Askergan at all, save for once again seeing it recede in his rearview.

It was difficult for him to open his eyes, especially given the fact that in addition to a cruel pounding behind them, the lids were gummed shut. At first, he'd tried to reach up with his left arm to wipe the substance away, but that arm felt heavy and ungainly and he'd quickly abandoned the effort. His right arm felt strange too, but this was a familiar strangeness, one that he knew was the result of recently having injected into the crook of his elbow.

As his slender fingers finally managed to wipe away thin trails of mucus from his eyes and the lids slowly separated, he quickly closed them again.

It was bright outside—too bright. The sun felt like shards of ice jammed into his retinas.

His eyelids fluttered, and he tried to concentrate on keeping them open, to fight the tears that first formed a film and then cascaded down his cheeks.

My heroin!

This singular thought kept his eyes open, but his vision was blurry and he had to blink rapidly several times before the world before him slowly came into focus.

Rainbows; there were rainbows everywhere, despite the fact that the air was hot and dry. The harsh sunlight separated as it passed through the hundreds of translucent cracker corpses, causing a slight prism effect.

It made him queasy.

Walter turned his head to the other side, grinding his cheek into several cubes of shatterproof glass that littered the road.

C'mon, where's the bag? Where the fuck is the case?

Then he finally spotted it: the black case was clutched between the fingers of... *his* hand?

The fingers looked familiar, thin and red, with nails bitten to the quick, and the cross tattoo in the webbing between thumb and forefinger was indeed his, but it didn't *feel* like his hand. It *was* his, it had to be, but he couldn't feel it at all; from the shoulder down, his arm was completely numb.

What the fuck? Is it broken? Dislocated? Fucking amputated?

He tried to force his fingers closed, to squeeze the case, to *feel* it, but nothing happened.

Walter tried to remember which arm he had shot into. It could have been his right, even though this would have been strange given that he was right-handed and preferred to inject into his left. But his arm had never felt this way, even when he had had no choice but to inject what he knew to be dirty drugs.

Infection didn't feel like this, not even the kind that turned his skin ashen and gave him palpitations. That was bad; this was *worse*.

Maybe I hit a nerve?

Walter finally mustered the courage to scan his numb arm, and when his gaze fell on the crook of his elbow, his heart sank: his pink, mottled flesh was relatively smooth and unmolested.

No infection in his right arm.

When his slow, rising gaze finally made it to his shoulder, Walter snapped to his feet so quickly that his head spun and he immediately fell back onto his ass. A bolt of pain flashed up his spine from his tailbone to the base of his skull, but it barely even registered. Instead, he began to frantically use his good hand to smack at his numb shoulder and arm, trying to brush off the cracker that was nestled there.

"Fuck!" he screamed, still swiping at the characteristic shape.

Every time his hand passed over the spot, he felt the creature, but no matter how hard he swiped, the irregularly shaped *thing* was still there.

With a grimace, he took another look at his shoulder, forcing his chin to his chest to get the best possible view.

Walter's heart nearly stopped.

It was patently obvious that no matter how many times he swatted at the cracker on his shoulder, it would not be brushed away like a pesky spider; no, it was clear that this cracker was more permanent.

With his lower lip dripping blood and spit, Walter somehow mustered the strength to inspect the shape buried beneath his skin.

The cracker was smaller than he had first thought, but the characteristic oval-shaped outline of the shell still covered most of his left deltoid. He could also make out the creature's six legs, all folded and articulated so that they were completely pressed against his... well, against whatever was *underneath* his skin.

"Fuck!" he swore, looking skyward, his eyes once again watering in the bright sun.

Then he turned back to the shape and used a trembling thumb to apply some pressure to one of the thing's legs. It was surprisingly pliable, despite the rigid outline beneath his skin.

A quiver ran through his entire body as if he had just experienced a minor electrical shock.

"Oh God," he whispered, tucking his chin against his collar to get an even better look.

The hard outline was horrible, of this Walter had no doubt, but there was something far more disturbing.

The thing's mouth, a small, silver-dollar-sized orifice, was directed out of a fairly smooth circular opening on his skin. Inside this hole, he caught sight of a horrible set of tiny, reciprocating teeth. Worse still was the fact that his skin around the hole seemed to be *fused* perfectly around the orifice. It was as if his pale flesh seemed to be part of the cracker's mouth — some sort of macabre, surrogate lips.

It was almost too hard to stomach, so instead, Walter tried to squeeze the case again. He was surprised to find that this time his fingers responded, even if this response had been reduced to only a pathetic twitch.

Maybe I'm just high.

Walter looked skyward again, staring into the sun until black specks clouded his vision.

Oh, he was high alright, but this was still happening.

Sudden movement in his right shoulder, an odd puckering sensation, drew his eyes back.

Even through watery vision, Walter could see the cracker quivering slightly, thrumming like a plucked violin string. The feeling made him nauseated; it felt like there were hundreds of spiders crawling under his flesh, all milling about, trying to find a good spot to lay their eggs.

His stomach lurched and his fingers squeezed the leather case, only this time he wasn't sure if this was a reflex caused by the cracker's movement in his shoulder, or if he had sent the command himself.

If he had thought it.

Another thing struck him then; he thought that he could actually feel the texture of the leather case in his hand.

He tried to squeeze his hand again, and this time his fingers actually closed.

He supposed that relief should have washed over him, that he should have felt relief, gratitude even. But the fact that he had regained control of his arm didn't matter as much as it should have.

There was only one thing that mattered. And it was the same thing that he had done daily for as long as he could remember, long before he had even had a son.

Walter squeezed the case again and a smile crossed his lips.

He was still high, but one could always get *more* high.

4.

THE THIRD CAR THAT Walter tried was unlocked, and he climbed into the backseat, first unzipping then unfolding the leather case without even bothering to close the door behind him.

It took less than a minute to load the syringe full of heroin. His first attempt to inject using his left hand was a failure; he was not as dexterous with that hand, and he had been so scared of losing any heroin that he couldn't even manage to press the plunger. Still, he persisted, driven by the hope that injecting into his right arm, close to the cracker, might cause the thing to curl up and die.

An image of the translucent crackers, their six pointed legs aimed skyward, littering the road outside, came into his mind and he shuddered.

Maybe that wasn't something that he wanted to happen beneath his skin.

Without further delay, he plunged the dull needle point into the skin on the inside of his right elbow. With his belt firmly clenched between his brown and yellow teeth, he tried to make the fingers on his right hand open and close, to repeatedly make a fist, as was his ritual, but his hand was still refusing to cooperate fully, and he could only manage a crooked claw.

Annoyed, Walter let the belt fall from his mouth, and the drug simultaneously spread from the crook of his elbow to the smallest capillaries in his tingling fingertips and up his arm to his heart, where it was shuttled to his entire body. He pictured the yellowy substance flowing through him, and when the substance hit his brain, a sigh escaped his chapped lips and his eyes rolled back. Walter slumped against the seat, the cracker-induced anxiety leeching from every pore like a toxic sweat.

As his eyelids began to flutter, he waited for the sweet bliss, the all-encompassing feeling of euphoria that he knew would soon overwhelm him, turning his mind and body into liquid, turning him into an unfeeling, unthinking memory of a man.

But the familiar wave never hit Walter.

Instead, *nothing* happened.

Walter blinked and turned his head to look at the open case on the seat beside him.

It was his gear, he was sure of it. And it was *good* gear, straight from Sabra, the same gear that had gotten him high as a fucking kite before all of Askergan had started going to shit.

But now he felt... *nothing.*

Could someone have switched out my gear for something else?

He glanced out the open car door, his eyes falling on serenity baked in a hot yellow glow.

No, there's—

A scream bubbled up from somewhere deep within him.

There was a clenching sensation in his shoulder as if an iron clamp had suddenly started to tighten on his deltoid.

It felt as if his entire shoulder was being crushed.

"What the fuck!"

Panting with the pain, he turned to the cracker and saw that it had become seemingly more defined, the ridges outlining the knobby appendages and the circumference of the shell now hard and thick beneath his skin as if etched in charcoal. The mouth or orifice or whatever the fuck the thing was with all the teeth that pointed out through the hole in his skin appeared be quivering as if it were excited.

Walter clenched his rotting teeth and turned his gaze back out the car door and stared at the six or seven cracker corpses in plain sight. They were most definitely dead, reduced to hard, translucent shells upturned on the hot black asphalt.

And this morbid scene extended as far as he could see.

The hundreds of crackers that had flowed—that he had shouted to *join him*—down the street before his car had been rocked by the shockwave of the exploding gas station had all stopped moving.

They were dead.

But the cracker buried beneath the skin on Walter's shoulder most definitely was not dead. This one was very much alive, and now that he had injected the heroin, it was thriving.

5.

CARTER DUKE PULLED THE plastic letters out of the sign placard and tossed them into the bag with the others that he had found in the church office. When the sign was completely devoid of letters, he stared at the empty space for a moment.

It's only fitting, he thought as he stared at the blank sign. *Askergan's message is waiting to be written — waiting for me to fill this blank canvas.*

Carter took a drag of his cigarette and continued to stare, enjoying the emptiness that seemed to transcend the sign and unexpectedly enveloped him as well.

It was strange, this psychological silence. For once, thoughts weren't coursing through his head, and he wasn't running through dozens of hypothetical conversations, continually coming up with and rehearsing answers to potential questions. Questions that would threaten to usurp his authenticity — that were *designed* to do just that, to poke holes in his universal condom of truth. Sure, this *emptiness* would only last a moment or two, but it was a welcome relief nonetheless.

Ah, the pressure of always being something else.

Even now, dressed as a priest, of all things, he knew what he really was: a con man through and through.

And it was psychologically exhausting.

The sign, on the other hand, couldn't answer back. It couldn't judge his response; it couldn't try to tease out the truth hidden between, behind, or *within* his words.

It was a sign; just a simple fucking sign, and he could write what he wanted.

For a split second, he debated putting up something stupid, some inane commentary that served no other purpose but to incite idealistic hope in the insipid: *Make Askergan Great Again.*

Ironic, pithy, on point.

Carter looked into the cloth bag, his eyes scanning the dozen or so plastic letters.

Pity, he thought. *No 'k's.*

Carter pulled his head out of the bag and looked around. It was late dawn, and the sun that crept over the horizon was hot but lazy. The church behind him was a pale white, but it had long ago fallen to neglect, and long strips of paint peeled down its length.

A simple structure, essentially just a large triangle—not much to look at, really. For a place that claimed it paid homage to the Almighty, it lacked a sort of panache; it looked more a pauper's shack. Oh, sure, there was the humility and humbleness and all that, but with all the money they had found in the church—a little over fifty-six grand—and the drugs, the least that Father Stevens could have done was to put a new coat of varnish on the old tradition. Even the church's steeple looked bent, although he couldn't be sure if it was truly crooked or if it was simply an illusion from the wavy lines of heat. But alas, the man had had other priorities, and fixing up the church clearly hadn't been one of them.

Carter spat onto the ground at his feet, generating a small puff of dirt.

Could have fucking paved something, though.

There was no church parking lot, just a patch of hardened dirt and clay off to one side where the parishioners parked.

Carter cleared his throat and turned to Pike, who through all of his contemplations had been standing silently beside him. It made him wonder, with everything that continued to whirr in his brain, what was going on in his friend's mind.

But that was a tough nut to crack.

"Not much to look at, is it?"

Pike's response was immediate.

"No."

Carter shrugged, but his indifference was short-lived. He knew that to convert the Askergan citizens, to *fully* convert them, this terrible excuse of a church wouldn't do. They needed something new, something modern. Something that would not only support a new identity, a new culture, but one that would promote it.

And the name—*Askergan*—that wasn't helping either. It was either a name recycled from some old city back in the days of horses and when life expectancies barely tickled double digits, or someone had taken a bag of letters like the one in his hand and shaken it, pulling them at random.

Askergan; no, that won't do. None of this will do.

For as long as he could remember, he and Pike had been on the run, snatching and grabbing what they could in an attempt to extort their way into some semblance of normalcy. But despite their scores, which were usually small but occasionally substantial, they would soon thereafter be on to the next town.

This was the life that Carter had chosen for them, but with every town sign that reflected in the rearview, he left something other than victims behind.

He left a little bit of his soul. And Carter wanted to change that before there was nothing of the real him left.

And there was also the practical matter of running out of leads, of having used up any and all of the contacts he had massed over the years. Case and point coming all the way to this remote county to extort a scumbag priest based on some information Pike had found on the internet and a few photographs that he had discovered simply by accident.

Yeah, things were getting lean.

But now they were *here*, and there was something about Askergan, something that had struck him the moment he and Pike had rolled into town.

Askergan was like the beauty queen whose jealous boyfriend had splashed acid in her face: once beautiful, but now scarred. Scarred, but still with enough underlying charm to get by in life.

We can stay here, he thought, his mind drifting to Pike as a young boy, punching and kicking his way through grown men, trying not only to break their bodies, but to also bury whatever it was inside of *him* that was already broken.

No, running wasn't going to be in the cards for them anymore. No more—he could sense a time when they no longer had to resort to blackmailing undercover police officers to relieve them of their pathetic pensions.

This was a new beginning—*the* new beginning.

And there was work to be had in Askergan, in case they ever got bored, in case all else failed. There was work, money, and drugs in Askergan.

Carter turned his attention back to the letters and then ironically gave the bag a shake. As the letters settled, a smile split his dark beard.

Yes, he thought as he began picking out the letters one by one. *This is a new beginning, a time for a new Askergan—a new time for a Modern County.*

6.

WALTER LUCKED OUT. AFTER the pain had subsided somewhat as the cracker relaxed following the injection, he found a red flannel shirt in the backseat and quickly pulled it on, desperate to hide his hideous shoulder. It wasn't so much that he was concerned about what others would think if they caught sight of it—Lord knows, he had stopped caring what others thought about him long ago—but more to hide the thing from his own eyes. To offer himself a moment unburdened of disgust, however temporary, so that he could try to contemplate what had happened—what the thing was doing in his shoulder, and why injecting nearly two grams of heroin had failed to get him high.

But before all that, he had to get out of there, to get far away from this horrible place with the idiot cops that were likely out looking for him as he sat baking in the sauna of a backseat. He put little stock in their policing skills, case in point the drugs that he had managed to keep on his person even after being thrown in jail, let alone his rather simple and even predictable escape.

But, shit, even a blind squirrel found a nut once in a while.

A quick glance into the front revealed that the keys were still dangling from the ignition, a fake casino chip fob hanging limply from the keyring.

Someone must have been in one hell of a hurry to abandon their car if the keys are still in it, Walter thought.

His mind flipped back to the scene that had unfolded after slipping out the police station window.

Yeah, seeing those horrible crackers would make normal, rational people do irrational things.

And boy am I grateful, he thought with a smirk as he forced his thin frame between the front seats and climbed over the center console. With a sigh, he collapsed into the driver's seat and turned the keys.

To his surprise, the car started on the first try.

The tightness in his shoulder continued to ease as he put the car into drive with his right hand; either that or he had simply become accustomed to the sensation. Either way, he wanted the thing out… the fucking thing had stolen his drugs, stolen his high. And if there was one thing that Walter would not stand for in this world, it was someone—or something—messing with his drugs.

He would amputate his arm if he had to get high, although he was acutely aware that this would cause some complications when it came time to inject again. But that was just a minor detail, something that he could work out later.

Details.

The word resonated with him.

Details… like what the hell happened in the Askergan Police Department. Details like where the fuck had all of these damn parasites had come from. Details like what had become of his son—what had happened to Tyler.

Sweating profusely in the flannel shirt, Walter Wandry gritted his teeth and slammed his foot on the gas pedal. The tires screeched, and the car lurched forward.

As he sped down Highway 2, swerving to avoid the parked and abandoned cars while simultaneously trying to crush as many of the cracker shells as possible, his mind was preoccupied, trying to remember how sharp the cooking knives in his drawer back at his dilapidated apartment were.

And wondering if he really could cut off his arm without killing himself.

*   *   *

Walter's entire body was soaked with sweat, partly from the sun that had nearly reached its zenith and had quickly heated the stolen car with a broken air conditioner, but mostly due to the fact that he hadn't gotten high in at least seven or eight hours.

Maybe even longer.

Still, he was happy to be out of the shithole that was Askergan County. He had only been to the place a handful of times in his life, despite living only about an hour and change away. And with each of those visits, the most recent one notwithstanding, he had just been passing through, using it as a throughway to Darborough or another adjacent county to score. So now, as he pulled into the small parking lot of his apartment complex in Pekinish, something just felt right—it felt *right* to be home.

But then his mind flashed to being thrown in the jail cell, crawling through the police station window, being nearly blown up, and then having that *parasite* in his shoulder, and things didn't feel *right* anymore. Instead, they felt horribly *wrong*.

Walter tore the casino chip fob off the keychain and threw it out the window.

"A lot of luck this brought you… can't even afford a goddamn car with AC," he grumbled as he scooped his drug case up and shoved the car door open.

Squinting hard, Walter quickly made his way across the tarmac to the back door, rhythmically squeezing his right hand as he walked, trying to force more feeling into the limb. The pain in his shoulder was almost completely gone now, but he was still experiencing something of a phantom limb sensation—his arm was there and it was his, but it also *wasn't*.

Like the drugs; they were in him, but they just weren't doing anything.

There, but not there.

The door to his building wasn't locked, as the last person to enter or leave had simply ignored the handwritten sign on the door that said, *'Please always make sure to loke the door'*.

Loke. *For fuck's sake, even I can spell 'Lock'.*

But there really was no need; why lock the door to this place—this housing unit with cramped apartments that were but a haven for drug users, prostitutes, and other high-ranking and contributing members of society?

The lobby was dark, as several of the pot lights buried in the popcorn ceiling had long since burnt out and hadn't been replaced. And despite the bright sun outside, the windows had been painted with a thick black paint, one that not only served to keep the offending light out, but also as a glue to hold the smashed pieces of glass in place.

Cheaper than replacing the broken panes, which would only be broken again in a few days.

Walter made his way across the trash-littered foyer to the elevator, jamming his left thumb into the up button. While he waited, watching the LED lights above the metal box change from 4 to 3 and then to 2, he clucked his tongue against the roof of his mouth and then licked his chapped lips.

Drink. I need a fucking drink.

Sweat trickled down the inside of his armpits before being soaked up by the flannel shirt he had stolen from the car, but

even that was near saturation and had been reduced to a
soppy mess.

Stolen.

He couldn't help think about the hard outline of the cracker
buried in his shoulder.

Stolen—like this fucking creature did to my high.

Walter shook his head and tried to distract himself from
the thought by bringing a hand up to his cheek and inspecting
the damage from the glass that he had landed on after being
ejected from his car. His fingers probed the deep pockmarks
on his cheeks, moving from one blood-caked divot to another.
He picked idly at the crusty sores, inspecting the brown scum
beneath his too-short nails after each satisfying peel. He
brought his hand to his beard next, trying to force his fingers
through the tangled mess of wiry white hair that traveled
nearly to the hollow of his throat. This proved impossible: the
coarse beard hairs were a knotted mess, and the dried blood
had stiffened and glued the strands together.

As he continued to pick at the cuts on his face and tug at
his beard, his eyes remained fixed on the sign above the
elevator.

It was still on the second floor.

"Come on, hurry the fuck up."

He licked his dry lips again and jammed the *UP* button
three or four more times. Each time he pressed the button, the
red light around it lit up, but then went dark a second later.

"Fuck off," he muttered, finally giving up and kicking the
metal door.

It wasn't the first time that the elevator had broken, or was
being held on a particular floor, and it certainly wouldn't be
the last. Not here—not in this shitty place.

Walter made his way to the stairs, throwing the door wide in frustration.

By the third floor, he was completely out of breath, and he came to a stop, grasping the metal railing tightly as his narrow chest heaved.

He coughed loudly and then spat a thick wad of yellow-brown mucus onto the stairs before pulling himself onto the next step.

By the fourth floor—his floor—he was so utterly covered in sweat that he debated tearing off the flannel shirt and leaving it in a damp heap right there in the stairwell. But a quick peek, a passing glance, at the mark on his shoulder, and he quickly decided against it; not only could he still clearly make out the dark outline of the cracker, but he could see the teeth again, rotating and gnashing, as if trying to take a bite out of the flannel fabric. He compromised by simply opening his shirt all the way.

Breathing heavily, he made his way out of the stairwell and down the hallway, and then stopped in front of his apartment. The door was slightly ajar, but this wasn't terribly unusual, especially not given the circumstances in which he'd left the previous day.

It had been his ex-wife that had called him, letting him know that Tyler had never returned from a fishing trip—he was surprised that the fucking drunk had even realized he was missing—and that the Askergan cops weren't telling her shit.

Her calling had been strange enough—he hadn't spoken to her in a number of years—but her calling about Tyler? That had been odd enough to get even his dulled intuition working.

"Why you calling me?" he had demanded.

When she had failed to come up with a reasonable
response, his mind had really started to churn.

Insurance; life insurance.

Like an omen from a God he didn't believe in, the words
had seemingly come out of nowhere. Maybe he had heard
something about collecting life insurance on a TV show, on
one of those true crime shows, but regardless of where they
had come from, when he had asked about a life insurance
policy on his estranged son, his ex-wife's answer had been
curt, to the point.

"There is, but if Tyler's dead, I get it all."

Fat chance.

He laughed at the absurdity of the conversation now, but
given what he had seen back at the station and what was
happening to him… well, maybe wishing his son dead wasn't
the worst thing in the world. And if he got some money out of
it, so what? Was that so wrong?

Walter pushed the door to his apartment wide and stepped
inside. Almost immediately, some of the anxiety of the last
few days flowed out of him and was replaced by the feeling of
just being home—even if home for him was a shitty apartment
with peeling beige paint, a dirty mattress on the floor, and a
tube TV that was still on and blaring shopping network
reruns.

"I get it all."

Walter laughed at his ex-wife's words now, knowing that if
there was any insurance money in this deal, she wouldn't be
getting a fucking penny.

He opened the cupboard above the sink and rooted around
for a clean glass.

But either way, dead or alive, he needed to find Tyler.

And he knew just where to start. The black cop. The black cop with the bulging biceps that had dared to grab him by the throat.

"Fucking prick," Walter grumbled, grabbing a glass that didn't appear clean so much as less dirty than all the others. He used his thumb to wipe away a brown smudge that went all the way around the rim of the glass, then proceeded to fill it with water from the tap.

The water tasted foul and did little to quench Walter's thirst. What he needed was a drink—a real drink. He turned to the fridge, grabbing the grease-smeared handle with his left hand, the drug case still clutched between the numb fingers of his right. He had only pulled the fridge partway open when he froze, his heart catching in his throat.

"Welcome home, Walt," a voice from somewhere deeper in the apartment said.

Walter's hand, numb or not, squeezed the leather case so tightly that he felt his fingers start to burn. Instead of panicking, he slipped the case into the fridge without opening it any farther, sliding it onto the shelf beside a half-empty bottle of beer. Then he closed the fridge and stepped out into the open.

Despite being seated, it was clear that the man in Walter's favorite chair at the back of the room was large. He had an almost comically square head, and the tightly cropped blond hair that clung to his large forehead did him no favors. The man's ears were cauliflowered, the tops of which were so thick that they pulled away from his temples, which only added to the immense size of his head. He was wearing a patent leather jacket, which must have been ridiculously hot given the weather, and his thick, knobby hands were resting comfortably on his knees. As Walter's gaze drifted downward, a sneer began to form on his narrow face. There was a matte black of a pistol in the man's lap, and it was aimed directly at him.

The door to the bathroom suddenly opened and another goon stepped out. This man was shorter than the one in the chair, and he had dark black hair instead of blond, but they were the same nonetheless; thick men in leather coats with big heads and ugly ears.

Thick men that were here for only one reason.

These men were here to collect.

"Why don't you sit down?" the man with the short blond hair asked. His thin lips curled into a smirk. "I think it's about time we had a little chat, Walter."

7.

REFUSING TO SIT HADN'T gone over well with the hitman. In the end, the man had forced him onto a wobbly wooden chair and had proceeded to tie up his wrists behind his back with telephone cable so tightly that Walter could barely feel his fingers.

Despite his predicament, he couldn't help but laugh in response to the man's most recent demands.

"Look around, you fucking moron—I have no money."

The man sitting in the chair in front of him bent forward, his expression souring.

He leaned in so far that their foreheads nearly touched.

"Don't fuck with Sabra," he hissed. His breath smelled of stale bread. "Sabra wants his money. He gave you the product, and now he wants his money."

Walter pulled as far away from the thick man with the short blond hair as possible, which, granted, wasn't even far enough to breathe fresh air, given the telephone cord that dug into his wrists before twisting through the back of the kitchen chair on which he sat.

Sabra.

An image of the massive, fat man, like a humid pile of uncooked pizza dough, flashed in his mind. Sabra, with a mouth foul enough to rival his own stench. Sabra, who controlled nearly all of the heroin distribution in the Northeast. Sabra, of the infamous torture methods that involved a man's scrotum.

Fucking Sabra.

The man had stupidly given Walter an 8-ball of heroin to sell, most of which he had promptly injected, and what little remained he had stuffed into his fridge a few moments ago. A part of him knew that he should be frightened, or at the very least concerned. He had heard stories of men who had crossed Sabra, men who—

Walter felt a twinge in his shoulder as if someone had prodded his flesh with a cattle gun. The sensation fired all the way up to his throat, causing the cords in his neck to stand out.

He gritted his teeth and fought the urge to cry out.

Something told him that he needed to get high again soon, only this time it wouldn't only be for him, but for the cracker as well. As much as he wanted it out of him, he was fairly certain that having it curl up into a translucent shell like the rest of them on Main Street was likely a worse proposition.

Walter blinked, trying to keep his head relatively clear. The man before him, mistaking his expression as one of fear, smirked.

"What's a matter? You think—"

Walter didn't let him finish. Instead, he lunged forward, tilting onto the chair's front two legs, and drove his forehead into the bridge of the unsuspecting man's nose.

Blood immediately gushed forth from the gash on the bridge of the man's nose and from both of Walter's nostrils at the same time. Hot liquid sprayed Walter's face, and he rocked backward, teetering before his chair finally settled.

The man made an *ungh* sound and instinctively brought a hand to his face, trying to stem the bleeding. "You motherfucker!" he yelled, his voice coming out thick and nasally.

Now it was Walter's turn to smile.

There was a commotion behind Walter as the other man, the shorter one with the dark hair, stopped rooting through Walter's things and started to come over toward them, but the man with the blood seeping out from between his knuckles and dripping onto his chin held out the hand with the gun. Walter noticed that the barrel was longer than expected, and it took him a moment to realize that there was a silencer on the end of it.

"Stay the fuck over there, Sherk. Just keep looking," he instructed. Then he turned to Walter and stared directly into his eyes. "I'll take care of this bastard."

Somewhere behind him, Walter heard one of his cupboards being thrown wide, followed by the tinkling of glass. He couldn't turn to see what the man was doing, his tightly bound hands so restricted his range of motion, but he hoped to Christ that the man stayed the fuck out of the fridge.

I need to get high.

The bruises from being launched from the car following the explosion at the gas station, the cuts on his cheek and face, his stiff leg—all this pain was coming back now, and he needed something strong to mute these sensations.

When he turned back to the blond man with the bleeding nose, Walter was surprised to see that he was once again smiling.

"So"—his voice sounded strange and muffled what with his hand still trying to stem the bleeding—"you're a tough guy now, Walter?"

He laughed and then pulled his hand away and spat blood onto the carpet.

"Good, good—tough guys are always the most fun."

When the man leaned in this time, he made sure to keep enough distance between them that Walter couldn't reach him.

His smile vanished and a coldness returned to his eyes.

"This is how it's going to work, Walter—I'm going to get that money for Sabra. I'm going to get whatever product you have left as well, and I'm going to give it to him on your behalf."

He leaned away, his leather jacket crinkling loudly.

"I'm going to give Sabra both the money and the product as a token of your"—he waved the barrel of the gun in a small circle—"appreciation."

Walter said nothing and the man shrugged.

"That's okay, you don't need to say anything. I am just telling you what is going to happen. Now—"

There was a tapping sound from behind Walter, drawing the blond-haired goon's attention. His eyes floated above Walter and landed on something behind him.

"I see you have a son," he said with a smile, his gaze returning to Walter.

Walter's expression remained flat.

"Ah yes, I can see it in your eyes… you love your son, don't you, Walter? Who would have thought that a fucked-up junkie could love another person, much less a son? And a woman? How did you get a woman to fuck you?"

The man raised an eyebrow.

"You rape a bitch, Walter?" His voice was a mocking whisper. "Yeah, I bet you raped some bitch."

Again, Walter resisted the urge to reply.

"And I see that he got your looks, Walter. How unfortunate. So now"—he waved the gun in a circle again—"we have added another element to this equation."

Walter finally understood; the man with the short black hair and the scar across his throat, the one who didn't speak, the one called Sherk, had found the picture of Tyler on top of his TV.

Took them long enough. Geniuses, these men ain't.

"We know about your son, so maybe you can simply tell us where the product is? The money? Unless, of course, we have to search for your son *and* the gear, Walter..."

Walter couldn't hold it any longer. His cheeks puffed and he suddenly burst out laughing. He laughed so hard that tears started streaming down his cheeks. At some point during his outbreak, he realized that the man in front of him was saying something, but he couldn't make out any of the words—he was laughing too hard.

The man eventually gave up and leaned back in his chair and waited for Walter's fit to finish. For a hired gun, a debt collector, he certainly had more patience than Walter had expected. Walter didn't know if that was a good thing or a bad thing.

"You fucking moron," Walter finally managed, still chuckling slightly. He blinked hard, clearing the tears from his vision. "You find my son, and *then* I'll be able to give you the money."

A confused expression crossed the blond man's face.

"You find my boy, and I'll find the money to pay you," Walter repeated, still fighting back laughter.

The confusion on the man's face contorted and into a mask of anger.

And there it was: the anger.

Walter knew that the man wouldn't be able to keep his cool for much longer. Patient or not, he was still a hired gun with a job to do, and he would only put up with so much shit before he acted out.

End it, Walter willed sourly. *End this shit.*

As if reading his thoughts, the man reached behind his back and withdrew a pillow from the chair. In one fluid motion, he placed the pillow on top of Walter's thigh, then brought the gun around and placed the barrel roughly six inches above his knee.

Walter gritted his teeth.

Without so much as a word, the hitman with the military-style haircut smirked and then pulled the trigger.

8.

THE SHOT WAS NEARLY deafening in the small apartment, even with the silencer on the end of the gun and with the pillow as an additional measure to keep the noise down.

The pain, on the other hand, wasn't all that bad.

Walter felt a burning sensation as if a lit cigar were being extinguished in his thigh, followed by a dull throb that seemed to flush through the entire muscle.

He had been through a lot in his forty-some-odd years, including being stabbed in the ribs, the result of another drug-fueled spat that had nearly killed him, and he, in turn, had dealt his own damage, including whipping his son until the boy's back was raw and peeling.

But he had never shot anyone, nor he had ever been shot.

Never too old for new experiences.

He opened his eyes and stared at his assailant, his breaths coming in abbreviated puffs.

"You—" Walter began through gritted teeth.

You piece of shit, was what he had wanted to say, but something happened before he could finish the sentence.

There was a tightness in his chest, and it was suddenly difficult to draw a breath. At first, Walter thought that he was having a heart attack, that all of the years of abusing his rail-thin body were finally coming back to haunt him—that the devil had come to take his one hundred and forty-five pounds of flesh.

But after only a few seconds, he realized that the pain wasn't *coming* from his chest, at least not directly; the pain was originating from his shoulder.

To Walter, it felt as if metal bands had been wrapped over and around his shoulder muscles, and with every breath, these bands were being tightened. This squeezing and constriction radiated in thick ribbons across his narrow chest.

A heart attack… it is *a heart attack.*

A scream bubbled to his lips as the pain intensified, and he dropped his chin to his chest. With his lower lip curling in horror, Walter took in his own body. Through the open flannel shirt, he could see his pectorals—no more than thin membranes of muscle—clenching so tightly that veins he didn't even know existed had pushed their way to the surface and jutted out.

He screamed again as the pain was ratcheted up another notch; it felt as if his arm were being torn completely from the socket. And as this pain radiated through him, he turned his head skyward, shut his eyes against the pain, and clenched his entire body, trying to fend off the agony that enveloped his torso.

"Not so tough now, Walter?" the blond man spat through a sneer.

Walter opened his eyes and looked at the man.

The man's words seemed appropriate, seemed right for a hitman such as this, but his eyes were just a little off, the inner corners lifting ever so slightly. Clearly, Walter's visceral reaction to being shot, although desired, was overwrought.

He squeezed his eyes closed again as another wave of agony overcame him. Spit dripped from his lower lip and fell to his reddening chest.

What is happening to me? his mind screamed.

The pain in his shoulder and chest was so intense that the gunshot wound to his upper thigh was but a mere afterthought. And even that was offering it more credit than it probably deserved; it may have occupied a part of his mind, but it was a very small part, an ant inside the whale of his shoulder pain.

Something cold tapped just below his chin. If it weren't for the fact that his teeth were so clenched that the cords on his neck jutted out, the tapping might have caused his teeth to click together. As it was, the only reason he noticed it was that it was cool—and he was burning up.

He lowered his head, but kept his eyes firmly closed.

What the fuck is happening to me?!

It couldn't be a heart attack—after all, a heart attack couldn't hurt this badly, could it?

The tightness was spreading, radiating from his right shoulder across his chest and back, eventually making it to his other arm. Both arms were nearly completely numb now.

"Walter?"

Another wave of pain bubbled and frothed inside him, and he squeezed his eyes so hard that he saw stars. He opened his mouth just wide enough to slide his tongue between his teeth. He had meant to just put his tongue there, for something to bite down on, to focus his pain, but he was overzealous, and a small piece of flesh dislodged from the tip. His mouth immediately filled with the coppery taste of blood.

But this didn't matter.

What mattered was the pain.

And when it came again, it was unbearable.

A scream wouldn't cut it this time; instead, Walter's jaw went slack and a moan veritably fell out of his mouth, a horrible, undulating sound as his head rolled uncontrollably on his neck as if his muscles had suddenly turned to jelly.

"Walter?" the man asked again, far away this time, his voice sounding as if whispered in a tunnel.

Somewhere hidden in the deep recesses of his consciousness, Walter understood that the hitman had pulled the pillow from his leg and was now examining his thigh, prodding the torn flesh with the barrel of his gun.

"Sherk! Get the fuck over here," he hollered to his partner. "I think he's having a heart attack or something... this shouldn't kill him. We can't let him die, Sherk! Sabra wants him alive!"

A shadow passed over Walter's face as the man stood and blocked the light from a bare bulb overhead, a sensation that barely registered with his eyes so tightly closed.

"Come take a look at his leg!" the man sounded anxious now.

Clearly, no matter how tough this hitman was, he was obviously terrified of what Sabra might do to him if Walter died.

This shouldn't kill him...

Walter dead meant no product *and* no money. Walter dead meant Sabra had no more need for a blond, square-headed collector of all things human and illicit.

And this said nothing of his sidekick with the dark hair and thick pink scar across his throat.

Eventually, Walter's pain subsided, blending into the background like an oppressive, yet palatable darkness. Even though he was terrified at the prospect of its inevitable return, for some reason a moment of clarity washed over him.

He knew what was causing the pain, and it most definitely wasn't the gunshot wound in his thigh.

"Look," he heard the blond man say.

Walter felt something prodding his thigh, a sensation that registered only as a non-specific pressure. It should have hurt—the man digging about in his bullet wound should have more than hurt; it should have been excruciating.

But this wasn't.

"See? This shouldn't kill him… right? It's a fucking leg wound."

There was a pause, and even with his eyes closed, he knew that the other man was also inspecting his leg.

"See? Fuck! *Fuck!* What do we do? Lie him down, try to stop the bleeding? *Fuck!* Wake the fuck up, Walter!"

Walter's breath was coming out in short bursts from between clenched teeth. The pain, like high tide, was building, on the verge of returning; he could feel his shoulder muscles tightening, their fatigued fibers twitching from their previous session.

"No," he managed at last, eyes still closed. "Not my leg."

He tried to take a few deeper breaths, but his body was so tense that his diaphragm seemed to have lost its ability to relax.

"What?" the man with the blond hair asked.

"My shoulder," Walter whispered. "It's my shoulder."

The air around Walter got hot and smelled of stale bread again as the man with the broken nose leaned in close. Any recollection of doing this but a few minutes ago, of getting his nose smashed by Walter's forehead, had clearly been forgotten.

"What?"

"My shoulder," Walter repeated.

Then the pain exploded again and he screamed.

Moments before he was once again forced into the dark recesses of his mind, Walter felt hands grab either side of his flannel shirt and tear it away.

The sound of ripping fabric was followed by a sharp intake of breath.

"Oh my god—oh my god!"

9.

WALTER'S SHOULDER PULSATED, AND then the skin started to stretch. Although he couldn't place exactly where this stretching sensation originated, it seemed to be somewhere on his left side, and not the right where the cracker was buried. It felt like there was something buried beneath his skin, something hell-bent on trying to force his insides out.

"Oh my god." He heard the words again, but this time he wasn't sure if he was saying them, or if they had come from the blond goon that had slumped back into the chair, eyes wide in horror.

Whimpering, Walter could no longer resist the urge to look down at his sweat-soaked chest, even though every fiber of his being was telling-him to keep his eyes closed, to wait for this moment to pass, to wait for whatever was going to happen to occur in blissful ignorance.

To die in relative peace.

But he couldn't resist; he just *had* to see.

Nearly immediately, he wished he hadn't looked.

With his arms still bound by the telephone cable behind his back, the cracker on his right shoulder was even more prominent, the thing's thick legs jutting up a few inches from the rest of his skin, the razor-like teeth in its mouth oscillating with increased fervor.

But this wasn't what made his breath catch. That honor was bestowed upon the half dozen or so thick red striations — stretch-marks, maybe, or blood vessels — splaying from the outline of the cracker shell and traveling across his chest, making it to his sternum before receding somewhere deep inside.

These vessels—if indeed that was what they were—were thick, like horrible varicose veins, twisting and turning in tight loops as they meandered their way across and protruded from his pasty white chest.

But despite these obvious marks, it was clear to him that they were not the source of his pain. No, it was now his *other* shoulder that was causing white-hot daggers to shoot throughout his entire left side.

Walter slowly turned his neck to that side and glanced at his shoulder.

There was another cracker embedded there, a smaller one, not quite half of the size of the one that had crawled up his hand on Main Street before latching on to his shoulder.

Where did that come from? he wondered absently. His entire world had started to quake, and he was suddenly overcome by a bout of dizziness.

He tried his best to keep his eyes on this new cracker as it became more prominent and then started to push against his skin from the inside, puckering, stretching, *probing* like a chick trying to hatch.

"Ungggh," Walter moaned as he lost complete control of his body. His head rolled back, and his eyes followed suit.

The cracker suddenly extended its six legs, tearing small fissures in Walter's shoulder. When it pushed against his skin once more, it budded and then tore through Walter's skin, sending his body into another tremor.

"Oh god," he whimpered, his body thrashing against the chair, its four legs tapping repeatedly against the ground with an almost rhythmic quality.

This time when Walter shuddered, it wasn't in pain; rather, it was sheer, unaltered relief, as the pressure from his stretching skin had finally released.

Walter felt his consciousness begin to fade, but he forced the gray away and regained focus, knowing that it wouldn't be long before he passed out.

The man with the blond hair stared at Walter, his square features frozen in horror as the bloody cracker trailing tendrils of pink skin climbed clumsily down Walter's arm.

"What is this?" the man cried, leaning back in his chair. "You're fucking infected! With—with—with *parasites*!"

The man went to stand when the cracker made its way onto Walter's lap, its movements becoming more coordinated, its limbs articulating in a more rhythmic sequence.

Lip curling, the man tilted his head and craned his neck, trying to get a better look at the pale creature that perched on Walter's lap.

"What the fuck is that?" the man whispered. He raised his gun, intent on prodding the creature that hissed rhythmically, the tiny holes on its back fluttering.

"Sherk? I think you should—"

The cracker suddenly flung itself at the man, landing against his leather coat.

"Fuck!" he yelled as he swatted it to the parquet floor with the back of his hand. He jumped to his feet, toppling the chair behind him in the process.

The cracker landed on its back, but then quickly flipped over. As Walter watched, the cracker closed the distance between it and the hitman in seconds, moving so quickly that it was already up the man's pant leg before he could react.

"Fuck!" he yelled. "Sherk! Sherk! Get the fuck over here!"

The man began shaking his leg furiously, trying to rid himself of the creature. When it quickly became clear that the cracker would not be swatted away like a pesky spider, he switched to trying to smash it through his pants, first with his thick fist, then with the butt of his gun.

But despite his best efforts, the thing kept on moving upward—Walter could see the disc-like outline at the man's calf, nearing his knee.

The hitman abandoned attempts to crush the thing and instead turned his attention to undoing his belt while he hopped up and down like a lunatic.

"What the fuck is this? Walter, what the *fuck* is this?"

A small smile spread across Walter's thin lips. As the pain in his shoulder—both shoulders, now—strangely began to subside, he was reminded of the numbness in his leg, of the fact that the half-undressed man with the square head and equally square body before him had shot him.

Serves you fucking right.

He had no idea what the cracker was going to do, if anything, but he hoped that at the very least it would clamp down on the man's balls.

Only now did Walter risk a glance at the arm from which the new cracker had budded.

There were thick lines of blood on his elbow and the part of his forearm that he could see before it receded behind him, still bound with the telephone cable. And there was blood on his shoulder, too, but what there wasn't was a tattered hole in his flesh from where the small, almost translucent cracker had burst forth.

There was only a patch of pale white skin, a milky membrane that looked even more sickly than Walter's normal pallor—as if the skin that the cracker had budded from had already healed over.

What the hell?

Before he could contemplate this any further, the man with the short blond hair screamed, drawing Walter's attention back.

The man's pants had gotten stuck around mid-thigh. Walter could see the cracker—which was translucent bordering on transparent, and much smaller than the crackers he had encountered on Highway 2 outside of the burning shithole that was Askergan—suddenly clamp down on the man's quad.

The man threw his head back and howled.

Sherk finally came into view, running in front of Walter's now teetering chair, a black leather bag clutched in one hand, a pistol in the other.

No!

During all of the commotion, the man must have found Walter's drug case in his fridge—which is presumably why he didn't come to his colleague's aid right away.

No! Put it back, you fucking cunt!

The blond-haired man was grabbing at the cracker on his quad with both heads, trying desperately to pry it off. Cords stood out from his neck, and the man's face was starting to turn a beet red.

The second hitman, the man named Sherk, dropped to one knee in front of his partner. To Walter's delight, he tossed the black case to one side and then he too tried to pull the cracker off.

From behind, it looked like the shorter, dark-haired man was going to town on the bigger man, sucking his dick, and

Walter imagined for a moment that the man's agonizing cries were actually born of ecstasy.

The bizarre scene almost drove him to laughter.

Then, as if the man had climaxed, he toppled, another howl filling the small, decrepit apartment. For a brief moment, Walter wondered if someone might come running in to help or if someone would call the police.

But he doubted it.

Not in this place.

Walter suddenly felt the tightening sensation again, only this time it was coming from slightly higher than where the other cracker had ruptured from, near the thin skin between his neck and shoulder.

The pain came next, the excruciating sensation of something forcing itself out of his skin. As before, his eyes rolled back, but he bit the inside of his cheek as hard as he could, tasting more blood. It would do no good to pass out now.

Besides, he wanted—he *needed*—to see this.

Sherk had managed to remove the blond-haired man's leather jacket and had pulled his pants all the way down now. But the cracker had already torn a hole in the man's leg and had embedded itself beneath his skin; a small, apple-sized outline like a second kneecap. The man, flat on his back now, was shrieking in pain, his meaty hands grabbing at the shape, and all the while Sherk kept pushing his hands away. The man reached into the back of his pants and pulled out a thick black handle. As he moved the handle in front of him, he flicked a switch and a gleaming six-inch blade popped out.

The pain on Walter's shoulder got so intense that he had no choice but to close his eyes. The new cracker embedded beneath his skin would bud at any moment now, and Walter knew that when it did, it would offer him relief… sweet, sweet relief.

As the pain reached a climax, Walter forced his tearing eyes back open for one final glance.

Sherk was still poised to drive the blade into the man's leg, but as he reared back, the blond man stopped grabbing at his thigh and instead began clutching at his chest.

"Get it out!" the man roared in a guttural tone. "Get it out!" he yelled again, only this time the words were garbled and difficult to make out.

Froth began to build at the corners of the man's mouth, and his eyes suddenly rolled back as he fell into a seizure. The contrast in reactions, from the frantic, yet purposeful pulling at his quad to his sudden lack of control of his limbs and neck, was so polarized that Sherk froze, the knife held in midair.

Another few seconds of staring and Walter realized that not only was the man's entire body shaking, but that his skin was also quaking—roiling, as it were. All of his exposed flesh, his arms, legs, face, and now exposed belly, was undulating like a rippling pond.

Sherk lowered the blade and scrambled from his knees back onto one foot, and when the massive, muscular blond man suddenly stopped shaking and his back arched as if being gripped by tetanus, he quickly stood and took a step backward.

Without so much as a gasp, the blond man's chest suddenly exploded, the skin tearing first, followed by his cotton t-shirt in at least a dozen spots at once. From the gaping wound rushed at least a hundred of the plum-sized, nearly transparent crackers.

Walter could see directly into the man's chest; his ribcage had been torn wide like a mortician's cornucopia. There was less blood than he would have thought, just enough to pool inside the cavity, the red line slowly rising until it covered his pink lungs. The crackers climbed off the corpse, but stopped moving once their pointed legs touched the bloodstained parquet. They were silent, poised, attentive—it was as if they were awaiting further instruction.

Walter turned back to the blond hitman. He could clearly make out the man's heart inside his open chest. As he watched, the slimy red organ took one beat, then another, then began twitching madly.

A second later, it stopped completely.

Walter had never witnessed a man die before, and he thought it would have affected him more.

It didn't.

Serves you fucking right.

Sherk took three quick steps backward, and on the fourth, he bumped into Walter's leg. The stocky man whipped around, crouching into a poised position as he did, making Walter think that the man still held a gun in his hand.

But it wasn't in his hand; the gun was on the floor beside the black leather drug case. Instead, he was holding the knife.

It looked pathetic, like a tiny child's knife clutched between chubby fingers—if the gun hadn't killed him, then what harm could a puny knife do?

Besides, what *he* had was so much more… *powerful.*

Walter smiled, blood from the wound on his tongue and the inside of his cheek throbbing, blood that stained his teeth a dark red, a subtle contrast from their usual brown.

A quick glance revealed that the translucent cracker that had emerged from his shoulder remained perched there.

And then it cracked once, instantly drawing Sherk's horrified gaze.

"Go," Walter instructed, his smile widening. "Go get this fucker."

The man tried to scream, but his voice box had been ripped from him years ago.

In less than a minute, his skin would be torn from him as well.

10.

"AND THE SCHOOL? HOW'S the school? All cleaned up?" the sheriff asked, trying to keep his tone direct but at the same time sympathetic.

Deputy Andrew Williams nodded slowly.

"Passable," he said. "We tried—"

"The bodies? What about the bodies?"

Williams swallowed hard and began toying with the pen on his desk. Like the sheriff, of the many things that had affected them after the crackers had infested the town, the footage that they had seen on Nancy's cameraman's viewfinder showing what had happened at Wellwood Elementary School had been one of the most disturbing.

And sad—definitely one of the saddest.

"Yeah, we moved them to the morgue, as you instructed. Only needed one bus, though, they were just—just—"

The sheriff laid his hand on the deputy's wrist, stopping him from twirling the pencil. The man immediately looked up at him with his small, dark eyes.

"—their bodies were just so small," he finished.

The way he said small—whispered the word—nearly brought tears to the sheriff's eyes. As he fought them back, he tried to think of something else, something less depressing than the thought of an entire school of children being decimated by an infestation of some sort of alien parasite.

Only this was impossible; the only things that rattled around in his skull were thoughts of the attack. Eventually, his mind turned to Mrs. Drew, and how she had sacrificed herself so that they might try to get to the source of the problem.

Sacrificed.

Such a terrible word, conjuring images of ancient altars covered in dripping blood from the *sacrificed.*

But without her, Paul doubted that he or Williams would have been here today.

He wiped his eyes.

Fuck.

"Thank you," he said, trying hard to sound strong. He lost the battle, and his voice wavered with the final syllable.

For a second, another emotion surfaced, one that surprised his tears away.

Anger.

Anger directed at Sheriff Dana Drew, anger for leaving him, for leaving all of them, when they needed him most — when they needed his radar, his ability to pick out the good boys from the bad. For his unique way of always seeming in control, keep everyone cool, knowing how to settle the masses, knowing what the fuck to do next.

And he was furious at Coggins, too, for being so selfish. For leaving.

Sheriff Drew would have stayed; no matter what he lost, if he were alive today, he would be here, standing beside me.

But Coggins wasn't the sheriff — he knew that now. Coggins had left him alone again, and Dana Drew would have never done that.

For a brief second, Paul was back in the room again, the hot, stinking room of his nightmares, the weight pushing down on him, the fire burning just outside the door. Like always, he was unable to push it open and to see; to see what had really happened inside the Wharfburn Estate, the event that had precipitated this all those years ago. The imagery was so powerful that it was like a memory rather than a dream.

And yet he had never been inside the Estate...

It was like someone *else's* memory. Or a story... had Coggins told him that much about what happened in the Estate all those years ago?

Coggins had been tight-lipped about the whole ordeal, but maybe... maybe back at the biker bar he had said something?

Paul couldn't be sure, but he thought he must have. Because if it was only a dream, then it was stronger and more *real* than any he had had before.

He shook his head and breathed deeply in through his nose.

Keep it together, Askergan needs you.

"Thank you, Andrew," he said. "What about the crackers, how's the cleanup going?"

Deputy Williams's eyes remained downcast.

"Surprisingly well. The gas station fire is out, and the majority of the crackers on Main Street have been destroyed—incinerated, as you asked. The rest, well, the rest will take time—there are just *so* many."

The sheriff nodded, and he let go of Deputy Williams's arm. He immediately started twirling his pen again.

"They all dead?"

The deputy hesitated before answering.

"As far as I can tell." The man swallowed hard before continuing. "Are we gonna get any help here, Paul? I mean, there are just so many dead..."

Sheriff White knew that he should say something motivating, even if his words were a lie about how they weren't on an island, that the choppers would soon fly in and bring with them the help that Askergan needed.

But he couldn't lie; it just wasn't him.

"I tried, Andrew. I called and I called, and I tried. FBI, CIA, fucking even neighboring counties. Best I could get was a damn pathologist, someone to come look at the—" He swallowed hard. "—the bodies. Try to figure out what the hell those cracker things are."

He sighed and looked away from his friend's dark brown eyes. "We're alone, Andrew. Askergan is going to have to get through this alone."

Like in his dreams, there was a weight on him, one that prevented him from taking a full breath, only now it wasn't someone from his past on top of him.

This time it was the entire weight of Askergan bearing down.

"I tried," he said quietly. "And that's all *we* can do."

The deputy nodded slowly.

"So what do we do now, then?"

What would Sheriff Drew do?

Paul chewed his lip.

WWSDD.

Sheriff Dana Drew would calm the masses, inspire confidence in them, keep things from getting out of control during this chaotic time.

At the very least, the man would try.

"Call Nancy. Let's get a news conference set up. Askergan needs us now."

Sheriff Paul White chewed his lip again.

Askergan needed *something*, of that he was certain.

He just wasn't confident that *he* was what they needed.

11.

THE APARTMENT HAD BEEN foul-smelling to begin with, but now it was unbearable.

It was the crackers, the tiny transparent ones that had promptly curled up and died mere seconds after tearing out of the chests of the two square-headed hitmen.

And it was the blood.

Together, the blood and dead crackers stunk of rotting meat tinged with metallic undertones.

The two crackers that had budded from him were gone; after burrowing into the two men and causing the rush of new crackers to be birthed, they had apparently remained inside their corpses, presumably dead as well.

Walter felt sick to his stomach. He had seen two men torn apart from the inside, and a horde of tiny white crab-like creatures spew forth and then die before all of them had even cleared their victims' body cavities.

He had no idea why those crackers had died—indeed, why any and all of the crackers on Main Street and Highway 2 had died—yet the one embedded in his shoulder continued to live. And that said nothing of the fact that the one in his skin had managed to raise another cracker—no, two more crackers—to attack the hitmen, and then those had started to proliferate…

His stomach lurched.

Why did they attack the hitmen? Why did they cause the small crackers to bubble forth and die? Why couldn't they survive for any significant time away from their host… from him?

The drugs, maybe? Was that altering their behavior?

Just thinking about all of this made Walter dizzy and he gagged, his focus shifting from trying to understand what sort of parasite was leeching his drugs from him to fighting back the bile that filled his mouth. As he pressed his chin to his chest to try to suppress the urge to vomit, he finally got a good look at his own body. The blood vessels or stretch marks or whatever the fuck they were that spread from the cracker still embedded in his right shoulder had now acquired a dark purple tinge. And their varicose paths seemed to extend now; they passed all the way over his chest and onto the other side, circling his left nipple.

He wanted to touch his skin, to feel it, but his hands were still strapped behind his back, tied to the chair.

And he still couldn't move.

The smell.

The blood.

The bodies.

The carnage.

And still, despite all this, his searching eyes didn't first look for a way to free himself, but to find the black leather case.

The drugs; maybe the drugs are keeping the thing in my shoulder alive when all others seem to just die.

Walter grimaced.

The drugs; maybe the drugs are what is keeping me *alive.*

It didn't matter; it was all rhetoric.

He needed his drugs either way, and he would soon have them.

Walter's first intuition was to stand, to run backward as best he could and drive the chair against the wall, hopefully splintering the thin wood.

But Walter had been shot in the leg.

A laugh burst from him.

"Shot," he said to the empty room. "I forgot I was shot."

But when he looked down, he was surprised that his blood had stopped flowing from the wound, and that he could no longer quite make out the ragged hole in his skin.

His mind flashed to the white patches of skin on his shoulder, the area from which the strange, translucent crackers had sprung forth.

Did it… heal me somehow?

He shook his head.

That was absurd—but this was all insane, wasn't it?

"I have to get the fuck out of here," he said out loud.

His wandering gaze eventually landed on Sherk's six-inch knife lying in a pile of congealing blood. And at long last, Walter mobilized.

That will do.

With a grunt, he managed to prop himself onto his toes, wincing at the dull sensation in his quad. Gritting his teeth, he stumbled forward, barely able to avoid falling into the two men's still warm corpses that lay beside each other like bizarre lovers. Walter shifted his weight onto his good leg and then pivoted toward the knife. This time when he felt the chair teetering, he went with the fall, twisting onto his back as he did.

The chair toppled, and Walter went down with it.

The fall didn't hurt as much as it should have, especially considering the loud rap the back of his head made when it went bouncing off the parquet. He saw stars for a brief moment, but his body had been so racked with pain—first with the gunshot wound, then with the stretching and tearing of his skin when it birthed the crackers—that bonking his skull barely registered.

His head still swimming, he turned so that he was partially on his side, and then tried to stretch his hands and fingers as far as the telephone cable would allow.

They came up short.

"Fuck," he swore, reaching again, his outstretched fingers desperately trying to grab the knife that was just a few inches from his grasp.

Again his hand grabbed air.

He grunted and closed his eyes, slowly turning his strained neck back to a neutral position. Three ragged breaths later, with spit and blood now beading on his long gray beard, he turned it in the opposite direction. Then he opened his eyes and found himself staring directly into a miniature harbinger of death.

A small, transparent cracker lay on its back only a few inches from his face. It looked hard, like a dried clamshell, the six small legs pointing toward the ceiling as if in prayer. Staring at the center of its mass, Walter could make out the small opening and the hard white teeth inside, but he didn't see much else. The shell was almost completely transparent, and although he could see right through it, it didn't appear to have any organs, much less a brain. It had a network of vessels—some blue, most red—seeming to branch from the thing's mouth, but that was pretty much it.

Walter instinctively glanced at his shoulder with the hard shell of the cracker still buried beneath and instantly recognized the similarities between the dark purple lines that radiated from the embedded cracker and now traveled completely across his narrow chest, and the ones inside the upturned crab inches from his face.

His head started to throb, so he shut his eyes again. Keeping them tightly closed, he stretched out once more with his fingers, and this time he felt something wet on his palms as the telephone cable cut deep into his wrists. When his fingertips brushed against something hard, his eyes snapped open.

Ignoring the blood now dripping down his forearms, he stretched even farther, grunting with the effort. This time, his right hand wrapped completely around the handle of the blade.

He grinned, exposing his crooked, bloodstained teeth.

The next part was easy, for as awkward as it was to turn the knife inward toward his wrists, the blade was so sharp that it easily sliced through the cable.

Walter sighed as the pressure in his wrists and forearms instantly relented. Still, the first thing he did after his hands were freed wasn't to rub his wrists, but instead, he brought his right hand up to the strange white skin on his shoulder. His fingers palpated the spot, curious at first, as if he were touching some foreign substance instead of a piece of himself.

The newly formed skin was oddly soft and cool to the touch. And smooth—it was impossibly smooth. And while he could feel the texture on his fingertips, the skin itself didn't seem to register his touch.

A shudder ran through him, and he pulled his hand away.

Intent on ignoring the patches of white skin on both his shoulders, let alone the cracker embedded in his skin and the thick network of veins that spider-webbed across his chest, Walter slowly eased himself into a standing position, keeping the leg that had been shot out in front of him protectively. Although slightly numb, he found that he could bend his knee with only mild stiffness.

How is this possible? This can't be what it feels like to be shot... can it?

He debated probing this wound as well, but the uncomfortable lack of feeling in the new skin on his shoulder lingered, and he decided against it.

Besides, there was a more pressing matter at hand.

When Walter reached down to pick up his case of drugs — *good Lord, how long has it been since I got high?* —he felt a strange taste in his mouth. Or, more appropriately, he felt *less* strangeness in his mouth.

In fact, it almost felt normal.

He clucked his tongue, and this felt normal, too. Sure, his tongue felt a little numb, but when he reached up to grab it between two grimy fingers, it was all there; the tip that he had bitten off seemed to have been regrown.

A small smile crossed his lips.

Healed. The thing is healing me somehow.

His hand, now wet with saliva and blood, went to his cheek next. The pockmarks from the glass that had been embedded there after being thrown from his car after the explosion at the gas station were gone—smoothed over. In fact, he realized as he further probed his face, several of the lesions that had seemed ubiquitous following his foray into intravenous drug use were gone too.

His skin seemed soft and smooth; it felt so completely normal that he was taken aback. It was *all* normal, except for the patches of white skin that had healed over after the crackers had been born.

A strange expression crossed his face.

With the hand not gripping the leather case, Walter undid his pants and slid a hand down his leg. He could still feel dried blood around mid-thigh, but the hole he'd expected to find simply wasn't there.

"What the fuck?"

He could feel a protrusion, something hard deep beneath his skin, but there was no ragged bullet hole. Although the healed wound prevented him from digging deep enough to actually feel it, he knew what this hard object was: the bullet.

It was the pain; it had to have been the pain. Whatever had happened when he had been shot and then bitten off a piece of his tongue had fucked with his brain.

Or maybe he had imagined this, all of it—maybe he was still lying in the back of the stolen car, a needle hanging out of his arm, and this was all just a nasty trip.

It was also possible that he had suffered a severe head injury when he had been thrown from the car after the gas station exploded, and that he was in some sort of dream-like coma.

Or maybe he was dead already.

Walter squeezed the fake leather case in his hand.

"Well, only one way to find out."

The cracker buried in the skin on his right shoulder twitched.

12.

IT WAS NEARLY DARK outside, yet Walter Wandry hadn't moved in many hours. He was sitting on the couch, staring at the TV without actually watching it. The black leather case was spread out in front of him on the rotting coffee table, several used syringes resting beside it. The small plastic baggie was open, and it was empty. His lighter, a cheap yellow BIC, was also spent, and the spoon that he had used to boil the heroin was marked by a dry brown smudge.

He had injected all of his heroin, more than he usually consumed over an entire weekend, let alone one afternoon, and he still felt nothing.

His tongue darted from his mouth and skipped across chapped lips. He was thirsty again.

Well, maybe not exactly nothing; his shoulder, the one with the embedded cracker that he had since pulled the flannel shirt back over to cover the hideous sight of, and the network of purple vessels that marred his pale, inverted chest, had stopped hurting.

It was as if the cracker had been as hungry for drugs as he was, and now that he had obliged, the greedy fucker had taken it all from him, somehow redirecting the flow to *it* rather than to his brain.

Walter had first injected into his right arm, then his left, but it made no difference; the moment before the surge that he expected as the opioid hit his brainstem, the feeling passed. Just like that, it fucking passed, as if his tolerance was suddenly so high that it would take a truckload of the stuff to get the feeling he so relished.

But, paradoxically, at the same time, the rest of him felt pretty good; in fact, he felt more alive than he had for a long, long time. His thigh where he had been shot now felt as if nothing had happened, and his tongue and cheek—both inside and out—had completely healed over. In his elongated reflection in the television screen, he had several times poked his tongue out and had noticed that, like the skin on his shoulder and above his collarbone, it too was a strange milky white.

But this didn't matter.

Walter balled his hands into fists. The strength that flowed in him was so odd, so foreign, that he had a hard time comprehending what he was feeling.

He was going on at least an entire day now without getting high—from precisely the moment before he'd burst through the Askergan County police station until now, despite his best efforts.

This was his longest sober streak in more years than he could remember.

Walter felt his eyes drifting upward for some strange reason, drawn to the photograph of a much younger version of his son, the one that the two hitmen lying dead on the floor had proposed to use as leverage to get what they wanted.

But Tyler was no pawn.

Walter felt a slight quiver in his shoulder, and he pulled his flannel shirt away from his body to look at the cracker. It had shifted a little, a sensation that Walter was having a hard time getting used to. It reminded him of the time as a young boy when a small larva had burrowed into his ear when he was sleeping. It was almost a month before he had been able to convince his father that there was actually something in there, and a few more weeks before it had grown large enough for his father to grab it with a rusty set of needle-nose pliers. And during this time he had had to live with it inside his ear, it had become a part of him—something, as uncomfortable as the idea was, that he just had to endure. But while the sensations were similar, he was not naïve enough to think that the end result would be the same; needle-nose pliers wouldn't help him this time, and besides, his father was locked away for life.

Still, this realization offered him negligible solace; the small mouth with the oscillating teeth that was fused to the opening in his skin and the dark purple lines radiating outward from that spot was something that Walter knew he would never get used to.

He might have to live with it, but he would never get *used* to it.

Did something like this happen to you, Tyler? Is that why Griddle was called in? Something to do with Kent?

He had heard the police officers—especially the big black fucker, the sheriff—talking in hushed voices about Tyler's disappearance. But at the time he had just been trying to get out of there, to get back to his car and get high, and he hadn't really paid attention to their words. Besides, any comments that they'd made had been overshadowed by his desire to get paid—to get the insurance money before his fucking drunk of an ex-wife did.

But that was *before.*

Things were different now. One glance down at his body in the torn flannel shirt that he had stolen from one car or another indicated as much.

Walter clenched his fists, enjoying the way that his knuckles turned white.

So much strength; so much power.

At the time, insurance money had been all that he'd needed or wanted.

"Fuck," he swore, looking away from the picture of his son's face.

The scar on his son's cheek was a reminder of what he had become—of what he had done.

His shoulder twitched, which he now recognized as a pang similar to what every junkie felt, regardless of the source.

"Fuck," he swore again. "I need to get high."

But it would take more than his few ounces of heroin that he had already injected to take him to that place—if it was indeed possible to get *there* with the greedy cracker sucking up all of his pleasure.

Walter slowly rose to his feet, a surprisingly fluid act considering that he had been sitting for so long.

The first thing he did was pick up the knife. Then he reached down and grabbed the blond man's pistol and tucked it into the back of his pants, flipping the flannel shirt over.

He would need a truckload of drugs to get high.

And he knew exactly where to get it from.

"Okay, Sabra, you fat fuck. I'm coming for you," he said through gritted teeth. Then he reared back and kicked the man that had shot him. The man's body rocked with the impact, and several of the dead, white crackers on his chest fell to the floor, their limp bodies quivering until they became still again, their six multi-jointed legs aimed upward.

The blood that had pooled in the hitman's body cavity leaked out of one side in a thick stream.

"*We* are coming for you," he corrected. His eyes flashed over to the photograph of his son.

And then for you, Tyler—if you're still alive, I'll find you.

13.

WALTER NOTICED THE CASINO chip even in the darkness, the cheap yellow bulb in the heavily frosted light fixture outside the entrance of his apartment complex reflecting off of it like a beacon.

He picked it up and rolled it between thumb and forefinger, enjoying the way that the pads of his fingers moved across the slick surface.

"Maybe you are lucky after all," he grumbled.

The car that he had stolen earlier that day—or perhaps it was the day before; time had since melded together—was still parked where he had left it, perpendicular to the entrance, blocking the passage of at least a half-dozen other rust buckets in the lot.

There was a note on the windshield, and Walter leaned in close to read it.

Move your car, you fucking douchebag—parasites are taking over the world.

Walter smiled and left the note where it was.

It would be a long drive to Sabra's place, which was good, as it would offer him some time to figure out what the fuck he was going to do once he got there.

*   *   *

Walter parked the car a block and a half away from the long, winding drive leading up to Sabra's mansion. Located at the top of a small hill, the mansion was isolated, with all of the neighbors occupying houses below it separated by both a grass-covered embankment and a wrought-iron fence that surrounded the property.

Strategically located, no doubt, but knowing Sabra the way he did, Walter also assumed that it was part of his strategy to impose some sort of psychological superiority.

Probably also why the man is pushing three-fifty... bigger, badder, better.

His thoughts turned to the hitmen Sabra had sent to his place, who were now lying dead.

I bet they thought they were bigger and badder, too.

Before parking, Walter had quickly cruised by when he had first arrived, taking note of two guards, one sleeping in the booth out front, the other standing by the gate, the chest of his black blazer jutting out unnaturally from the gun that was buried inside.

From his previous visit, he knew that there was more protection in the form of bikers and ex-military that now served as security guards than he could see—many more men like the ones by the gate, hidden in and around the house, ready to come to the fat prick's aid should he mumble an order.

If there was one saving grace, it was the fact that at nearly three in the morning, the rest of the street was quiet.

Walter's shoulder twinged, prompting him to action. With a deep breath, he shut off the car and stepped out into the night.

*   *   *

It took less than five minutes.

Five minutes for Walter to abandon the car at the end of the street, to walk to the fence that lined the property, to peek through the bars of painted steel. It took only a few seconds more until he felt a gun barrel press up against the side of his head.

Unlike his earlier encounter with the hitmen, this probing with the gun wasn't violent, or even particularly aggressive. In fact, it was almost sensual the way it first brushed the lobe of his ear before nuzzling against the base of his skull.

"I knew we would be seeing you today," a voice said. "I just didn't think you would come alone."

Walter, hands still grasping the bars, didn't respond at first.

His plan—if his ill-formed idea of traipsing up to the bars and squeezing through, sneaking in through an open window like some sort of ninja, could be called a 'plan'—was ridiculous.

And it had taken five minutes for someone to spot him and predictably put a gun to his head.

Fuck.

What made his thought processes even more insane was the fact that he had been here less than two weeks ago, desperate, sweating, shaking, begging for some product. Which Sabra had eventually given him, after making him dance, of course—and not without explicitly stating the consequences should Walter not sell the product and repay what he owed. And during this time at the mansion, he had seen at least forty well-armed bikers in and around the place.

Fuck.

For some reason, his thoughts turned to the fake casino chip in his pocket—the one that had been hanging from the keyring of the abandoned car. So strange, having a fob like that in Askergan where he had stolen the car. After all, there was no casino for miles.

Not so lucky after all.

He felt the gun press into the back of his head.

"All right, I can see that you are in a bit of a zone, Walt. Why don't you slowly take your grubby paws off the fence and come with me? Don't make this a thing." The man cleared his throat. "Sabra's waiting."

Walter obliged without hesitation. He did, however, shrug his shoulders slightly, making sure that the flannel shirt with the torn buttons fell over and covered his shoulders.

The man with the gun looked very different than the two hitmen that had visited him at his apartment. While they had obviously been professionals, perhaps of Serbian or Eastern bloc descent, this man was clearly a biker. He had long gray hair tucked up into a ponytail, and a rather predictable handlebar mustache, the color of which matched his hair.

It was strange, Walter surmised, that the man's voice, so oddly polite given the circumstances, was in such contrast to that of the 'professionals'. Wearing a cutoff jean vest exposing wiry forearms adorned with multiple tattoos, this man was a biker through and through.

And left-handed, Walter noted. But as his gaze went to the man's other hand, he realized why the man was holding the gun in his left hand.

The first three fingers of his right hand ended just shy of the first knuckle.

"You got a little blood there on your forehead," the man informed him. He took a step backward and Walter hopped off the ledge.

Walter said nothing, but a grin started to form on his pale face.

Why do I need a plan? he thought, again remembering the two dead men back in his apartment. *Even if there are forty men here, my little cracker friend will take care of them.*

Maybe.

The man wagged the gun, indicating that Walter should turn and walk ahead of him, down the flagstones that led to the entrance of the palatial estate.

"Did Sherk or Barney rough you up a bit?"

Barney. The guy with the square head and blond hair was named fucking Barney *of all things—like a big purple dinosaur.*

It was a ridiculous name for a hitman or debt collector.

The image of the man lying on his back, his face frozen mid-scream, his chest blown open, his heart twitching then stopping, came to mind.

A big, fucking dead *dinosaur.*

"Where are they, anyway?"

Walter shuffled forward on the dimly lit walk, fighting the sudden urge to answer, to yell at this biker that both Sherk and Barney were fucking dead, and that Sabra and he were about to meet the same fate shortly.

Instead, he said nothing.

"You know, Walter, I think you better start answering questions—or at least get used to the idea of answering them. 'Cuz Sabra has a way of making people talk."

The man hesitated.

"Turn right here," he instructed, and Walter obliged.

He was suddenly awash in bright lights that marked the top of huge metal gates with ornate, rounded tops. He tried to get an idea of how high they reached into the night sky — twelve? Fifteen feet high?—but the light was so bright, and in such stark contrast to the dark surrounding sky, that it was impossible to tell. Off to one side was a plain square structure that was an eyesore compared to the wrought-iron gates. Walter peeked inside and noticed another biker in there, but he was slumped back in his chair, arms crossed over his burly chest, and was dead asleep.

"Keep moving," the man behind him instructed, but this time Walter hesitated.

Go where? Through the gates?

For a moment he thought that maybe the man behind him had the same plan that he had formulated on his drive from Askergan: to slide *through* the gates.

But that was ridiculous.

The gun prodded his skull again, and Walter had no choice but to take a small step forward. As he did, like the doors of heaven, the tall wrought-iron gates opened. Just looking at their massive size, Walter thought that they might have creaked and groaned when opened, but that wasn't the case. They slid silently through the night.

Expecting me, are you?

A quick glance around, first at the sleeping guard, then at the corners of the building, revealed several video cameras aimed in his general direction.

Yeah, Walter. Just sneak right on through the gates of Fort Knox.

The driveway on the other side of the gate was much better lit compared to outside. The pavement expanded from a simple single lane to a large, flat parking lot. There were at least a dozen bikes parked on the lot; their chrome reflected the lights like stars.

And there were four bikers all hanging out with them, their eyes trained on Walter.

None of them were smiling.

"What'd you find there, Dirk? Got yourself a good ol' junkie to give to Sabra?" one of them asked, flicking a cigarette to the pavement.

The man behind Walter answered.

"Came on his own accord, it seems."

The man who had asked the question raised an eyebrow.

"Where are Sherk and Barney?"

There was a silent exchange before the man in front of him spoke again.

"You think—"

"Who? Barney and Sherk? No way," Dirk answered quickly. Walter felt the gun press into his spine. "Care to chime in here?"

Walter ignored the request and continued to walk, his eyes trained ahead even as the bikers stared at him. Unlike the last time he'd been here, they didn't make fun of him or shout insults, call him a junkie or a crackhead. This time, they kept their mouths shut. And this made Walter smile even bigger. He didn't know if it was his bizarre confidence following what he had done to the two hitmen or if he was just getting loopy after being sober for so long. Whatever it was, it was affecting the bikers as well.

Walter took another few steps forward and then shook his head, trying to clear it.

It didn't matter. He was going to get high this day. And Sabra was going to facilitate this, whether he wanted to or not.

When they had made their way most of the way up the long, winding driveway that led to the house, Dirk finally spoke up again.

"You know, Walter, you'd be better off talking now. Better answer my questions before Sabra starts askin'. I mean, you came here by yourself, so you must want something, don't you?"

Walter couldn't hold it in anymore. He took one additional step toward the large wooden door, the entrance to Sabra's lavish estate, then turned to face the man that led him at gunpoint.

"I'm a junkie, man," he said, still smiling. He held his arms out to his sides. "What could I *possibly* want from Sabra?"

Dirk's thin lips twisted into a grimace.

"I was afraid you were going to say that."

Walter laughed. The other man did not.

He wagged the gun.

"Turn around and go inside, Walter."

14.

"WELCOME BACK, WALTER," THE fat man said, rubbing the sleep from his eyes with a thick fist.

Slouched in a massive chair before Walter sat the morbidly obese drug lord of the tip of the American Northeast, covering a territory that included Pekinish, Darborough, and, of course, Askergan. Although still considered a small-time drug pusher on any national scale, Sabra and his empire was growing. And after recently teaming up with the notorious Skull Crushers biker gang, and subsequently rebranding them his own, his reach wasn't only expanding, but it was doing so at an alarming speed.

Part of the reason for this rapid growth in territorial stronghold was the unilateral way in which he ruled. Like an alpha predator, Sabra would first encircle and then corner other dealers, smaller dealers, ones that didn't have their own biker gang at their beck and call, and politely ask them to join the fold.

The smart ones surrendered. The stupid or the brave — typically one and same, Walter was slowly realizing — became horrific reminders to the others of what happened when they failed to fall in line. And, like his burgeoning drug empire, Sabra's cache of creative ways of imposing his will was also expanding.

Walter pulled his eyes away from the man and glanced around quickly, trying to catch his bearings. He was in a large, dimly lit room — some sort of office, he supposed, although truth be told, it was larger than his entire apartment. The thick rug beneath his feet was illuminated by the ambient yellow glow emitted from a large chandelier high above his head, which also cast the thick wooden desk before him in a strange light. Dirk had holstered the gun when they'd entered the room, and now he was standing two feet behind him, arms folded across his chest. At some point during their walk to this room, another biker had joined them, a man that looked far meaner than Dirk. This man had a thick black mustache and eyebrows of similar intensity, likely hiding scars like the ones that seemed to mark his entire face and shaved head. But it was his eyes that were worrisome: just pinpricks in the dim lighting, these were the eyes of a man who didn't ask twice when he wanted something. And he looked none too pleased to have been awoken at this hour.

Even so, he wasn't the most dangerous person in the room. Instead, that honor was bestowed to the behemoth of a man that sat on the other side of the desk. As Walter took a seat in the metal chair that was bolted to the floor with large metal rivets—such a strange chair, so plain in this room of extravagance—he tried to fully take in Sabra's impressive, if disgusting girth.

Easily topping the scales at over three hundred pounds, the man's doughy head peeked up from behind the desk. His skin was deeply tanned, and his neck, a giant waddle of a thing, was covered in unsightly skin tags. His hair was slicked back, a dark black helmet of a do that looked strong enough to withstand gale-force winds. Around the man's neck were several thick gold chains, and when he raised his pudgy hand as he did now, Walter noticed that every single one of his sausage-like digits was adorned by a massive gold ring.

With his other hand, Sabra grabbed a sandwich from atop a golden plate and took a hefty bite. Either he didn't notice the lettuce that fluttered from his mouth and landed on the wooden desk, or he didn't care.

Disgusting slob.

Although Walter had seen the man not a fortnight ago, Sabra's incredible size was still a wonder to behold.

Walter's shoulder suddenly seized, and he fought hard to avoid doubling over. His molars ground together as he resisted the urge to cry out.

He needed to get high soon.

Walter's eyes scanned Sabra's huge desk before him, his gaze eventually falling on the mirror covered with several thick lines of cocaine.

True to form.

Not his drug of choice, but it would do; in a pinch, it would do.

And this most definitely qualified as a pinch.

Evidently, Sabra noticed his gaze.

"You need something, Walter? Need something to take the edge off?"

The man laughed, his huge chins shaking madly, flecks of half-chewed salami spraying from his wet lips.

It was revolting; the man had clearly just been awoken from his slumber, and yet somehow had a sandwich at the ready.

Disgusting.

Walter fought the urge to respond or comment, deeming it better to keep his mouth shut at this juncture. Seeing the coke had done something to ease the pain in his shoulder, but it was still there. And he knew that if he didn't get high soon… well, he didn't *exactly* know what would happen, but if the men in his apartment were any indication, it wasn't something that he wanted to find out anytime soon.

His life had changed this morning, that much was certain. This morning, he had wanted nothing but to get high, had known that dying in the back seat of a shitty champagne-colored Chevy wouldn't have even made him burp with indifference. But after being imbued with this… this *power*, that, coupled with the sight of his son's scarred face, had inspired change in him.

No longer was he preoccupied with insurance money from his son's death. Now he wanted to see Tyler again, to see if he too had been given this gift, so that together they could… well, he wasn't sure what, but exploiting Sabra and his resources—primarily the bikers and their extended reach—was a start.

Still, he wanted to get high.

Needed to get high.

Sabra shrugged.

"Ben, come over here, grab the mirror. Give the little man a little hit."

The man with the mustache immediately stepped forward. Walter offered a quick glance at Dirk and noticed that the man's eyebrows were raised in obvious confusion. Ben, on the other hand, was as loyal as they came, and he headed toward Sabra without hesitation. He picked up the mirror and made his way back toward Walter, his heart rate increasing with every one of Ben's slow, methodical steps.

There were four thick lines of coke on the mirror, each one at least three inches in length—a *lot* of coke. Even though Walter preferred heroin, he knew that Sabra only had the good shit. And this was Sabra's shit.

"Just a little hit, Ben. We still need the man to be able to *feel*."

Sabra laughed again, a thick, bubbly sound like a child struggling underwater.

Despite his anticipation, the sound nearly curdled Walter's stomach.

Thankfully, Ben stepped between Walter and Sabra, blocking his sight of the horrible Jabba the Hut creature. He held the mirror in thick, hairy-knuckled fingers in such a way that the largest and thickest lines of cocaine were closest to him.

Walter's shoulder seized again, but this time he was able to ignore it. Like a ravenous dog, he leaned forward, driving his nose into the mirror that was still clutched in Ben's hand. His enthusiasm was so great that the man almost dropped the mirror. Walter didn't care; he brought a finger to his nostril, pinched it tight, and then snorted an entire line in one go.

As expected, his nose instantly caught fire, and he pulled back, holding his head high, staring at the brass chandelier above him.

But that was it.

There was no rush, no immediate pupil-dilating, pulse-pounding surge of ecstasy. There was only a calming feeling in his shoulder; a calm, slow, pulsating feeling as the drugs coursed through the thick red and purple veins that crossed his chest and fed the cracker.

Frustration taking hold, Walter turned his head back forward and reached out, trying to grab the mirror from Ben and to get at the other three lines.

The other man was too quick. He pulled the mirror away, and from somewhere behind him, Walter heard Sabra shout, "Just a taste! Just a taste!"

Walter snarled at the man with the mustache, and pushed upward, intending on lunging from the chair.

He didn't even make it to his feet.

With his free hand, Ben reared back, and with lightning speed his thick fist came forward, smashing Walter in the nose. A spray of blood immediately gushed from his nose, gushing all over the undoubtedly expensive carpet in front of his chair. Walter brought both hands to his face, trying to stem the bleeding.

It hurt, but what hurt more was not being able to get high.

Eyes watering, he stared up at the man with the thick mustache who was staring down his thin nose at him with his odd, flat eyes.

You are going to pay for that.

Then it was his turn to laugh. Realizing that the blood flow was already starting to slow, he pulled his hand away from his face.

"Just a taste," he said, his words coming out wet. "Oh, I'll have a taste, alright."

Walter felt a stern grip on his shoulder, almost pre-emptively convincing him that staying seated was the best course of action. It was Dirk, and for a brief moment he felt bad for what was going to happen to this man—he was different from the others, and maybe he didn't deserve the same fate as the hitmen back at his apartment.

Walter took a deep breath and sat back down. It didn't matter anyway. He wasn't going to fight these men, at least not in the traditional sense.

As if understanding his plight, his shoulder started to tighten and he felt a strange pressure in his left bicep.

They're coming.

When Walter raised his eyes again, Sabra was no longer smiling.

"I don't know what the fuck you did to Sherk and Barney," he hissed, "and I have absolutely no clue why you came here, of all places. But I can promise you one thing: you are going to wish you hadn't."

The big man slowly brought himself to his feet, the white silk robe that he wore flowing all the way to the ground. The sash had come slightly untied, revealing the man's massive breasts, which were completely smooth and hairless—like the rest of his chest—and, of course, a deep bronze.

Sabra made his way around the side of the desk.

"I was going to let you live, Walter. After all, it is poor business for a dealer to kill off his clients, even ones that have difficulty paying."

Ben stepped to one side, allowing Sabra's large body to pass by him. Walter's eyes followed Ben's hand as he put the mirror with the lines of cocaine, amazingly still piled up like neat snowbanks, even with a spray of his blood marking half of the surface, up in front of his face.

A pudgy hand reached out and grabbed his chin and squeezed tightly.

"But now look what you done. You went and ruined my fucking carpet, Walter." He glanced at the blood droplets by the front two feet of the chair bolted to the ground. "And this ain't no cheap rug."

The man had power in his hands, owing most likely to his immense size. Walter tried to shake the fingers away, but found himself unable; Sabra's grip was just too strong.

"I'm going—"

Sabra tilted his head to one side, a slight, barely perceptible movement, and it was clear that he was staring at Walter's nose.

He had seen the blow Ben had delivered, and selecting him to guard his room was an indication that he was more than aware of Ben's strength. Even though Walter couldn't see his own face, he could tell by the way the bridge of his nose had started to itch and how the bleeding had stopped so suddenly that the man was in awe of the fact his face was healing. Still, Sabra went to great efforts to avoid interrupting his planned diatribe.

"—to make you pay for your transgressions, Walter. You could have given me the money you owe me and I might have let you keep one of them. But now…" The man leaned back and sighed as if these subtle movements were taking much out of him. "But now I will have to take both."

Both? Both what? What the fuck is this slob talking about?

It was all Walter could do to ignore the increasing tension in his shoulder, hoping that whatever semblance of control he had exerted over the cracker at his apartment was still buried within him.

"Both what?" he demanded through gritted teeth.

Instead of answering, Sabra's thick lips broke into a smile, and Walter felt something snake its way up the inside of his thigh. He immediately tried to close his legs, but Ben was on him, grabbing his knees and holding them apart.

At the same time, Dirk's grip on his shoulders tightened. Walter was going nowhere.

Sabra's other hand, the one not still gripping his face, made its way to his jeans, and then the man grabbed his balls tightly.

Even Walter, recently accustomed to pain, couldn't help but wince.

"If there is one thing I have learned maintaining control of this drug empire, it is that there are two parts of the body that, when threatened, make even the toughest of men buckle. Strangely, they are much the same shape and the same size." He let go of Walter's chin, which was red and raw where he had grabbed it. Then he traced a line beside Walter's temple, and Walter whipped his head to the side.

Sabra pulled his hand away and leaned back.

"One, are the eyes. But you see, the thing about the eyes is that once you fuck with them, then they can't see what else you do to them. And sight is a powerful sense."

Lowering to eye level, Sabra came within inches of Walter's face.

"The balls, on the other hand…"

When he spoke again, his voice was different, deeper.

"I could pop your balls like fucking grapes," Sabra hissed, his breath reeking of deli meat.

Go now, my —

But then Sabra pulled his hand away and took a step back. Both Ben and Dirk's grips loosened as well, and Walter kept the thought at bay. He had no idea how many of those crackers he could send forth, *if* he could mentally make them burst from his skin, and he didn't want to risk fucking this up.

"But I am no savage, Walter. No, I am a refined man of great taste and style, and I will not resort to brute strength to punish those that cross me." Sabra turned his back to him and sauntered toward his desk. "I am also a creative man, you see. And I have other ideas for how to deal with you."

The man pressed a button beneath the lip of his massive desk, and the sound of creaking chains suddenly came from above them. Walter's eyes flicked upward, and he saw the large bronze chandelier with the weak orange bulbs and the thick chain links slowly begin to lower.

"Stand him up," Sabra ordered, his back still turned.

Walter didn't need Dirk to help him to his feet, but the man facilitated the process nonetheless. The man then guided him off to one side, directly beneath the chandelier that continued to descend slowly from the ceiling.

What the fuck is going on?

Walter watched as Sabra leaned both hands on the table, and then, as if saddened, he said, "Take off your clothes, Walter."

Walter froze.

"Walter, take off your clothes." His voice was almost pedantic, bored even.

When Walter still didn't respond, Sabra turned and nodded at Ben.

The man, who had stood and backed away when Dirk had directed Walter to beneath the chandelier, reached out, grabbed his flannel shirt, and promptly tore it from his body.

"Jesus." The word just slipped out of Ben's mouth, and he instinctively took a step backward.

Walter smiled as Sabra turned, a look of confusion and anger crossing his fat face.

"Ben? What—?"

But then he too caught glimpse of Walter's chest and his eyes went wide.

15.

"FUCKING CHRIST," SABRA MUMBLED. His eyes had grown to charcoal briquettes protruding from his toasted meringue face. It was clear that he was trying to maintain the facade of being in control, of being the giant, larger-than-life drug lord in a silk robe.

"What's wrong with your skin?"

But this was too much, even for him—Walter didn't even have to look down at his body to know that. He could feel the cracker pulsating in his shoulder, and a pressure was building in his left bicep and just below his ribcage.

It was almost time.

The crackers were coming, and they were coming for the fat man, the mustached man, and the one named Dirk.

Walter's smile grew.

"Just a taste," he said, licking the blood from his brown teeth.

Sabra frowned. He was not used to being mocked.

"Any word from Sherk or Barney?"

Dirk shook his head.

"Where did they find him?"

"Don't know. But they went to Askergan first."

Sabra nodded, his chins wobbling.

"Turn on the TV, Dirk—go to the news. And Ben, strip off the rest of this filthy bastard's clothes."

Dirk moved quickly around both Ben and Walter, picking up the remote and turning on the large TV mounted off to the side of Sabra's ornate desk. Ben, on the other hand, so eager to please Sabra just a few moments ago, was no longer so obsequious. The man's dark, beady eyes were staring at the network of vessels that crisscrossed Walter's chest, veins so thick that they stood out from his pasty flesh. When his eyes met the cracker's oscillating teeth in his shoulder, he paused completely.

"Ben! Take the fucker's pants off, now!" Sabra's voice, nearly musical when he had been sitting behind his giant desk, was now loud enough to make Walter's ears ring.

Ben finally set to motion, but he was still hesitant, making sure to stay on Walter's left side, his eyes locked on the cracker even as he yanked down Walter's jeans and then his crusty underwear.

"There has been a—a—an infestation of sorts in Askergan County," a female voice suddenly flooded the room. "The county was overrun by some sort of—ugh, ugh—crabs."

Walter glanced at the TV and caught a brief glimpse of a blonde woman, pretty even with dirt and soot smeared across her forehead, before the camera cut away to a shot of the smoldering gas station, and Highway 2, littered with the white, upturned corpses of the crackers.

"It seems as if the infestation of these parasites originated in Askergan..."

Sabra looked away from the TV and turned back to face Walter, a look of sheer disgust on his face.

"Looks like you spent a little time in Askergan, didn't you, Walt?"

Walter shifted his hips, swinging his naked cock at the fat man. Ben grunted and moved farther away. He looked like he might be sick.

Sabra laughed.

"Funny guy, I like that—I like funny people." Then he turned to Ben, who had risen from his feet after stripping Walter. "Grab the chandelier, Ben."

The man with the bushy mustache swallowed hard.

"Sab, I ain't—"

Sabra pushed his thick lips together so tightly that they became wrinkled.

The fat man's words echoed in Walter's head.

I could pop your balls like grapes.

Standing there naked, he watched as Ben finally pulled the chandelier all the way down from the ceiling. The chain clanked noisily as it piled onto itself, and when Ben grabbed a fistful of the chain and walked behind him and the metal chair, Walter figured that that was enough.

It was time.

Go now. Go now, and take them out.

Nothing happened.

Ben dropped to his knees, and Walter saw that the length of chain now went from the chandelier on the floor in front of him, to around and behind him where it was clutched in the mustached man's fists. The other end of the chain, looped through the chandelier and extended high above them, didn't seem to be affixed to the ceiling as he had first thought, but appeared to be attached to some sort of winch mechanism.

Go now! Go!

This time, something happened, but it was far from the excruciating pain he'd expected from stretching skin. The pressure in his biceps and triceps increased, a similar feeling to what he had felt before the crackers had budded and attacked Sherk and Barney. But instead of growing in intensity, as his brown gritted teeth could attest to in anticipation, it seemed to quell and then subside.

What the fuck? Go, you fucking crab motherfuckers! Go forth! Get this fat man and his biker friends!

"Jesus fucking Christ, you ever even wipe your ass?" Ben muttered. Walter had forgotten that the man was behind him, crouching between his legs. When he felt the cold chain touch the back of his scrotum, he had an involuntary intake of breath.

"Dirk! Point your gun at him. If he moves, shoot him."

I could pop your balls like grapes... but I'm no savage. I'm a creative man.

Dirk's face had turned an ashen shade that matched his mustache and hair, but he held the gun out in front of him as instructed.

Get the fuck out! Get out, you goddamn parasites!

Walter barely resisted moving when the chain was wrapped around his ball sack and then was pulled tight behind him, through his legs. He felt his balls trying to resist, to suck back up into his abdomen, but the way that Ben had looped the chain—*how did he do that? The chain links were so thick*—they were locked in place.

Walter felt panic begin to set in.

"I'm going to fucking burn my hands," Ben grumbled as he stood.

"You see, Walter," Sabra began, his massive face transforming into a smile. "There are things in this world that you just don't do."

The fat man with his tits hanging out of his silk robe reached over and pressed the button on his desk again, and the crank on the ceiling started to whir. The chain began to suck back into the ceiling, one link at a time. Looking at the loose coils on the floor and gauging the rate that the chain was moving, Walter figured he had two, maybe three minutes before his balls were ripped through his asshole. For once, Sabra's flair for the dramatic—in this case, using an extremely slow motor to raise and lower the chandelier, presumably to make the person sitting in the bolted chair squirm—was going to work in Walter's favor.

His gaze left the chain and traveled to his biceps. He could barely make out the outline of a crab shell, but it wasn't raised as the others had been. Instead, it was just a dark smudge.

"You don't sleep with your sister," Sabra continued. "That's a no-no. And you don't eat on the can—even I know that."

The man's face turned hard, all of the doughiness seeming to somehow vanish.

"And you don't *fuck—with—Sabra*."

With the final word, Walter looked up.

"You—" he said, struggling to get the word out. Even though the chain was far from taut, it was heavy, and he could feel his scrotum stretching to impossible limits. This Sabra was one sick fucker.

"—don't fuck with the parasite."

He spat blood onto the carpet.

And then it happened.

16.

SABRA STUMBLED BACKWARD WHEN the first scream erupted from Walter's mouth, his large hips bumping into the heavy desk. Any normal table would have toppled from his massive girth, but this table was up to the challenge and stood fast.

Judging by the expression on the fat man's face, it appeared that he would have liked it to do just that, if nothing else but to put some space between himself and Walter.

"What the fuck!" Sabra managed to blubber. His back against the table now, he was so confused and distracted that he was trying to hoist himself on top of it, over it, instead of just going around it.

Walter shut his eyes, his lids fluttering wildly. The pain was intense; regardless of his previous injuries—being shot, punched, having his scrotum stretched—there wasn't anything to prepare him for *this*.

It was as if his entire body had been set alight.

He spread his arms wide, for no other reason than he thought it might somehow cool himself, or... or *something*. It just felt strangely natural.

The veins in his chest—thick, corrugated ribbons of blue and red and purple—pulsated, and the cracker in his shoulder clenched down hard on something deep inside him.

And then there was the stretching, the tearing sensation that originated from his left bicep and below his ribcage at the same time. After a moment, however, the feelings became decentralized, and pain radiated throughout his entire body without a recognizable source.

With every eyelid twitch, his vision went from intermittent rays of yellow light to narrowing darkness.

Emptiness.

Death.

Go forth, he pleaded for what felt like the tenth time, knowing that if the newly born crackers didn't bud soon, he would pass out.

And then he had no idea what would occur.

"Fucking Christ! What is happening to him?!"

He thought it was Sabra's voice again, but now someone else was shouting too—Ben, maybe? It all sounded so far away that it wasn't possible for him to discern who was yelling.

"Just fucking shoot him!"

There was a moment of clarity right after Walter's pain reached a climax, and then the pressure in his arm and stomach relented with two consecutive wet pops, and he let out a sigh reminiscent of his first orgasm.

A shot rang out in Sabra's office and he felt something strike him in the calf.

The feeling barely registered.

"Unghhhh," he moaned, the sound rolling off his tongue.

"Fuck, Dirk! Shoot the fucking things! Shoot them!"

More gunshots rang out, but this time he didn't feel them plunk against him. Instead, they hit somewhere around his feet, making loud *thock* noises as the bullets embedded themselves in the hardwood floor.

"Fucking shoot them!"

And then the guttural cries started and Walter finally opened his eyes.

17.

BEN WAS STANDING TWO feet to Walter's right, tearing desperately at his jean vest, scratching at his chest as if he had been attacked by a swarm of bees. The man's normally tiny eyes were wide, the lids red.

"Get it off me!" he bellowed. "Get it the fuck off me!"

Walter saw movement beneath his shirt and knew that one of the crackers had reached him and had maybe crawled up the leg of his pants like it had done with Sherk.

"Get it the fuck—"

But then the movement beneath the man's shirt stopped as the cracker clamped down. Ben bent over as if he had been punched in the stomach, his mouth extending into a capital 'O' shape.

"Jesus, fuck!"

Sabra, now… the man still had his back against the desk, his silk robe having come completely undone, revealing not only his bronzed belly, but also what looked like a pink thong.

I'm going to enjoy watching you eaten from the inside out, you fat bastard.

He watched the translucent cracker pause on the floor halfway between himself and Sabra.

The man's big eyes were locked on it.

Dirk squeezed off another round, but the cracker lifted three of its legs and the bullet missed.

"Dirk!" Sabra shouted. He shifted his body to one side, as if feigning to run in that direction, but the cracker followed him by leaning that way. "Dirk! Shout the fucking thing!"

Walter wanted to watch this, needed to watch it, but he suddenly became aware of a change in the lighting in the room.

He glanced around and saw that the chandelier had started to drag across the floor.

Then he felt the tightness in his groin and looked down.

The first thing he noticed was the thick veins in his chest; they looked darker, thicker, had more relief to them now. There was also blood on his left biceps, thin streams of it that traced lines all the way down his outstretched arm to his armpit. And there were more of those white patches as well on his biceps and on his stomach, where the skin had rapidly healed after the crackers had budded.

Finally, there was the bullet hole in his calf, but this had regressed to a mere sting, and Walter expected that it would be completely healed in a few minutes.

But his balls, on the other hand, were another matter. The chain that Ben had wrapped around them held fast, and a quick glance upward revealed that it would only be moments before it became completely taut. And after that, well... Walter didn't want to think about *that*.

Dirk squeezed off one more shot, aiming the round at the cracker, but when he missed, the man simply bolted from the room, offering none of the other men so much as a second glance.

"Dirk! What the fuck!" Sabra shouted.

The man made a move as if to run—or shamble—after Dirk, but before he took a step, the cracker seized this opportunity and lunged. It flew through the air with amazing speed and purpose, landing directly on Sabra's massive bronzed belly.

"No!" he screamed. His pudgy hands went to his stomach and tried to swat the cracker away like a large spider.

But this cracker wasn't having any of it. Its oscillating teeth clamped down immediately and it started to dissect its way beneath the man's skin with unprecedented fervor.

Sabra howled something unintelligible.

A heavy sound came from Walter's right, drawing his attention.

Ben had collapsed to the floor, his eyes completely rolled back in his head, froth at the corners of his mouth, coating the edges of his black mustache.

The other cracker had gotten to him.

There was a tearing sound, and then Ben's body arched. A second later, his chest was torn open, blood soaking his t-shirt and then his jean vest. There was a flurry of movement beneath the wet material, like hands trying desperately to escape from muddy earth, but this quickly faded away, coinciding with Ben's lifeless body collapsing to the hardwood.

Sabra, who had started to sweat and go red from the exertion of trying to pull the cracker from his burgeoning gut, was wheezing now, the effort taking a toll on his giant heart.

For some reason, amidst the pain that was now encompassing his entire lower half, Walter thought of the white patches of skin as he stared at Sabra.

Such smooth skin. So perfect, so brown and even. I could use your skin, you—

Then Walter felt something between his legs tear and his world faded to black.

18.

A WOMAN'S VOICE... SOFT, sweet, but direct.

Why is there a woman in here?

Walter opened his eyes and was surprised that the light in the room had gone back to the way it had been before the chandelier had been lowered.

Which meant...

Walter gasped and unfurled his body from the fetal position, reaching down between his legs tentatively, his fingers gently prodding the area like the crown of a baby's head.

The surface was wet and tacky with blood, but thankfully he found no sign of an open wound.

Had the chain broken?

His eyes flicked upward, and he cringed at the sight of blood and gore hanging from the chandelier chain.

"In a few moments, we will have the sheriff of Askergan County on to tell us a little more," the woman on the news droned on, "but it appears as if this house—what residents refer to as the Wharfburn Estate, even though both Mr. and Mrs. Wharfburn have been deceased for nearly a decade—this once palatial and yet now burning ruin of an estate was the source of the infestation. Authorities say..."

Walter looked away from the television and returned his attention to his own body.

Nude, he lay in a pile of blood—his own, or maybe that of the two other dead men in the room. He had no idea how much time had passed, but assumed that it couldn't have been long—an hour, maybe, or two. If the news on the TV was indeed live, then the woman was standing in morning dusk— two hours, tops. And then there were the gunshots. Although he doubted that the sound would have made it to the bikers outside, Dirk most likely had. And even if the man had simply ducked his head and fled without addressing any of them, like he had done in this room, just seeing him in such a sense of panic would have likely inspired a visit to Sabra.

Sabra.

But before searching for the big man, Walter ran his fingers over his left bicep. It was smooth there, smooth and white, just like the other spots on his body that the crackers had erupted from. Just like...

His hand went back to between his legs, his breathing becoming shallow.

Smooth.

At first, he'd thought that his fingers had found his scrotum, and relief had washed over him. The skin was smooth and soft... but a quick second of probing and he realized that it was too soft.

His testicles were gone, ripped from his body by the chandelier chain.

Walter stopped breathing entirely.

The skin down there, like on his chest and arms, had healed, leaving behind what was undoubtedly a pale patch of skin.

Neutered.

He had been neutered like a fucking mutt.

A shudder ran through him.

Walter closed his eyes and spread himself out on the carpet, arms wide.

What the fuck is happening to me?

Time seemed to stop, and Walter considered, seriously considered, that he was, in fact, dead—that what he had experienced today was the hell that he was going to have to endure for eternity.

And if it wasn't? Then he could just press the button beneath Sabra's desk, only this time he would wrap the chain around his neck and not his balls.

But then the cracker in his shoulder quivered, bringing him back to reality—whatever reality it was.

Why end it now? Why now, after you have been given such power?

Walter forced his self-pity away, his thoughts briefly turning to his son's scarred face.

Whatever hell this is, you earned it.

Walter groaned and pulled himself to his feet. He was still sore, but he suspected that, like his broken nose and two gunshot wounds, the cracker would deal with this new pain soon, no matter how cringe-worthy.

Walter walked slowly over to Sabra's fallen body. The man's ribcage was blown wide, revealing blankets of thick yellow fat covering his organs—his heart, his lungs, his liver— like bubble wrap. He stood over the body for a moment, staring at it.

Again he was struck by the crackers' strange behavior— this wasn't at all what he had seen throughout Askergan.

They're evolving somehow… that must be it. Somehow the drugs are causing them to change.

Some of the crackers that had erupted within his chest were still in the cavity, their translucent bodies covered in blood, while others had escaped the man's massive chest only to die after straying too far from their host.

These were a completely different animal than what he had seen littering Highway 2, and before that, in the sheriff's office before he had forced his way out the window. These were different, and somehow the drugs coursing through his system seemed to keep them—or, more specifically, one of them—alive. The others, for whatever reason, were not so lucky. They didn't even seem capable of surviving in Sabra's body, the gigantic incubator that was no doubt also flush with drugs.

Only the one in his shoulder seemed to live on.

Walter kicked one of the small crackers' chitinous bodies across the hardwood.

Parasites—all of you.

Aside from the gaping hole in Sabra's chest, the man's perfectly smooth, perfectly bronzed skin was otherwise untouched.

Skin, so smooth and soft. I might have a use for you yet.

He thought about his own mottled flesh and how the man had insulted him for it.

A smile crossed his face.

Yeah, I think I have a use for your fake-and-bake skin.

But first things first, he thought, and the first thing for Walter was, and always would be, drugs.

He hobbled awkwardly to the man's desk, offering a wide berth around Ben's body, and immediately grabbed the mirror with the still perfect little mounds of coke. He was about to indulge when he caught a glimpse of Sabra's massive chair— more of a throne, really—only a couple of feet to his left.

"Why the fuck not?" he said to the empty room.

The chair was so heavy that he doubted he would have been able to move it; thankfully, Sabra was so fat that this was unnecessary. Walter could just slide his rail-thin body in between the desk and chair without moving it.

The first line of cocaine didn't even so much as burn his nose, let alone get him high. But the cracker in his shoulder noticed; it noticed, and it liked it.

"Now, Sheriff White, can you tell us a little more about what happened here? What happened in Askergan over the last forty-eight hours?"

Walter's eyes shot up at the sound of the word 'Sheriff', and then they immediately narrowed at the sight of Sheriff Paul White's black face.

"Well, Nancy, as you've said already, Askergan was infected by some sort of crab-like parasites. There was a nest"—he gestured to the smoldering ruins behind him—"in the basement of the Wharfburn Estate. We are still totaling the loss and injury due to this, ungh, *infestation*, and can't release any more details at this point in the investigation."

The burly sheriff then turned toward the camera, his expression suddenly stern—too stern, maybe, like it was an act, like there was a specific image he was trying to portray. Regardless, when he spoke again, it was as if he was speaking directly to Walter.

"I want to assure the Askergan citizens that we have everything under control. I repeat, everything is now under control. Please stay in your homes. A deputy will be going door to door to answer any of your questions and to make a list of the missing or lost. Again, I want to stress that the situation has been controlled."

Walter wasn't sure if the cracker in his arm heard or understood what the sheriff was saying, or if it was simply a coincidence, but it pulsated when the sheriff uttered the word 'control'.

"We are still—"

The blonde woman turned and interrupted the sheriff.

"Do you know what kind of creatures they are? Or where they came from?"

The sheriff made a face.

"We are still working out the details, Nancy."

Odd. 'Nancy'. He should have just said, "Please, no more questions at this time", and walked off. But he hadn't. He had called her by her first name, and stared at her as if he was angry.

Something suddenly clicked in Walter's brain. It was the sheriff's words and the way he looked at the woman, with soft yet hurt eyes.

He's fucking her.

"And body count? Do we know how many citizens were attacked by these creatures? How many are dead, Sheriff White?"

Sheriff White's lower lip curled, and Walter thought he even saw the man cringe.

"The creatures caused several accidents as well as numerous fires across town. There were deaths, to be sure, and we are very sorry for the victims of this horrible accident. But at this time, we are unable to provide any further details."

Nancy, clearly unsatisfied with this response, continued to press despite the fact that the sheriff looked as if he was nearing his wits' end.

"There were rumors of a missing boy—"

The sheriff's eyes went wide in surprise.

"Nancy, as I said—"

Walter started to snort another line, but hesitated; it was like watching reality TV—*real* reality TV. The asshole sheriff and his fuck toy having a spat on camera.

"Are the rumors true? Is it true that one missing boy, Tyler Wandry, died here at the Wharfburn Estate?"

Walter's entire body started to tingle.

Tyler!

There was a long and awkward pause, something that seemed to stretch on and on as Walter gaped, barely able to swallow let alone breath.

Tyler!

So much had changed since he had first burst into the police station demanding that his son's body be retrieved, even though he hadn't even been sure that he was dead yet.

Now, however, things were different.

Walter's hand instinctively went to the spot where his balls had once been. Yes—things were very different.

"As I said," the sheriff began slowly, "there were numerous casualties last night, and we are still taking a look at exactly what happened."

"And—"

"I'm sorry, no more questions at this time. Thank you."

The sheriff gently pushed the microphone away from his face, and the camera, after lingering for a moment on the big man's sour expression, moved as well, panning out to get a shot of the smoldering ruins behind them.

Dead. My only son is dead.

Walter leaned forward and snorted a line of coke.

And thanks to Sabra, there is no way I will ever make another.

He turned back to the image on the television, barely noticing the fact that his shoulder had started to quiver again. His eyes were red, his vision blurry. Rage built inside him.

"I'm coming for you, Sheriff. You killed my son and I'm coming for you."

Walter leaned down and snorted the final line on the mirror, and then he tossed it to the floor in disgust.

"The parasites have not been controlled, you lying prick. I'm coming for you—I'm coming for you and for anyone you care about, starting with that blonde little bitch."

Walter spat on the floor.

When he turned back to the TV, the newscast had gone on to something else, but Walter only saw one thing.

His bony hands gripped the thick wooden armrests so tightly that they started to crack under his grip.

He saw the imprint of the sheriff's face, his big lips, his oddly sorrowful eyes, and he saw the blonde reporter looking up at him.

"I'm coming for you, Sheriff. I'm coming for you and I'm coming for *Askergan*."

PART II – GRIDDLE

19.

"NANCY! WHAT THE HELL were you thinking?"

The question didn't draw an immediate answer. Instead, the woman seemed content in ordering her fat cameraman to get another shot of the burning wreckage before they packed up.

"Make sure you get a good panorama of the fireman trying to put out the fire. And I want good framing, get it all in the same shot. No chopping off their fucking heads like last time."

Paul reached for her arm.

"Nancy, what were you doing?"

The woman turned to face him. She had cleaned up amazingly well after what they had experienced, including changing her outfit and doing a half-decent job of at least appearing as if she'd slept last night and hadn't spent the entire time blowing alien crabs into white smears. But even with makeup, the soot that seemed permanently tattooed on her forehead had been impossible to conceal.

"I'm getting a shot of the burning house before they put out all the flames," she stated matter-of-factly.

Paul shook his head.

"No, what *were* you doing? Why did you ask about the Wandry kid? You saw what I saw, Nance. You know about the fucking crackers, the shit that happened at Wellwood Elementary School, Tyler Wandry, and fucking Mrs. Drew, for Christ's sake."

An image of the woman fleeing from them, drawing the crackers momentarily away before Greg Griddle had shot her in the head, flooded back to him, and an incredible sadness washed over him.

He forced the tears away.

"Why do you need me to say it? And on TV, for Christ's sake!"

Nancy tried to keep a stern expression, but he could tell that she too was nearing a breaking point.

"People need to know, Sheriff. They have a right—"

Paul cut her off. He wasn't in the mood to buy any of her reporter or newscaster babble.

"After all you've seen, do you *really* want Askergan to know?"

Nancy seemed to contemplate this for a moment.

"Yes—I dunno. Does it matter? I just put the news out there. I told you this"—she gestured to both of them—"was important, but so was this." This time she indicated the microphone and her cameraman.

Paul made a face. She was telling the truth, of course; Nancy had made it exceedingly clear that her career was important to her.

Maybe even the most important thing to her.

"Still, Nance, this is fucked. What happened here… what happened in Askergan, this isn't normal. And you and I both know that this is the first time that something of this…

nature… has happened here. Do you want to send everyone into a frenzy?"

Nancy shrugged, and she averted her eyes. It was clear now that she hadn't meant to put him in the position she had, but that her instincts had taken over.

"But it's over, right?" she said softly. "I mean, the things are all gone, right?"

Paul placed his hand on her chin and raised her eyes to meet his. Her green eyes were soft and bright, despite the gray smudges that peeked through the makeup on her cheeks and forehead. She was scared, he saw.

Nancy, who less than forty-eight hours ago had been shooting a pistol at crackers in a lemon-yellow dress like some sort of female James Bond, was scared.

She was one tough bitch, but she still *felt*.

I love her, Paul realized at that moment. Despite their mutual agreement, that her work would come first and his own was of paramount importance, he *loved* her.

When he spoke again, his voice was soft.

"I don't know. I think so."

They had killed so many crackers and blown up thousands more.

But it had been what Coggins had done, Coggins and Greg Griddle, that had really put the nail in the proverbial coffin. Whatever they had done at the expense of Tyler Wandry and Kent Griddle had caused the vast majority of the crackers to just curl up and die.

Kill the queen—the *king*—and the hive will die.

"What the fuck were they, Paul?"

The sheriff looked around at the upturned cracker corpses that littered the Wharfburn lawn. As he had told Deputy Williams earlier in the day, he had called every bureau he could think of, trying to get an expert out here—looking for soldiers, police, even a goddamn forest ranger—and all he had managed to procure was a fucking pathologist.

Not even an entomologist, microbiologist, or a fucking *crab*ologist.

In the past—during Dana Drew's reign—Askergan had been content in doing their own thing, taking care of their own people. After all, Askergan County always was a little different, even before all of *this*. Shit, they had a sheriff's department mixed in with the PD. And he, Sheriff Paul Lee White, was the top dog. Still, this was too much for *them*.

It was too much for him.

Paul looked skyward, trying to retain his composure.

"Sheriff? *Sheriff!*"

The urgency of the voice drew Paul's attention not to Nancy, who had felt his pain and had stepped toward him, slipping a comforting hand around his waist, but to Deputy Williams, who was hurrying toward him.

The man was waving his arms madly as he ran toward them, while at the same time somehow pointing to the rubble behind him.

Paul's gaze followed Williams's wild gesticulations, eventually landing on a fireman hoisting a body out of the Wharfburn rubble.

"Paul!"

He'd known there would be bodies in the house, but the shocked expression on his deputy's face immediately sent the alarm bells in his head ringing.

He gently peeled Nancy's arm from around his waist.

"Andy? What's wrong?"

A horrible thought crept into his head.

He swallowed hard, and his hand went instinctively to the gun at his hip.

"Are there more of *them*?"

Deputy Williams stumbled, breathing hard. When he looked up, his eyes were not so much scared as surprised.

"No," he gasped. "Not more of them. But we found somebody."

Paul raised an eyebrow and he took two steps toward the other man.

Found somebody? You mean found some bodies.

Interpreting the expression on the sheriff's face, Williams shook his head back and forth vigorously.

"No, we found somebody, and they're *alive*."

20.

'YOU THINK HE LOVES *you more than me?'*

The boy with the dark hair turned to face his brother.

'I don't know.'

There was an honesty in the boy's voice that could not be faked, and it gave them both pause.

Walter and Donnie Wandry were sitting in the branch of one of the tall oak trees at the back of the property, roughly fifty or so feet from the small farmhouse they called home. It was far enough to be out of earshot and to be out of sight for anyone that might just be casually glancing out the back of the house, but not so far that if their father whistled they wouldn't hear.

Not being able to hear when Dad called wouldn't be a good thing. Indeed, not showing up a few moments after the high-pitched sound would be a very bad thing.

'Was it always like this?' Donnie asked. He was gently probing the bruising on his cheek as he spoke, as if trying to reaffirm that it was still there.

Walter shrugged.

'I was three when you were born; I don't remember much about what happened before then.'

This was only a half lie; while it was true that he didn't remember anything specific about his life back then, he remembered how he'd felt.

He had been happy, and Mom and Dad had been happy, too. Although he was only fourteen, the boy was mature enough to know that life had a strange way of shifting, of memories changing from one moment to the next, and that one could never be completely sure if what they remembered was actually true.

Still, while memories could be faked, feelings were less easy to manipulate. His life had been happy before Donnie was born, he was sure of it. It just didn't feel right to say so.

Not now, anyway.

'I don't get it. Why does he hate me so much?'

Tears were beginning to spill from Donnie's large, dark eyes now, making wet track marks on his face. His nose was getting red, too, and they both knew that it would only be moments before the two of them were racked with sobs.

'He doesn't hate you.'

Another lie.

'Then why does he hit me? Why? I'm not any worse than you... I mean, you do bad stuff too, and he never hits you.'

Walter wrapped his arms around his brother. As predicted, they both started crying, their bodies heaving as they held each other.

Then a whistle cut through the warm evening air and they immediately disengaged.

'Hurry, help me down. We can't be late!'

Less than five minutes later, they were in the kitchen, huffing from running as fast as they could.

'Sit down.'

Both boys pulled their chairs out from the table and sat down.

The man in the blue overalls did the same. He wasn't a particularly big man, and if the boys continued to grow at their current pace, adding three or four years to their already fourteen and eleven, it wouldn't surprise anyone if they outgrew their father. The man was short and thin, but hard, too. Hard in a way that boys, even the mean boys that teased them at school, just couldn't muster, despite their intentions. He had dark eyes, a small mouth, and thick, knotted hands.

The boys' father was hard in a way that extended from his callouses to his heart.

At least, when it came to one of them.

The other person at the table had already been seated when they had come in from outside. The boys' mother was an equally small person to their father, which lent to jokes at school about how the boys resembled the mailman. They were always being picked on, mostly because they spent their evenings mowing the lawn or collecting eggs from emaciated chickens, while the others did normal things like play soccer or go fishing.

But unlike their father, their mother wasn't hard. She was, in fact, a sweet person.

But that wasn't quite right; that was another one of those little lies again, like the one about their father not hating a favorite punching bag — that he didn't hate Donnie.

Their mother was sweet, but only in the past tense sense. For whatever had irked their father when the youngest boy had been born, for whatever had turned his fury on him, it had had the opposite effect on her. Slowly, as the beatings grew more regular, she became more and more abject — indifferent. But like Walter, the thin man with the rough hands never laid them on her, either.

'Say grace.'

It appeared like an open invitation, that anyone was entitled to chime in with the word of the Lord.

It wasn't.

'You, boy,' the man asserted, his red-rimmed eyes glaring at the boy with the bruised cheek.

Donnie averted his gaze and clasped his hands together, and the rest of the table followed suit.

After the prayer, the family ate in silence, the sound of heavy masticating filling the space that would in a normal household have been consumed with conversation — idle chatter about how their days had gone.

Dinner ended calmly enough, but when the man at the head of the table instructed Donnie to clear the table, things quickly took a turn for the worst.

The boy dropped a fork, and the entire house went silent while the tines rang out in prolonged vibration. Donnie cringed as he stared at his father's face, watching as the man closed his eyes and then took a deep breath in through his nose.

Then he shot out of his chair with such speed that it toppled loudly behind him. The boys watched as their mother bowed her head and began to move her lips silently.

Perhaps this was her turn to pray.

Donnie started to whimper.

'What's wrong with you, boy?' the man shouted. He reached over and grabbed the boy by his long blond hair.

Donnie screamed.

For some reason — for an unknown reason that even many years later would still remain unresolved — Walter also rose from his chair.

'Don't," Walter whispered, tears streaming down his face now.

The man in the overalls turned, his thick fingers still twisted in the younger boy's hair. He seemed to tighten his grip as he eyed his eldest son. Donnie cried out again and twisted to look at his brother.

'Please,' Donnie mouthed, but it wasn't clear if he meant 'Please, stop him,' or if altruism had sunk in its often dulled teethed and he meant, 'Please, don't anger him further; don't let you become the focus of his rage as well.'

But the thin, balding man would never challenge his eldest son, for reasons that would never become clear.

Why not me?

That was another question that would forever rack his brain.

'Don't,' Walter repeated.

'What did you say to me, boy?'

He let go of his youngest son, and Donnie fell to the ground in a heap.

'What—did—you—say?'

Walter held his ground.

'Leave him alone.' His voice was still but a whisper, but his words were powerful enough.

His father clenched and unclenched his fists, but the anger in his face was already fading.

The man turned to watch Donnie clamber to his feet and almost reached out to grab him as he hurried past. But Walter held his gaze until his brother was safely behind him.

'Go, Donnie,' Walter said over his shoulder to his brother. 'Run and don't ever come back.'

Something flicked across his father's eyes, but neither brother was sure what it was.

Shame. It had to be shame. After all, it couldn't be satisfaction, could it?

21.

THERE WAS A MASK on his face, and although it only covered his nose and mouth, it pushed up against his bottom eyelids, blurring his vision.

Help me, he tried to say, but the only thing that he could manage was a weak gasp that fogged the mask.

His throat burned, and his mouth tasted as if he had lunched on ashtray full of cigar butts. The man blinked hard, trying to clear the clouds that drifted across his vision.

The last thing he remembered was running into a burning house, searching for his…

"Kent!" he shouted, and this time he managed to force the words out in a throaty gasp. The mask fogged, and he suddenly reached up to tear it off.

He only got as far as pulling the left side away before someone grabbed his hand and stayed his progress.

"Kent!" he shouted again. He was suddenly overcome by a coughing fit, and his body was racked with shudders. The mask slipped back down over his nose and mouth, and he breathed deeply, trying desperately to catch his breath.

When the feeling finally passed, he brought his hands to the mask again, but this time he remained outwardly in control.

On the inside, though, his mind was as frantic as ever.

Please. Please tell me that they got Kent out!

He blinked hard again, trying to stem the tears that threatened to once again cloud his vision.

This time he managed to slip the mask down off his face and breathed in slowly through his nose.

"Kent?" he whispered.

A face suddenly filled his vision, one that he recognized, one that he had first seen what seemed like months ago when he and Kent had made their way to the police department to tell what then seemed a fantastical story.

After what they had seen since, however, it now seemed almost benign.

A dead girl, a cellar full of ghosts.

"I'm sorry," Sheriff White said, shaking his head slowly.

The man started to cry.

"I'm sorry," the sheriff repeated. "I'm so sorry, Greg — your son didn't make it."

"No," Greg moaned. "Nooooo!"

His mind, like his vision, started to narrow into a black void. His hands started to shake, and the rest of his body followed suit.

As Greg Griddle faded into unconsciousness, he heard Sheriff White shout.

"Help! He's seizing! Let's get some help over here!"

22.

GREG KNEW THAT HE was in a hospital room. He knew not only because of the ubiquitous beeps and boops, or because of the fact that there was a respirator on his face and a crisp white sheet pulled up to his armpits. He knew because of the smell—the slightly aseptic, rubbing alcohol scent tinged with a pureness that only meant one thing: hospital.

He heard another sound, and his eyes snapped open, half expecting a cracker to be at the foot of his bed, staring up at him with that horrible, oscillating mouth.

But the room was empty, a white void of which he was the only inhabitant, save, of course, the box of medical machinery and the IV bag jammed into the back of his hand.

Kent. My boy, my champ.

Greg started to cry. He remembered the fire and running back into the burning house after pulling the girl with the fake leg out of the basement. And he remembered ignoring the deputy's pleas, his words shouting that Kent was gone, that he was dead.

And then he remembered waking up, being pulled from the soot and ash, rising like a phoenix.

He had conceded his death.

And he had lost.

"Kent," he whispered. Then he brought a hand to his face and wiped the tears away.

The door to his room suddenly opened, and a woman stepped through. She was attractive, with short blonde hair tucked behind her ears and round red lips. She looked tired,

though, with dark circles under her eyes. For a second, Greg
didn't recognize her—the last time he had seen Nancy
Whitaker, she had been filthy, her face and hair smeared with
grease and grime, her once yellow dress covered in cracker
blood or guts, or whatever the white stuff was that oozed out
of them when they were shot.

*Crackers—where did they come from? And… and… did they get
Kent? Is that what happened to him?*

Greg closed his eyes again, and when he opened them,
Nancy was hovering over him, a sad expression on her pretty
face.

"Do you remember me?" she asked softly.

Greg nodded and wiped away more tears.

"I'm very sorry to hear about your son, Greg, about Kent.
So, so sorry."

Just hearing his late son's name brought about another
bout of tears.

*Kent—my champ. Dead before his sixteenth birthday. Dead
before he went to college, had his first bender, and probably fucked
his first girl. Christ, I don't even know if he even got a chance to kiss
a girl.*

His mind wandered to his son's round face, his freckles, his
short red hair. He thought about the way Kent had a hard
time making decisions, how he was still finding out who he
was, but despite this, he always had a half smirk on his face.

His smirk.

The Griddle Grin.

Nancy leaned down and hugged him as best she could
given that he was lying in the hospital bed.

But the Griddle Grin was gone now, vanished—gone when
Kent had disappeared, after an Askergan police cruiser had
come to pick him up.

Gone now that Kent was dead.

Greg kept sobbing and reached up to hug Nancy back.

It was all his fault, of course; after all, he had been the one that had taken Kent fishing, and then he had taken him to the Askergan Police Station to tell his story.

And Tyler—he'd also taken Tyler.

"What about Tyler?" he managed, and Nancy pulled back a few inches.

She shook her head slowly, and Greg's tears returned.

It was all his fault.

"What happened?" Nancy asked when they finally let go of each other. Greg thought that she had been crying too, but wasn't completely certain.

"I don't know," Greg replied, turning to look out the hospital window. Rays of sunlight leaked through the double-paned glass, but he couldn't tell if it was dawn or dusk outside.

"What do you remember?" Nancy prodded.

Greg continued to stare out the window, contemplating, for a moment, what she meant by the question. Nancy had been there when the crackers had attacked the police station—she knew about them, as did most Askergan residents, provided they had eyes at the front of their heads.

No, it was clear that she wanted to know about something else; she wanted to know what had happened at the abandoned house. The one that Greg knew was at the center of all of this shit...

"The crackers," he whispered at last. "They were everywhere. They seemed to be either coming from the house or coming to the house." He swallowed hard. "We tried to burn the house down—wanted to burn it down, to put an end to it all—but then we heard a voice... there was a girl and she was shouting at us, 'down here, down here', or something like that. And we got her, pulled her out of the basement. But Kent—Kent, he—"

Greg shut his eyes, unable to continue.

Nancy nodded as if she understood his plight, as if anyone could, and then she reached for his hand.

"Do you know what happened to your son? To Kent?"

Greg shook his head.

"Maybe, maybe—no, not maybe, *she* knows. The girl from the basement knows. Crackers, maybe? Probably."

"Corina," Nancy whispered abjectly.

"Corina?" he repeated.

In his mind, he had always referred to her as *the girl*. He might have heard her name once, from Jared or Coggins, or someone else, but the smoke and fumes from the burning Estate had done something to his memory. Either way, the name was new to him now.

Nancy looked at him, her expression confused. Evidently, she had assumed Greg had known her name, maybe even knew her.

"She knows what happened to Kent," he said. "What's her last name?"

Nancy tried to withdraw her hand and step away from the bed, but Greg grabbed her, holding her fast.

"What's her name?" he asked again, anger creeping into his voice.

A pained expression fell over Nancy's face, but Greg refused to let go.

"What's her name?" he demanded.

"You're hurting me."

Kent was hurting too, most likely, before he died—and so what's a little pain to you? Why should you get to live, while he dies?

Greg ground his teeth and squeezed Nancy's hand even harder. Tears formed in her eyes, but he knew they weren't from pain—it would take more than a sore hand to make this woman cry. No, the tears were from something else.

Reality suddenly hit him like a ton of bricks.

What am I doing?

Greg immediately let go of her hand, and Nancy promptly pulled it to her side and stepped back from the gurney.

"I'm sorry," Greg grumbled, averting his eyes. "I'm sorry."

It finally dawned on him how strange it was that she was here. After all, she wasn't ACPD or from the sheriff's department, although Greg was beginning to think that they might somehow be one and the same here in Askergan. And she wasn't a friend—they had only met a few nights ago. They had been through a lot together, but she must have had family to attend to, somewhere better to be than here with a near stranger.

Nancy Whitaker—a name he only knew because he had overheard the sheriff or deputies use it when referring to her.

So why was she here?

Greg opened his mouth to ask her as much when her eyes suddenly went soft.

"Lawrence," she whispered.

"Pardon?"

"Her name is Corina Lawrence," she repeated, and then quickly turned and left the room before Greg could ask her anything else.

For a moment, he just stared at the door as it swung back and forth before coming to a rest.

What a strange visit.

"Lawrence," he whispered into the empty room. One of the machines to his left answered with a *beep*.

Greg's eyes slowly closed, and he breathed long and deep, trying to bring on sleep. He tried to picture his son's face, but the only thing that came to him was the girl's dirt-smeared face as he pulled her out of the basement.

Corina Lawrence.

Large green eyes, scared, but also somehow guilty.

Corina Lawrence knows what happened to my son.

Greg's eyes snapped open.

He yanked the IV out of the back of his hand and removed the monitor from his index finger. As he swung his legs over the side of the bed, his head spun a little, and he paused.

The machines around him were beeping more frantically than usual, drawing a portly nurse through the door a split second later.

"Mr. Griddle, you need to lie back down!"

Corina Lawrence, you know what happened to my son, don't you?

"Mr. Griddle?"

You know, and you are going to tell me. I need to know.

Greg stood, putting a hand on the bed for support. He spied his clothes, all covered in smoke and ash, in the corner, and he hobbled over to them and began getting dressed, completely ignoring the nurse.

His throat burned and his head was still spinning, but he thought he could manage, that passing out was not imminent.

He would find Corina Lawrence, but first, he would find his son. He would find Kent's body, and then he would find the girl.

"Mr. Griddle?"

The nurse wasn't really there of course, no one was there.

Only Greg and Kent were real.

Only Greg and his champ.

Greg left the hospital room without looking back, knowing that there was one place that he could go to find some answers.

23.

CARTER DUKE BROUGHT THE bottle of beer to his lips and leaned back in his lawn chair so that he didn't actually have to expend the effort to raise his arm further and tilt his head back.

Naw, this was better; this was easier. And God, did that beer taste good—cold, bubbly, and *fucking* good.

He licked his lips and spoke to Pike, who sat quietly beside him.

"You think this'll work?"

Carter stared out at the barren expanse in front the church. A slight wind picked up some loose dirt and tossed it into the air like confetti.

Carter chuckled.

And I bringeth the wind, he thought, fingering his white collar.

He took another sip of beer and then pulled on his cigarette, watching the dirt as it swirled and then dissipated. Only after the dirt was completely gone did Pike answer him.

"This is a dangerous place, Carter."

Carter turned to his friend and partner.

"You clairvoyant now?"

The smirk was still on Carter's face, but the man's words were troubling. After all, nothing scared Pike.

Nothing.

When Pike continued to stare off into the distance, Carter took pause. He wondered briefly if his reaction had something to do with the priest—the fact that he had been attacked by those crab-things, whatever the fuck they were.

He shook the silliness from his head.

That wasn't it; no matter how strange the creatures were, they were gone now. And the priest? Well, fuck him, he got what he deserved. *Less* than he deserved.

So what was it, then?

Carter observed the man's face. It was surprisingly free of nicks and scars, given that Carter had first "rescued" the man from the underground fighting circuit nearly two decades ago. Pike had been but a boy back then, a young ruffian, untrained, undisciplined, but *my God* even back then he could fight. Back then, there was no one that could take Pike in hand-to-hand combat, and like a fine wine, or in this case like a wine soured, more vinegar than nectar, he was even tougher with years gone by.

Carter was happy to have someone as loyal as Pike by his side, irrespective of his skills. Still, he wasn't deluded enough to think that they didn't come in handy, that they weren't an amazing bonus. After all, in their line of work, they had many an opportunity to put his particular talents to use. And it went without saying that his skills would be needed again in Askergan.

Maybe even soon, because whatever Pike felt, whatever had inspired his comment, Carter felt something too. Maybe not danger, as Pike had proclaimed, but *something*. Good or bad, *something* was about to descend on this place, something that, despite what the townsfolk had already seen and experienced, would be eye-opening, to say the least. It was the dirt in the air, the charged atmosphere, the heat, the *tension*; something was coming.

Carter turned away from Pike and joined him in staring at the swirling dust. He took a final drag from his cigarette and then flicked the butt.

Becoming the priest incumbent in Askergan had been easy, just as Carter had predicted. It was human nature: tragedy, especially the kind that was difficult to describe or understand, pushed people to institutions that were born of secrecy and the supernatural.

In this case, it was religion, but Carter had also seen people turn to the dark arts, the occult, and other clandestine disciplines that could only be found with some serious internet digging.

Others still resorted to revenge, which was another human trait that he planned on exploiting, and sooner rather than later. In his experience, Carter had found that most people were intrinsically primed for revenge; they just needed some direction, a person or place to focus their rage. And after what Pike had found out about Askergan, the drug problem, Sabra's near-ubiquitous influence, and the cracker invasion, it was baby games for Carter to define the best target. Still, even one as silver-tongued as himself would need the support and backing of someone who was known to these people, who was in a position of authority, who was respected.

A smile slipped onto Carter's face, and he again adjusted the white collar around his neck, which seemed to be just a little too tight for his liking.

The man he had in mind was big, black, and had a star on his chest. Word was, the sheriff may need him just as much as Father Carter Duke needed him.

Ah, ye of mutual benefit.

Two of Carter's favorite words—*mutual* and *benefit*.

Carter finished his beer and stood, tossing the empty bottle on the dirt ground.

"Dangerous, sure," he said, the smile still plastered on his face. He gave Pike a friendly pat on the back. "But that's why I have you, isn't it?"

Pike looked up at him, but he still wasn't smiling. It was no matter; the man rarely smiled, and Carter didn't blame him for not smiling now. It was time to get to work.

24.

IT CAME AS A surprise to Greg Griddle as he made his way down the narrow white hallway that he was in Askergan County Hospital. It was a surprise because Greg didn't think that a place with a population of somewhere around three thousand warranted their own hospital. But it was an old building, which was evident by the peeling paint and the warped linoleum floors, and he assumed that it had been grandfathered in—a relic of times gone by that still maintained some utility. In a way, this was a blessing, because if he had been shipped to an adjacent county—Darborough, or maybe Pekinish—then his plan would have been more complicated. As it was, being in the Askergan hospital meant he was more likely to find out the answers that he sought.

Old hospitals like this one usually didn't have much in the way of security, or even key passes to gain access to the morgue. And they were almost always located in the basement in these old buildings.

Which was where he was headed now.

Greg passed a doorway, and his reflection literally stopped him cold.

Jesus, this can't be me, can it?

But as he brought his hands up to his face and pulled the sallow flesh beneath his eyes, it was obvious that this was, in fact, him.

Greg used his hands to try and part his hair, to make it settle down on his head. It responded, which at first was surprising, but as he leaned closer to his reflection, he realized that it was the grit and grime that made his hair so pliable. His first instinct was to use his t-shirt to wipe the soot from his hair and face, but a glance downward revealed that this would not only be futile, but it would make things worse — clearly, with the sheer volume of patients that had been admitted during Askergan's darkest hour, the nurses hadn't had time to strip him of his clothes and put him in a hospital gown. Greg was still wearing the same t-shirt and jeans that he had been when he had roared up to the station in his wounded Chevelle — which could have been two, three, maybe even four days for all he knew. His shirt was filthy, covered in not just dirt and ash, but also with a tacky white substance reminiscent of molten marshmallows.

Marshmallows… Kent had been so pissed when Tyler had stolen his marshmallow. So pissed, and he had been pouting again.

The fresh tears were helpful in that they cleared some of the black streaks on his face, but he quickly wiped them away.

Now was not a time for crying — soon, after he found out why Corina had made it out of the basement and Kent hadn't, there would be plenty of time to cry.

And reminisce.

"You're a master baiter, Kent."

The hallway was predictably packed after what had happened in Askergan, which was a blessing: no one took notice of the dirty man in the blackened clothes wandering around like a drunk. And the chaos also meant that he had no problem locating an abandoned nurse's cart pushed off to one side. A quick glance revealed a clean towel, and he immediately snatched both, barely pausing to spray it with some alcohol. He was about to continue down the hallway when he noticed a fresh set of scrubs on the lower shelf, sticking partway out of the half-closed sliding door. He grabbed these too, then ducked into the next doorway he passed.

The room that Greg entered—room 230—was identical to the one he had woken up in. A quick glance revealed that the only bed in the room, also identical to the one which he had lain in when Nancy had entered, was occupied, but the elderly man lying on it was breathing rhythmically, his eyes closed. The top line on the beeping monitor read, *Simon Bodkin, M, 68 y/o*, followed by a random stream of numbers that Greg didn't understand.

For a moment, the sight of the old man lying alone in the bed caused his heart to flutter. There were deep grooves etched on his wrinkled face, ones that were evidence of one of two things: a hard life, or wisdom and experience. Greg was tempted to walk over to the man, to get a better look at him, to maybe stroke his forehead and hold his hand. It was strange, this feeling, and somewhere deep down he knew it was a longing to feel something for an old man, someone that he might be able to love, to care for.

A father, one so very much unlike his own.

Years ago when he had left home, he had made a solemn promise to himself, one that until a few days ago he had diligently kept.

I will never treat my son the way I was treated. Not only will I not be the source of his anguish, I will protect him from everything.

But the crackers had stolen his boy from him, and *he* had let it happen.

Greg clenched his jaw.

"Fuck you, Dad," he hissed, then added, "Fuck you, Simon Bodkin, whoever you are."

Pulling his gaze from the man, he used the damp cloth to quickly wipe his face and arms, trying to clear off most of the grime. After a few strokes, however, the cloth had turned completely black and become useless. He glanced around the room for another, and while he saw a pile of fresh towels by the sink, before he could move, the man on the bed groaned and his eyes flickered.

Greg abandoned getting another towel and instead tore off his shirt and tossed it on the chair. Then he put on the top scrub. He debated putting on the bottoms too, but his jeans weren't that dirty, at least not compared to his shirt, and a quick tap on his back pocket revealed that his wallet was still there. The scrubs, on the other hand, didn't have any pockets.

Pockets… wallet…

A plan was already formulating in his mind, and he knew that if he wanted to get into the morgue to see his son, he would need his wallet and his business cards.

It dawned on him that he would also need his car, which was…

Greg racked his brain.

Did I drive it to the Estate?

He thought he might have—but whether it was at the Estate or back at the station didn't matter, he realized; either way, it was clearly no longer accessible.

Simon Bodkin groaned again, and Greg's eyes darted to his face. The man's sagging cheek was twitching in obvious pain. Allowing his eyes to drift, he spotted a set of car keys lying on the table beside the man's bed.

Jaw still clenched, Greg strode across the room and snatched up the sleeping man's car keys, noting the Mazda symbol on the electronic fob.

Wallet… cards… and now car.

He offered one final glance to the man on the bed and was shocked to see that it wasn't Simon Bodkin anymore, but someone else.

It was the face of his father, who for so many years had abused and tormented him, the underlying reasons for which had never come to the fore.

"Fuck you, Dad," Gregory Griddle spat, then turned and left room 230.

*   *   *

"Hi," Greg said, trying to lay on his most charming smile.

It was all for naught, as the woman behind the desk in the pink scrubs didn't even seem to notice him. Instead, she quickly flipped through a couple of pages on the notepad in front of her.

Her lips turned into a frown.

"Jane? Do you know what happened to—" She flipped another few pages. "—Mr. Simon Bodkin? Says here he's supposed to be in room 203, but the computer is showing that that room is empty."

For a second, Greg was taken aback.

Simon Bodkin.

That had been the name of the man in the room that he had changed in.

What are the odds?

Greg shook his head and tried to refocus as he waited patiently while another woman, an older woman with stark white hair, lifted her head from her computer screen.

"203? You sure? Computer is saying that Mr. Bodkin is in 302?"

"302?"

"302. Oh, and you have company."

The first woman, a thick-skinned black woman, finally lifted her gaze. Her eyes narrowed when she saw Greg standing in front of her. He tried his best to keep his winning smile plastered on his handsome face.

"Hi," he said again.

Sell… you're a salesman, for Christ's sake, now sell.

"Hi," she replied curtly, raising a painted eyebrow. "Can I help you with something? Are you looking for—?"

"My name is Greg," he interrupted. "And I know that you are really busy—I mean really, really busy—and my timing couldn't be worse."

He coughed into his sleeve; coughing and keeping a smile on his face at the same time was much harder than it looked.

The woman's eyebrow traveled so high up on her forehead now that he thought it might roll right over the top and become part of her hair that was pulled back in a tight bun.

You're losing her.

"But—" He rubbed a hand on his still dirty face. "—I've had one hell of a day. But I can see that everyone in Askergan has. See, I'm not from Askergan, I came here because Dr. Drake invited me."

He reached into his back pocket and pulled out his wallet. After flipping through several cards, he found his business card and held it out to her.

The nurse in the pink outfit just stared at it, making no move to grab it.

"I'm sorry, but this is—"

Greg held up his hand.

"The worst timing ever? I know, I know. But look at me. This was the worst time to come here. And I'm really in"—he lowered his voice—"deep shit here, if you catch my drift. I drove all the way from Lancaster, begged my boss to let me go. I've had three warnings already, missed my sales quota for three straight months. I just need to see Dr. Drake for a minute. Just a minute, to tell him about these new defibs that we are selling."

There was a pause, and Greg waited. He could see the woman's hazel eyes soften, but her lips remained pursed together.

"This is the worst time," she said simply.

Greg nodded.

"I know, I know. And I get that Dr. Drake won't be buying anything today, obviously. Still, I need to see him. If my boss calls and Dr. Drake says he never met with me, it won't matter if the apocalypse descended on Askergan, it'll be my ass."

He had debated using something other than defibrillators as the object that he was selling—after all, he wanted to get into the morgue, not the ER—but it wouldn't sound genuine. After all, that was what he sold. Besides, he doubted with what was going on that the nurse would put two and two together.

"I don't know a Dr. Drake," she said, then turned to her colleague, who had since receded behind her computer again. "Jane? You know a Dr. Drake?"

"Nuh-uh. Don't know a Dr. Drake."

The woman turned back to him and shrugged.

Greg raised his hand again.

"It's okay, I don't need to speak to *him*. I just need to speak to someone in the morgue, in case my boss calls. Doesn't matter who it is. And, again, I get it. Not selling today, and that's cool. I also know that you could care less about defibs. But, please, I've had one hell of a night, and I don't want to lose my job."

He could tell that the woman before him was torn, which was a good thing, and he debated adding more, but he didn't want to come on too strong.

Let her answer; let her come to me now.

There was an awkward pause, and Greg's cheeks started to burn from the fake smile he was still sporting.

"And you just want to see anyone in pathology? Dr. Gilbert should be around here somewhere, but I doubt she'll give you even a second. But if you wait here, you might be able to walk with her. No promises, though." She indicated a lone chair against the side wall. "You can wait there."

Not good.

Greg's gaze drifted to the door at the end of the hallway, the one with red block letters that read "AUTHORIZED PERSONNEL ONLY."

He shook his head slowly.

"This sucks, I know. Like, I really know. But if I could only go in there"—he indicated the door—"for a minute, I think I might be able to keep my job for another month. Please."

The woman looked at him quizzically, then turned back to Jane, who had an identical look on her face.

"Here," Greg said, holding out the card again. "Please, take my card."

When she turned back to Jane again and the woman shrugged, Greg knew he had her. His narrative had been nearly flawless; first convincing her that he wasn't some sort of pervert, and then disarming her. After all, what was the worst he could do? It was the morgue, and everyone in there was already dead…

The smile on his face had become genuine.

"There someone in there, Jane?"

"Yeah—the specialist that the sheriff called in."

The woman turned back to Greg.

"One minute," she said, her lips pressing together again. "Just one. Don't make me come in there to get you. In and out, that's it. Talk to whoever is in there about your defibs and then out again. And I'm only doing this so that you can keep your job. That's it."

"I swear," Greg replied, already backing toward the door. "And thank you, thank you so much." He turned to the door, but then paused. "Oh, and Mr. Bodkin is in room 230, not 302," he told the ladies, his hand finding the set of car keys in his pocket. A pang of guilt struck him, but this quickly vanished when he pushed through the doors marked "AUTHORIZED PERSONNEL ONLY."

25.

THERE WERE BODIES EVERYWHERE. And it was the sheer number of them, as opposed to the individual injuries—although, in some cases, these were horrible enough—that made Greg's stomach turn.

Unlike his son, he had seen his share of dead bodies, but this—this was too much.

Bodies were piled four or five deep on top of gurneys that were meant for one person. There were stacks of bodies on the floor, pushed up against the wall like dust or dirt swept to one side.

Greg swallowed hard. As a medical device salesman, he had seen dead bodies before, but not this many and not like *this*.

He tried to compartmentalize what he was seeing, trying to consider the bodies as items and not once living, breathing people. He tried to focus, to try and concentrate on the reason why he was here in the first place.

Kent. Where are you, Kent?

But this seemed a near impossible task. The piles of bodies weren't inventory like bonbons or rakes or pieces of lumber; these were loved ones. And there were so many of them—so many lives lost.

His mind flicked back to the woman in the lobby, the one that had hesitantly let him in the morgue. She could not have seen this—if she had, there was no possible way that she would have let him in here.

This was… it was *horrible.*

Greg saw men, women, even children, their tiny bodies placed—thankfully—off to one side by themselves. It wasn't really possible for him to count, but Greg thought that the room must have had forty or fifty bodies.

"About time," a voice from the back of the room sounded. Greg's blood ran cold. "I need all the help I can get."

Greg's mind churned as he decided what to do next.

"Hello?"

Greg finally spotted the woman, and he knew instantly that his defib 'help me keep my job' story wouldn't work with this woman. No, this woman was… different.

She had short brown hair that was tucked behind both ears, and vibrant blue eyes that stood out on her tanned skin. Pouty lips, a small upturned nose, and a figure that he could make out even beneath her lab coat: small and tight, but curvy, too.

She was cute, bordering on beautiful, but she was also smart. Greg could tell this just by looking at her—he could see it in her eyes.

No, the 'missed my quota' would never fly with this woman.

And when he didn't respond immediately, she sensed something was off and her eyes immediately narrowed.

"You're wearing scrubs… the top at least… but you aren't a nurse or doctor. And Sheriff White never said anything about another deputy." She looked him up and down. "Besides, no deputy would wear those filthy jeans in the morgue. So, who are you?"

Greg's face went slack. He was sick of lying and trying to remain calm. His son, his champ, was dead. And he had meant everything.

"Greg, my name is Greg—I'm just a father looking for my boy."

The woman's tight expression immediately softened.

"Did your boy go to the school?" she asked gently.

Greg looked up.

"School?"

"Wellwood Elementary."

He shook his head.

"No… he was… he was at the house."

The woman stared at him for a second.

The house.

Then she nodded.

"I'm so sorry—so sorry."

Then she gestured for him to move toward her, and Greg obliged, doing his best to avoid the piles of dead bodies. Out of the corner of his eye, he caught strange shapes buried underneath their dead skin, outlines that could only be one thing: crackers.

His breathing was coming in short, terse bursts.

The woman grabbed his hand when he was near, and then pulled him toward a gurney off to one side.

"You shouldn't be here," the woman whispered. "But I'm a parent too."

"Thank you…?"

"Eliza," she replied, looking up at him with her steel-blue eyes. "Eliza Dex."

Greg wiped tears from his cheeks and stopped next to the gurney. Unlike the others, this bed only had one form on it, that much he could tell despite the fact that it was covered by a blue sheet.

"I—I can let you look. But that's it. Eventually the body will be released to you, but for now…" Eliza's sentence trailed off, which was fine by Greg; he wasn't really listening anyway.

His thoughts, like the heart thumping in his chest, were racing, scenarios of the horrible things that had happened to Kent passing through him.

Why is there a sheet on him? Why only him? What did the crackers do to him — is it too horrible to show even in this place of mass death?

"The sheriff asked me to look most closely at your son," Eliza said quietly. "Said he was there first — got to the house before anyone else — and that he might have clues as to where they came from."

Her hand grabbed the plastic blue tarp and was about to pull it back when Greg spoke up, stalling.

He didn't want to see, not just yet.

"Are you a doctor?"

She nodded.

"Pathologist. I get called in sometimes when, ugh, weird things happen. Things that aren't in the textbooks, if you know what I mean."

Greg's heart skipped a beat as he thought of the battle with the crackers at the police station, then out at the Wharfburn Estate.

Weird things.

"Would you like to see your son now, Greg?"

"Yes," he said dryly. "I'm ready."

With that, Eliza Dex pulled the sheet back and Greg sucked in a breath, holding the air in before turning to see the horrors that had befallen his son.

26.

TRISTAN DEVON OWENS, CURRENTLY known as Dirk
Kinkaid, didn't look back when he bolted from the mansion.
Even when his biker brethren hollered at him, more surprised
than anything else, he kept his head dead and continued to
run.

At forty-two years young, he had kept in shape for
occasions such as this—well, situations *like* this; situations
from which he had to escape, but not to specifically run from
crab-like things that chewed you up and spat you out. At
forty-two years young, Dirk Kinkaid was his fourth
pseudonym, the prior others being Lucas Thomas Wright,
Steven "Stevie" Drew, and Elvis Giablini.

And of course, there was *his* name, the Owens name, the
one that somewhere out there a woman and a young boy
shared. Or maybe not. *Probably* not. If he put any thought into
it, he would have no choice but to assume that they had
changed their names, that the program had *forced* them to
change names. Still, he liked thinking that somewhere out
there his wife and son had his name: *Owens.*

Dirk was forty-two now, but back when he had been a
young man in his mid-twenties, he had been a rising star in
the New York detective ranks. So when a chance arose to go
undercover as a low-level soldier in one of the most notorious
Mafia brotherhoods in the United States, he'd had to say yes—
it was a compulsion, driven by some underlying need to strive
to be the best, to make sure none of the so-called bad guys
ever escaped.

Dirk had known the risks; he'd known that if he was found out, it would not only mean his death, but that he was putting his wife and newborn son in danger.

Besides, he had been told that he wasn't going to be alone in the ranks, that there was another officer embedded in the criminal enterprise.

Someone with the initials *CD*.

Not much to go on, surely, as the Mafia had numbers in the low four digits in New York alone, but it had given him comfort nonetheless. And besides, he was a star detective, for Christ's sake; he'd felt confident that he would be able to eventually figure out who his fellow undercover agent was.

The three missing fingers on his right hand ached at the memory, and Dirk rhythmically squeezed his palm as he ran.

Oh, he had found *CD* alright, but the man wasn't his friend. In fact, Dirk doubted the man was even a detective at all.

But it didn't matter; his missing fingers and displaced wife and son were proof enough that *CD* most definitely was not a friend, colleague, or confidante.

Both Dirk and *CD* had been forced to change their names and flee from the Mafia. The only difference being that while *CD* ran away, Dirk ran *after*. First combing the southeast, then slowly migrating north, Dirk had followed the man with the ever-changing name but constant initials, employing his honed detective skills to follow the man's trail of lies and deceit as he exploited, extorted, and blackmailed his way across the country.

There had been close encounters before, but Dirk was closest *now*; after infiltrating and then working his way up through the ranks of the Skull Crushers' biker gang, Dirk knew that *CD* was within his grasp.

But now *this*—this fucking freak Walter, who had revealed horrors of the like even Dirk was foreign to, and who had threatened to foil another one of his plans.

Walter had ruined his chances to catch *CD.*

Still, Dirk had no choice but to run from what he had seen; his viscera demand such a reaction. After all, staying meant almost certain death—a horrible death—and that would not serve his need for a pound of flesh.

Part of him expected the other bikers outside Sabra's mansion to follow him as he ran, but no one did. In fact, some men even went the opposite way, back into the palatial home, curious to figure out what had happened to Sabra.

Dirk knew that when they found him, some, if not all, would have the same reaction he'd had: to run. For those that stayed, it would be worse. Twelve years, the first five of which he'd served as an undercover agent, and the last seven as a… well, what was he now, really? No longer an officer of the law—that ship had sailed when he'd stopped his biannual check-ins. And that was more than a half-decade ago. But after all this time, he hadn't seen *anything* like what he'd seen inside Sabra's mansion.

If twelve years entrenched with bad men had taught him one thing, it was for him to recognize when bad men were about to do bad things.

And this man, this Walter, was one of the worst he had ever seen. Walter was the worst kind of bad man: the kind that had nothing to lose, that cared less about their own wellbeing than even that of others. He was far worse than even Sabra, who was keen on neutering those who didn't pay up in due time.

Dirk hopped on his bike and drove his foot onto the pedal, and it immediately roared to life.

"Dirk," a man hollered over the sound of the motorcycle engine. "What the fuck is going on in there? What's going on with Sabra? And where are you going?"

It was Mickey, one of the few bikers that Dirk had actually formed a relationship with. Like Dirk, the man had his demons, but he wasn't like the other brutes. For a moment, the two good fingers on Dirk's right hand simply hovered over the throttle, and he stared into Mickey's pale eyes.

He was scared, Dirk saw. Genuinely, unabashedly afraid — not a frequent occurrence for bikers, even one with Mickey's disposition.

Mickey felt that something bad — something worse — was about to happen here, too.

"Take off," he said as the two good fingers wrapped around the throttle. "Get out of here, Mick. And do it now."

And then he put the bike into drive and it shot forward, leaving Mickey, Sabra's estate, and the other bikers in a trail of dust and dirt.

For a brief second, he debated heeding his own advice: to flee. But as Dirk and his bike put distance from the horrors at Sabra's house, the visceral sensations that he had felt slowly subsided, and the reality of how close he was, just how very close he was to finding the man who had taken his wife, son, and fingers from him, the man with the initials CD, settled in. The man with the silver tongue. The fucking conman, the fucking fake, the phony, the fucking parasite with his deadly sidekick.

C fucking D.

And yet here he was, on his bike, tearing down Highway 2, leaving behind the bikers that were his best chance of finding CD.

Is this it? Has he escaped me again?

Dirk felt a pang of regret and remorse. But unwilling to succumb to these emotions, he cranked the throttle again and set his mind to motion.

Think—how can I salvage the last two years? How can I still use my leverage with the bikers to find him?

Dirk was so lost in thought that he didn't even see the police car coming toward him, traveling in the opposite direction. If he had, he most definitely would have slowed down, given that the speedometer on his motorcycle was closing in on triple digits. It was only when the police car passed him and then switched on its lights that he noticed.

"Fuck!" he shouted, his words swallowed by the roaring air rushing by him.

A quick glance in the rearview showed that while the cop had turned and was now heading back toward him, Dirk was putting a lot of distance between them, and fast.

He can't keep up.

Dirk leaned forward, ready to accelerate even more, to leave the officer in his dust, when a thought suddenly struck him like a slap in the face.

If I can't use the bikers to catch him, maybe it's time to switch sides. Maybe it's time to go back to my roots.

A smirk fell on Dirk Kinkaid's lips, and although it was barely visible beneath his handlebar mustache, it was there.

I have information they want, and they might be able to help me get what I want.

Maybe they can help me catch him.

Dirk let go of the throttle and gently brought the bike to a slow, allowing the twinkling red and blue lights in his mirrors to grow until they merged into one ubiquitous purple orb.

27.

THE GUT-WRENCHING REACTION that he'd expected to feel never came. Instead, Greg Griddle was beset with a sort of calm that defied the situation.

It was probably the fact that the horror, the devastation that he had prepared himself for, simply wasn't there. In fact, if Kent hadn't been buried beneath a sheet in the basement of some shithole hospital lying on a cold metal gurney, Greg might have thought him sleeping.

And then his mind pulled a fast one, forcing him to stand there and watch his boy's chest, to wait for the rise and fall that accompanied every breath, even though in the back of his mind he knew it wasn't coming.

He counted in his head.

One, two, three…

When he got to twelve, he forced himself to stop counting. With a trembling hand, he reached out to Kent and laid his palm on his unmoving chest.

Feeling the cold hardness of his skin, reality overcame Greg and he was struck with a deluge of emotions.

"No," he croaked. "No. No. No. No. No."

His strength drained from his limbs and he collapsed onto Kent's body, his back hitching with each and every one of his sobs. He tried to force these movements back into his boy, to give him the rhythmic up-and-down movements of his own body—the natural, organic movements of every living, breathing thing.

But that wouldn't work. His son was dead and gone, and that was the end of it.

It isn't fair.

Still crying, but with reality injecting him with some semblance of control, Greg pushed himself back to his feet and was surprised that Eliza was behind him now, offering him not only emotional support, but physical as well. Her hands that gripped his waist were strong, much stronger than he would have thought given her average stature.

"I'm sorry," he blubbered, not sure if the apology was aimed at Eliza, himself, or Kent.

The young pathologist rubbed his back, but said nothing.

Greg wiped the tears away, clearing his vision. And then he stared at Kent.

The boy's skin was pale and thin, and there was a smattering of burst vessels around his eyes. His cheeks were also a strange blue tone, and there was an indentation around his throat. But as far as he could tell, there were none of the impressions of the crackers, which had become almost expected in this place—in Askergan.

Greg pulled the sheet down a little more, down past the waist of his boy's jeans and to his thighs. Only then did Eliza reach out and lay her hand on his, stopping him from moving it farther. The boy's arms were clear—pale, dead, but he still couldn't see any crackers.

He hated the question, didn't want to ask it, but he had to know.

"What happened to him?"

Eliza replied almost robotically.

"Kent was asphyxiated."

At first, Greg didn't think that he had heard her correctly. Surely she hadn't said 'asphyxiated'; surely she had meant

some other technical term that meant killed by a parasite… a
fucking cracker, whatever the hell that was.

"What?"

Eliza nodded.

"Asphyxiated."

Greg turned to the doctor. For a brief moment, he thought
that maybe her eyes were watering too.

"Asphyxiated?"

"Yes. Do you want a moment to say goodbye? I can't—you
can't be in here. I'm sorry for your loss, but I can only give
you a minute with your son." She waved her hand over the
dead bodies in the room. "I can't even guess when his body
will be released, so I suggest you say goodbye."

Greg swallowed hard.

Asphyxiated? What the fuck is going on?

"But you said asphyxiated? Like someone choked him?
Who?"

Eliza shook her head.

"I'm sorry. Even if I knew more, I wouldn't be at liberty to
say."

But Greg's thoughts had already turned to the girl in the
basement with Kent when he had died. The girl with the
artificial leg.

Corina Lawrence… did she…?

It was almost unthinkable, but who else? Who else could
have killed… no, not *killed*, murdered… his son?

Rage began to usurp sadness and dismay.

Somehow, he managed to nod at Eliza, then he turned back
to Kent, eyes blazing.

"I love you, son. I love you more than anything."

He glanced quickly over to Eliza, who had taken a step
backward and was averting her eyes; she was giving him as

much privacy as she could manage in this room of dozens of ghosts. He leaned in close and pressed a kiss on his son's cold blue forehead.

"...and I'll find out who did this to you, champ. I'll find out and—"

And what?

Greg didn't know. But he would find out, if it was the last thing he did.

"—and I'll make them pay. I'll make them fucking pay for what they did to you," he whispered.

The anger in his voice surprised even himself, and he took one last look at Kent before pulling the sheet over his face again.

Then he left the room without even looking back, without even so much as a thank you for the woman who had done him the courtesy of allowing a final moment with his dead son.

A single thought ran through his mind.

I'll make them pay, champ. They will pay.

28.

GREG WAS SO CAUGHT up in what the pathologist had told him—*asphyxiated*—that he nearly tripped as he exited the morgue. The woman who had granted him access was still at the desk, but when she spoke, he didn't even hear her.

It wasn't until she was nearly shouting at him that he took notice.

"Mister! Everything all right?"

Greg looked up at her with red eyes.

"Corina Lawrence," he said, although he wasn't sure why. It was the only thing that was burning through his mind now, the only thing that made sense.

"What? You okay? What happened in there?"

When Greg didn't answer, she immediately turned to the phone behind her. She punched a few numbers, and then a second later started speaking.

"Hey, everything all right in there? What happened?"

Greg kept his head low and kept walking. Even when the nurse turned her attention back to him, he ignored her.

"Mr. Griddle? Mr. Griddle, come back here!"

Greg didn't stop—he didn't even look back.

Less than ten minutes later, he found himself in an absurd situation, driving toward the Askergan police station in a stolen SUV. This was not lost on Greg Griddle, only it didn't seem to matter to him as much as it should have. The only thing that mattered now was finding out what had happened to Kent. And although he was sure that it had everything to do with Corina Lawrence and not the crackers, the best way to find her, he knew, was to confront the man that only hours ago he had stood side by side with and fired bullet after bullet into a frothing sea of crackers.

Greg wasn't familiar with Askergan County, and the SUV that he had stolen didn't come equipped with a GPS, but what he was good at was retracing his steps. He simply ripped down Highway 2, taking pretty much the same route that he had taken with Reggie when they had raced to rescue the sheriff and his deputy.

And this is how the sheriff repays me for standing with him — by lying to me, by keeping this from me.

He was driving too fast, way too fast, but he didn't care.

Somewhere in the back of his mind, he registered the fact that there were far fewer crackers on the road than the night — or was it two nights? Three? — prior, and that the firemen were still hosing down what was left of the gas station. As he turned onto Main Street, he also caught sight of several bikers, more than a dozen, parked at the side of the road. He passed several more of them on the road, and on several occasions, he had to swerve to avoid them.

But none of this mattered.

A few minutes later, he pulled into the ACPD lot — or at least he tried to; the parking lot was jammed full of cars. In fact, there were so many cars in and around the police station that he had to park nearly a block away, and even then he did so in an area that was clearly marked as a tow-away zone.

Greg exited into the warm summer air, not bothering to lock the vehicle. Then he made his way quickly to the front of the station. The front window that had been blown inward by the crackers was covered with a patchwork of plywood, a tangible reminder of what he and the sheriff had been through together.

But what gave Greg pause was the people: they were packed outside the station, and he could see even more inside through the door that someone conveniently held open with their foot. Every walk of life was represented here in this crowd, from the elderly to the young, but they all had one thing in common: their eyes were red, their faces plastered in sadness. Some, like him, were obviously angry as well, but they were all somewhere on the spectrum of distraught to devastated.

For a second, Greg's mind turned back to the bodies that he had seen in the morgue, and couldn't help but think that if these people only knew what had happened to their loved ones, that they were, in all likelihood, dead, that most would lean toward the devastated end of the spectrum.

But unlike most of *them*, he knew—he knew what had happened to his loved one, to Kent, and that took precedence over all else.

Greg bullied his way through the crowd. At first, he tried to be relatively gentle, to grumble 'excuse me', avoiding physical touch as he made his way past and through the elderly, but there were just so many people that this quickly stymied his progress. Eventually, he digressed to sheer determination.

He was almost at the door when he elbowed his way past a particularly large man in a cut-off t-shirt.

"Hey, get in line, buddy."

Greg turned and looked at him, his eyes blazing. The man, catching this look, immediately clamped his jaw shut and stepped off to one side to allow him to pass. And pass he did. A few more strong elbows later, Greg was back inside the station, only this time, it was very, very different from what he remembered.

When before the place had been empty save him and a handful of others, fighting for their lives, the place was full now. Stepping on his toes, he caught sight of Deputy Williams's smeared face as the man tried desperately to keep the mob away from the inner part of the station, applying equal efforts into holding them back and placating them.

It didn't seem to be working.

But this didn't matter to Greg; it wasn't the deputy that he was seeking, but the sheriff.

Then he saw him, and he experienced an involuntary intake of breath.

Sheriff Paul White had his back to him, but it was clear that it was indeed the sheriff. It was his broad back that gave him away. That and his bald black head.

Corina Lawrence, Corina Lawrence, Corina Lawrence.

"Sheriff White!" he shouted.

But his voice was too quiet to be heard above the din of other shouts. Greg elbowed his way nearly to the very front of the crowd. Someone cried out when his elbow landed hard into soft tissue, but he ignored them.

"Sheriff White!" he yelled again. When this also failed to elicit a reaction, he raised his voice once more. "What the fuck happened to my son?"

And then it wasn't just the sheriff that turned, but most of the crowd as well. Eyes still red, Greg glared at the man.

Their eyes met and for a moment everything seemed to stop.

And then recognition and sadness overcame Askergan's sheriff.

Sheriff Paul White opened his mouth to say something, but movement distracted both him and Greg before he got the words out.

Another man who had also been standing with his back to Greg, standing right next to the sheriff, also turned.

The anger fled Greg's face.

"Reggie?"

29.

GREG GRIDDLE WAS USHERED and then pulled through the station before he had a chance to fully grasp what exactly was going on.

And then, before he knew it, he was back in Interrogation Room 1.

Full circle.

Only this time, Kent wasn't with him. This time, Kent was dead.

Murdered.

When the door shut behind him, he realized that it was just him and Reggie in the room—the sheriff hadn't joined them.

His burly friend stepped forward and surprised him with a strong embrace. Greg felt like this was the right time to cry again, but he was all out of tears.

He pushed Reggie away and stared up at his friend's concerned face.

"What the fuck are you doing here?"

Reggie looked shocked.

"I could ask you the same question."

Then Reggie went to embrace him again, but this time Greg pushed him back immediately.

"What are you doing here?" The words came out like an insult, and Reggie recoiled.

"I—I—they needed help, Greg. The sheriff asked me to stick around for a bit, to be an, ugh, impromptu deputy. Can you believe that?"

When Greg just stared, he quickly continued.

"I'm just glad you made it. The sheriff told me that they pulled you out of the fire. Man, that was…"

The words just dragged on, without Greg really hearing any of them.

When his friend had said the words, 'deputy', the man had had a hint of pride on his face. And this enraged Greg.

How dare he be proud at a time like this. How dare he feel that way when Kent is lying in a morgue, surrounded by the dead.

"How dare you," he barely whispered.

Reggie immediately stopped talking and stared.

"How dare you stand there and speak to me as if everything is normal. My son is dead, Reggie. Kent's fucking dead."

It was all he could do to prevent from lashing out and striking the much bigger man.

"Where's your son, huh? Where's Baird?"

There was a pause as Reggie, his face pinched now, debated whether this was a rhetorical question. When it became apparent that Greg was waiting for an answer, he finally spoke up.

"He's at home, Greg. Baird's at home. And I'm so sorry about—"

That was it. Greg blew a fuse, and his right hand fired out with speed and accuracy he hadn't known he possessed. His fist made contact with Reggie's face, and the man's head whipped to one side. A loud crack echoed throughout the small interrogation room.

As Greg watched, fists clenched at his sides, Reggie turned back to him, rubbing his cheek that had already turned a shade of pink.

He was crying, Greg saw, but this did nothing to temper his fury.

Kent's dead; asphyxiated.

The door to the room suddenly flew open, and both men turned to see the sheriff lumber in.

The man's eyes darted from Reggie to Greg, and finally to Greg's fists. Greg didn't know the man from Adam, he realized, but he could tell by his expression that he had guessed what had happened.

"You lied to me," Greg hissed. "You lied to me about Kent."

The sheriff looked confused.

"You lied to me… said that the crackers got him, that he fell victim to whatever the hell the things are that attacked this shithole of a town. But he didn't. He was strangled to death. *Murdered.*"

Both the sheriff and his "deputy" gaped.

"Murdered?" the sheriff gasped. "What? By who?"

There was genuine surprise on the man's face, but this wasn't enough to stop Greg.

"Why was he even here? Why was Kent back in Askergan?"

"Murdered? Greg—"

"Don't you fucking 'Greg' me!" he shouted. "One of your fucking men picked him up and brought him back here. Why, Sheriff? Why?"

Reggie and the sheriff exchanged looks, and Greg took an aggressive step toward the sheriff.

Reggie moved to step in front of him.

"Oh, now you're protecting him? After all, we've been through and you're protecting *him*?"

When Paul spoke again, his voice had lost some of the confused quality and had regained a modicum of authority.

"Calm down, Greg. I didn't know what happened to Kent."

"Calm down? Calm down?! Don't you fucking tell me to calm down! You killed my son! You killed Kent!"

Reggie had to physically get between the two men now as Greg was inches from throwing another punch. But this punch, he knew, wouldn't have been shrugged off like the one he had delivered to Reggie moments ago. This one would land him in jail.

Greg backed down; being thrown in jail would mean he might never get to the bottom of this.

"Corina Lawrence," he mumbled, his eyes remaining trained on the sheriff.

Something passed over his face, and Greg instantly knew that he was onto something.

"Where is she?"

The sheriff opened his mouth, then quickly closed it again.

"Where is Corina Lawrence?"

"I can't tell you that."

The sheriff looked away when he said the words.

"Well then tell me what the fuck happened to my son!"

Greg became distinctly aware that he was no longer the only one shouting. The mob at the front of the station must have been fueled by their argument, as their voices had started to escalate as well. Sheriff White glanced toward the closed door, concern on his face. After all Askergan had been through, after all it had survived—barely, by the skin of the County's proverbial teeth—it was all about to come crumbling down.

"I can't tell you where she is, Greg. I'm sorry. But I'll find out what happened to your son. I promise."

"Fuck your promises!" Greg screamed.

The tension in the room had reached a breaking point and was at a juncture.

When Greg made up his mind and stepped forward, the sheriff didn't back down. Greg didn't blame him; despite what was going through his mind, and undoubtedly how badly the man before him felt for what he had gone through, for what Kent had gone through, he still had a county to preside over, to protect.

Strong hands suddenly grabbed Greg by the shoulders, and before he could reach the sheriff, he was quickly guided to one side. He tried to shrug his friend off, but Reggie was too strong. The much bigger man exerted his will, and before he knew it, Greg was being forcefully shoved back into the hallway. He tried to turn, to confront the sheriff again, but Reggie's grip tightened and he was unable to stop his forward progress.

No, no, no. I need to find out what happened!

But he couldn't turn, couldn't do anything but continue back toward the mob of citizens. With a strong shove, Greg found himself being propelled into the crowd. When he was finally released, the people filled in his path, and he found himself unable to make his way back, even if he'd wanted to.

He turned and caught his friend's sad face.

Reggie was crying again.

But despite his tears, he managed to mouth the words, "the church—they went to the church".

For a moment, Greg did nothing; he simply stood still amidst the chaos even as his once best friend turned and tended to other Askergan citizens.

The church.

It felt like a curse word to him.

The church.

On some fucked-up level, it kind of made sense; after what Corina had done, after what she had done to *Kent*, she—anyone—would seek some sort of salvation.

Greg Griddle's needs were on the opposite end of the spectrum, but their basis in human nature was equally as primal.

Revenge.

He was seeking revenge for what had happened to his son, despite his promise all those years ago, despite trying with every fiber of his being to not treat his son or anyone else in the so utterly inhumane way that his father had treated him.

In a way, he too was seeking salvation, but his redemption would not come from God.

Gregory Griddle swallowed hard and then turned and left the Askergan County Police Station for the final time.

30.

"AND SO I ASK you this one simple question: where was God during the most recent crisis? Where was He when the Devil's parasites crawled forth and took so many of your loved ones?"

Greg slipped into the church when the pastor paused to take a breath. It was packed inside, and it was also hot and uncomfortable. The pews were filled with people, and there were more standing at the sides and at the back, whom Greg joined presently. It seemed unusual that, despite what had happened in the county over the past week or so, the place would still be so packed, but this congregation—coupled with the throngs of people back at the station—was clear evidence that people were seeking answers to things that they couldn't possibly understand. Still, he was amazed at the speed with which they had congregated. After leaving the police station, Greg found out that he had been out—unconscious—for nearly two full days, although he still couldn't ascertain if this had taken place in the basement of the house, or in the hospital. In fact, he remembered next to nothing after entering the house, only a strange dream, about his childhood, growing up with his brother…

"And when you ask yourself these important questions, I demand that you ask with conviction," the pastor continued with such vigor that it interrupted Greg's thoughts. He looked up at the man in the plain black outfit and the traditional white collar. He was younger than Greg would have expected, somewhere around thirty, but not much older. The man had a propensity to scratch at his short, yet thick black beard, which wasn't unlike his hair, and he had cool blue eyes that were strange for someone with such dark hair.

But it was the smile that Greg immediately gravitated towards. He recognized the smile because he had used the same one to gain access to the morgue; it was the smile of a salesman, the smile of a conman. This was no priest, Greg knew almost at once. The problem was, as he looked around at the parishioners staring at the preacher with rapt attention, no one else seemed to notice.

"With *conviction*. Because the Lord wants you to question what has happened here, what has happened to Askergan."

Greg raised an eyebrow.

Definitely not a priest... no priest would ask their parishioners to question; that flew in the face of all that the institution stood for.

"These beasts, these parasites that have invaded the town, came and took our loved ones with them—and for this, I am incredibly saddened. But you must ask yourself why—why would the Lord inflict such pain and suffering on this town? Why this town, of all towns?"

Greg caught several of the people look up quizzically with tired, sad eyes. He took this opportunity to scan the crowd, to try and locate Corina Lawrence.

The only problem was, he wasn't sure what she looked like. His memory of pulling her out of the basement was as clouded as the air had been in the house.

Black, obscured, toxic.

But he remembered she was young, had short hair, and, last but definitely not least, had an artificial leg.

"Why?" someone from the crowd shouted.

The wannabe priest nodded, and he proceeded to pace from one side of the altar stage to the other.

"Yes, go on, it's okay. Ask why."

Someone else shouted 'why', which was quickly followed by a few more inquisitive yells.

"Why, Lord? Why did you take Harvey from me?" an old woman shouted from Greg's right. She was so close that he could smell her lavender perfume.

And then it felt like everyone in the church was shouting, filling the rafters with their saddened cries.

The priest continued to nod as he walked back and forth, his eyes low.

This guy is good, Greg couldn't help but think. As a fellow salesman, even in his current state, he couldn't help but appreciate the pitch that he was seeing unfold before his eyes.

Several people broke into sobs, and the priest let this carry on until it seemed that things might get out of control. Just as the noise reached its peak, he raised his arms and slowly lowered them. Like a conductor commanding an orchestra, the shouts and cries quickly died down.

"You might also be wondering what happened to the cross with our Lord and Savior, Jesus Christ, that used to hang behind me."

The pastor raised a hand, indicating the empty space behind the altar. Greg squinted his eyes and thought he could make out the dark outline of a cross amidst the sun-bleached wood backdrop.

"And I am compelled to ask you to question why I, Father Carter Duke, am here instead of Father Peter Stevens."

Nearly everyone in the church nodded. This time there were no shouts, however, only hushed silence.

"I am compelled, because I asked those very same questions every night for the past week. And last night, God finally answered."

There was a collective intake of breath as Father Carter built the tension. When he spoke again, his voice wasn't quiet, subdued as before, but bombastic. He held his palms up to the rafters above

"And the Lord spoke to me, and he told me that the parasites that invaded Askergan were *necessary*. That they were part of His plan, that they were not the work of the Devil—oh no—but that they were His doing, that they were necessary to cleanse this town of the evil that had laid its roots. The drugs, the crime, the disease that was rampant in Askergan has been cleansed, my people, it has been cast out! Like the Devil himself, God has cast this evil out of Askergan!"

A cheer erupted in the church, making it difficult for Greg to make out what the pastor said next.

"… and we shall rebuild… former glory… idyllic Askergan will be reborn!"

Another cheer, this one louder than the first.

Greg tried to scan the crowd again, to find Corina in the throng of people. But it was too hectic inside the church, too hot and heated, for him to find anything but raised arms and the backs of desperate people's heads.

"And now we pray."

Silence again, accompanying bowed heads.

"As you pray, my colleague will be coming around with the collection basket. But this is no ordinary Sunday, my devoted disciples, but a new beginning. A modernization of Askergan, one without crime and without disease—without the influence of the Devil. I ask that you empower me with the financial resources to carry out God's word, to finish what He started."

With everyone else's bowed heads, their lips moving in silent prayer, Greg had a clear view as the man seated in the front row stood. He was sharply dressed in a navy suit jacket and maroon tie, which matched his slacks. The man had a large basket in his arms, which he held out to the first parishioners that he approached. As Greg watched, he noticed that not only did they empty the loose change from their pockets, but they also rid themselves of the bills in their wallets with such gravitas that it was as if they were on fire.

Amazing, he thought, taking a good look at the man in the suit's face.

He had a square jaw and deep-set eyes, complete with a stern expression that was in stark contrast to Father Carter's smirk. And, also unlike the pastor, it was obvious that this was no salesman. If Greg were put to the task, he would have said this man, as unimposing as he was in his slick outfit, was the muscle of the operation.

Still, despite these strange revelations, they held little meaning for Greg.

So what if this conman and his bodyguard were pulling the proverbial wool over all of Askergan's eyes?

This mattered little to him. What mattered was finding the only person who knew what happened to Kent. And that meant having to wait and watch the converted leave to find the person he was looking for—assuming, of course, that what Reggie had told him back in the station was true.

That Corina Lawrence was, in fact, here.

He would have to wait just a little while longer to find the girl responsible for his son's murder.

31.

GREG GRIDDLE WAS APPALLED by the uplifted expressions on the faces of the people as they left the church.

How can you all be so happy after what happened here? After what happened to this place?

It was all he could do to avoid sneering at those who passed him, their hands outstretched with the ubiquitous phrase, "the Lord be with you."

But he remained calm despite himself, watching each and every one of them leave like a disgruntled bouncer.

More than half of the three hundred or so people inside the church left by the time he finally spotted her.

Corina Lawrence was at the front of the church, her head hung low. A thin man with a cleft in his chin—her father, maybe, or an uncle who looked oddly familiar—had his arm wrapped around her for support. Greg immediately recognized her by her stiff gait, a dead giveaway that she had a problem with her left leg. Anyone else might have assumed based on her age that she had maybe suffered a sprained ankle or a damaged hip playing softball or soccer, but he knew better.

She had an artificial leg, Greg knew.

His eyes narrowed in on her, and he concentrated on her face. She was cute, with a dimple on her dirty chin, and large green eyes.

Corina didn't look like a killer, but this did nothing to deter Greg's fury.

He took two steps forward, intent on making his way to her, when an elderly woman—the same one that had shouted for her Harvey, perhaps—stepped into his path.

"Peace be with you," she said, holding her hand out expectantly.

Greg's intent was to step by her, but he caught several others staring at them and decided, with the energy in the air, that it would not serve him well to ignore the elderly woman.

Against his better judgment, he tore his gaze away from Corina and grabbed her hand briskly.

"And with you," he grumbled. When he went to pull back, she held fast.

He looked down at her arthritic hand and wondered for a moment where the woman's strength had come from. She was a little over five feet tall and was all skin and bone, hunched at the waist, but she was strong.

"I see your addiction," she said softly. "But don't you worry, son. Askergan will be clean again. The Lord is looking out for us now. You shall also be cleansed."

Greg stared at her pale eyes, and his first thought was that she was in some sort of trance. Again he tried to pull his hand away, but found himself unable.

"Yes, cleanse," he mumbled, and finally his hand was released.

"Revenge is but the Devil's fingers. Don't forget that."

And then she was gone, like the multitude of Askergans before her, she had vanished into the dirt-covered parking lot.

Greg instinctively wiped his hand on his soiled jeans and turned his gaze upward, again searching for Corina.

His heart skipped a beat when he didn't immediately find her. Desperation setting in, he pushed by a young couple and stepped deeper into the church.

Two more steps and Greg came face to face with Corina Lawrence.

The girl, with her head low, didn't notice him, and neither did the thin man that was helping her along. The two tried to step around him without raising their eyes, but Greg shadowed their movements, not allowing them to pass. He had had nearly an hour, what with the drive to the church and then the sermon, to figure out what he would say to her once they finally met, but nothing could have prepared him for the fury that he felt at that moment.

"You," he spat, and the girl finally looked up. She was younger than he'd expected, not much more than a teenager, really, and scared. She was really, really scared.

Not a killer.

"You killed my boy," he whispered, and Corina recoiled.

The man moved in front of her defensively, but Greg didn't even look at him.

"You killed my boy," he repeated.

Something akin to recognition passed over her small face, and Greg knew in that instant that his words were not without truth. Whether or not she looked like a killer no longer mattered; he saw in her face what she had done.

An innocent person would have looked confused, not guilty.

Why? Why did you kill my boy?

"I'm—" she started, but the doors to the church suddenly blew wide and the few remaining members inside the church, including Greg, Corina, and the man she was with, quickly turned.

"Oh, Father Peter! It's time to collect!"

32.

TWO MEN IN JEAN vests, one thin, one heavily muscled, both with bare arms adorned with tattoos, burst through the church doors. Unlike Greg, these men with their gaunt, hardened faces simply pushed the remaining parishioners aside as they moved into the church.

"Father Peter?" the larger one shouted again.

It wasn't Father Peter or even Father Carter who stepped forward, but the other man, the one in the double-breasted suit jacket.

"Calm, Pike," Greg heard the pastor say. There was a new sort of energy in the air, one not of salvation this time, but of something else; something more sinister.

The man named Pike stepped forward despite the pastor's words.

"Who the fuck are you?" the thin biker with a ponytail shouted, eying Pike.

The other churchgoers, sensing that something was going to go down, either quickly left the church or crouched back into the pews. Greg felt Corina doing the latter, but he reached out and grabbed her hard by the arm.

He wasn't going to lose sight of her this time.

She cried out, and the man at her side stepped to intervene, but again they were distracted by the bikers.

"Strong, silent type?" the thin biker sneered. "Don't matter. Where the fuck is that pedophile, Stevens?"

Someone in the gallery gasped.

"Father Peter Stevens is no longer with us," the man named Pike replied, his eyes narrowing. Greg watched as the biker with the heavily muscled arms slowly reached into the back of his jeans.

This was going to escalate, and quickly.

"Where is he?" the skinny one demanded.

Greg felt Corina start to pull away from him, and he retightened his grip.

"He's not here. Your business was with him, his debt with you."

The muscular biker made a face and pulled a large pistol out of the back of his pants.

"His debt, your debt, the church's debt. Either way, there is money to be paid."

Father Carter only smiled. He turned to the people that were still stuck inside the church.

"You see? This is the Devil in Askergan that we need out. This is the problem that the Lord wants me to extinguish. This isn't the old Askergan—this is the new, Modern County."

Modern County.

The way the pastor said it made it sound like a proper noun, like a name and not a thing.

The biker with the gun scoffed.

"Only thing you're going to see if you don't get our money is a bullet between the eyes, Father."

For a second, nothing happened, the men were locked in a stalemate.

It was Pike who finally broke the silence.

"Tell Sabra he can come get it himself."

The man wagged the gun back and forth as he chuckled.

"Tough words for a queer in a suit. Anyways, we don't serve Sabra anymore—he's long gone. Kinda like what I expect happened to our dear Father Stevens."

Father Carter raised an eyebrow.

"We serve the Crab now, and I'll give you a little tip, seeing as you can't seem to make up your mind: pay up. Pay up now, and continue to pay, because I don't care what God you pray to, He ain't gonna help save you from the Crab."

Greg couldn't believe his ears.

The Crab? What the fuck?

It sounded like a terrible Batman villain.

The Crab.

Under other circumstances, it might have been funny. But it wasn't, not with a massive silver pistol being waved around.

"Yeaahhhhh," Father Carter said. "I would. I would love to just pay you scabs so that you can keep this county in the dark ages. Seriously, that would be great."

He had a sarcastic smile on his face.

The bikers looked none too amused.

"But you see, there is one little problem with that."

"Oh yeah? And what's that?"

"My man Pike here won't allow it."

Three things happened next in such rapid succession that Greg didn't know which occurred first.

What was apparent was that the man with the gun squeezed off a shot and it echoed loudly in the church. But his bullet, clearly intended for either Pike or Carter, went awry. A man came out of the pews, a fat man with a red face and short brown hair that clung desperately to his forehead. His shoulder struck the biker in the kidney, knocking his arm with the gun in the direction of Greg, who was no more than a dozen or so paces away. There was no time to react, but thankfully the bullet whizzed by Greg's ear. It hit something with a *thunk* and someone moaned, but before Greg could turn, *Pike* happened.

The man lunged forward, closing the distance between him and the still standing biker with amazing speed. The way that the thin biker poised himself, by stepping forward with his lead leg and bringing his fists in front of his face to protect himself, it was clear that this wasn't his first fight.

But none of this mattered.

Pike was just too fast.

As Greg watched in amazement, Pike's left foot shot forward and hit the other man's lead knee head on. The biker cried out, and he doubled over, trying to protect his injured leg that was bent the wrong way. Greg was amazed that he was still standing. Pike struck again, only this time he did so with his fist. He delivered a devastating uppercut to the man's chin.

Even with the sound of the gunshot still echoing in his ears, Greg heard the man's jaw snap together. Shards of shattered teeth and blood flew from the biker's mouth as his eyes rolled back in his head. The man was unconscious the second the blow landed, and Pike quickly hopped back to avoid the man's bloodied face and jaw from ruining his suit.

If that wasn't enough, something even more bizarre happened next. The remaining church members suddenly rose out of their crouched positions and flooded toward the fallen man.

Then they were on him, delivering their own not as effective, yet damaging punches and kicks to the unconscious biker.

"A new Askergan!" Father Carter shouted. "A Modern County, where the Devil is exorcised from this land!"

Greg felt himself being yanked again and turned in time to prevent himself from falling on top of Corina.

"Jared!" the girl screamed, and Greg followed her gaze.

The bullet had struck the man that she had been supported by in the thigh, and he was on the ground moaning, using both hands to try and stem the bleeding.

Jared.

And then it hit Greg. He knew this man; he had fought beside him, and he had been at the house when they had burned it to the ground.

Jared had helped him fight off the crackers at the police station.

Greg's mind started to spin... there were too many connections, too many coincidences in this shithole of a county.

To steady himself, he squeezed Corina's arm even harder. Regardless of Jared, the man called Pike, Father Carter, or the two bikers, he would not let go.

Kent.

Thoughts of his son continued to run through his head, from the years he had spent raising the boy from a tiny red-headed baby through his awkward teen years.

Kent. Kent. Kent.

Then someone grabbed *his* arm, and he shouted.

The muscular biker had since dispensed of the man that had tackled him, and he had somehow crawled over to Greg without him knowing. And now he was standing directly behind Greg. His first instinct was to struggle, but the man's grip was iron, and he knew that it would be futile. Instead, he focused all of his efforts on keeping his hand locked to Corina's arm.

I found you, and I won't let you go.

But Corina had ideas of her own. She yanked her arm from Greg's grasp, and at the same time swung her leg around— Greg didn't get a chance to see if it was the artificial one or not—maintaining her crouched position. She instead made contact with the back of the biker's ankle, sweeping the unsuspecting man's legs out from under him. When he fell backward, the biker maintained his grip on Greg's arm, and together they toppled.

Greg landed hard on top of the biker, back to belly, and he heard the man's breath forced out of him in a *whoosh*. The back of his head cracked against the biker's teeth, and Greg felt four individual points dig into his dirty scalp and hair. Grunting, he started to roll off the man, intent on scrambling to his feet and grabbing Corina again, but this time she came to him.

Sliding across the floor, Corina shoved Greg off the biker with her feet and then slid her legs on top of the muscular man with all the fluidity of a highly rehearsed dance routine. Perpendicular to the biker now, she slid one leg over his face, and the other over his chest. Corina wrapped her hands around the man's wrists just before he rolled away from her. Then she lunged backward, pulling her body straight, and bending the biker's elbow joint in the most perfect armbar that Greg had ever seen.

All of this happened so quickly that the biker still hadn't had a chance to catch his breath from the fall before he was locked in the tap-worthy position.

Only this wasn't an octagon, and there was no tapping here.

Corina's face went red with the effort, and the man grunted beneath her, the sounds muffled by her leg that was laced over his face. Greg could see the inside of the man's elbow turning red with the pressure, but he was fighting the move using brute strength by flexing his biceps. But this could only last so long, Greg knew; eventually, his strength would run out and his arm would snap like a dry twig.

Greg went to scramble to his feet, but he froze. Although Corina had trapped the biker's left arm and was indeed in the process of hyperextending and without question leading to a break, it was the biker's other hand that gave him pause.

"You shot Jared!" Corina screamed, the cords standing out on her neck as she pulled even harder with her hands, arching her back for additional leverage.

The biker mumbled something in response, but Greg didn't catch it at first.

He was too busy staring at the gun that was aimed directly at his midsection.

The biker grunted and shouted again.

This time Greg heard the words loud and clear.

"Let me go, or I'll kill him."

Corina evidently heard this as well, as she temporarily released some pressure on the biker's arm. She didn't go as far as to let go of his wrist, but she did sit up a little to survey the situation.

Greg was still on his side, frozen during the process of pushing himself to his feet. The biker was in the cross position, ironic in this place of worship, one arm still locked between Corina's legs, the other outstretched and aiming the gun at Greg's gut.

Greg met Corina's stare, and guilt washed over her pretty, if tired, features. Then she let go of the man's arm, and Greg knew that his first impression—that this girl had, in fact, killed Kent—was completely accurate.

Once released, the biker quickly stood, keeping the gun trained on Greg at all times. His other arm, Greg noticed, hung a little lower, and he seemed reluctant to bend it.

"Get over here," the biker demanded, and Greg had no choice but to oblige. He stood, took one step forward, and the biker reached out with his injured arm and grabbed his shoulder, spinning him around. Clearly, although his arm was sore, to Greg's detriment, it was still functional.

Corina stood too, and Greg seized the opportunity to grab her by the arm as before, squeezing tightly, refusing to let go.

"Let her go," the biker hissed in his ear. He snaked his arm around Greg's throat, putting just enough pressure to make breathing uncomfortable and swallowing impossible.

An image of Kent, lying on the metal gurney, his face purple, burst blood vessels around his eyes, flashed in his mind.

This is how I die; asphyxiated, just like you, Kent. And while it isn't at the hands of Corina, she is here—she is here all the same. It is her fault once again.

"No," he croaked.

Even when he felt something cold and round against his temple, he refused to let go of Corina.

Instead, for reasons that could only be explained by guilt, Corina allowed Greg to pull her toward him, spinning her around as the biker had done to him just moments ago. And then he too put his arm around her throat.

It was a bizarre situation, a hostage taking a hostage, but Greg refused to let go.

During the entire scenario—from Corina putting the biker in an armbar and then letting it go, to Greg being taken hostage with a gun to his head and him grabbing Corina around the neck—Pike had remained calm, standing near the other biker's fallen body. The other parishioners had since risen from the fallen biker, their arms—all of them, from the men, to someone that couldn't have been into his teens yet, to an elderly woman—but sleeves of blood. Whatever instinct had had them cowering in the pews when the bikers had burst through the doors was gone now, and probably forever. Now they stood beside Pike, *with* Pike, their bloody arms hanging at their sides, awaiting instruction.

"Move one step and I'll kill him—I'll kill them both."

Despite the intimidating men and woman before him, the comment was not addressed to them, or even to Pike. Instead, he was speaking to Carter, who stood off to one side, the same smug expression on his face.

Greg tightened his grip on Corina's throat, and he heard the girl gag. It was amazing how quickly things in the church had changed, from uneasy parishioners listening to a very unconventional sermon, to standing at arms, willing to do anything that Carter bade.

Astonishing, really, what desperation could do to a person—especially if the person was being guided by a man such as Father Carter Duke.

Carter shook his head subtly, something that Pike picked up on, and he stood down, indicating for the parishioners to do the same.

When the men and women stepped backward, Greg realized that they had actually been standing on top of the downed biker, but he fought the urge to look at the mangled corpse. He had seen enough death for one day.

"Good," the man hissed in his ear. His breath was a sour mixture of whiskey and stale cigarettes.

And then they were backing toward the door. Before Greg knew it, the three of them were in the hot sun.

"Be gone! Like the Devil, you will pay for your sins!" Carter shouted, which was accompanied by an enthusiastic 'Amen.'

Squinting hard, Greg managed to turn his head a quarter of an inch to make out a faded blue van, the door thrown wide.

And then something smashed into his temple and the sun suddenly reduced to but a pinpoint of light.

The last thing he heard before being thrown into the van with Corina was the biker shouting back into the church.

"The Crab will come for you, preacher! The Crab will come for you all!"

33.

'WILL I EVER SEE you again?' the boy asked, his eyes downcast.

'I don't know. Maybe. I hope so.'

'I hope so, too.'

They were at the tree again, only this time they were standing by the trunk and not sitting on one of its branches. Using taking out the compost as an excuse, the boy who had just stood up to his father, who in that very moment had become a man, had found Donnie weeping by the tree.

There was something profound about this moment, a feeling that was only intensified by the realization that they might not see each other again.

Ever.

Donnie strode forward and hugged his brother.

'What will happen to you?' he asked.

Walter pulled away, confused at the question.

'Nothing… probably nothing. After all, he never hits me. What… what will happen to you?'

Donnie swallowed hard.

'I dunno. I just know that I can't stay here. He'll kill me if I stay, I think.'

They embraced again, and Walter whispered in his brother's ear, 'I'll find you. One day, I swear I'll find you.'

After a squeeze, the two boys separated. And then Donnie turned and started to run.

He never looked back.

"—and what do I want with two nobodies? A cripple and her father?"

Greg's head was spinning and his back and side hurt. He resisted the urge to open his eyes, knowing that this would only make things worse.

Instead, he listened.

"Do whatever you want with them... I needed them to get out of there. You should have seen it. The new priest... he has this guy that destroyed Rick. Like, *destroyed* him."

"Rick?"

"Yeah. Didn't even get a punch in. And this here *bitch* fucked up my arm."

The other man paid no attention to the complaints.

"And you came back with no money? What about the drugs?"

There was a slight hesitation before the biker from the church continued.

"Nothing. These aren't... they aren't normal church people. And the people there, the uhh, the uhhh, donators? Whatever the fuck you call them, the people watching the priest, well they fucking *tore* him apart. They ripped Rick to shreds when he was unconscious."

Corina. Kent.

This time Greg opened his left eye, but he did it slowly, careful not to make his captors aware that he was awake. The lids stuck together tightly, and he felt a crinkling sensation from his right eye all the way up his forehead.

Dried blood.

"And no money or drugs?"

For some reason, this voice also sounded familiar, but he couldn't quite place it.

"No." Unlike in the church, his voice lacked authority now.

The Crab—he had to be talking to the Crab.

Greg forced his eye open a little more, taking in some of the world around him. He seemed to be in a dimly lit room, lying on top of some sort of patterned rug. His left arm was beneath him, and it was completely numb. His left hip was also numb, but he could feel his left leg from his quad down.

Directly in front of him was the top of Corina's head, her short hair arranged in such a way that he knew she must still be unconscious.

"Well, then how am I supposed to pay you and your fucking group of Dixie Chicks? Huh? You had one job to do: get the money and the drugs. And you come back here with two fucking—what? Two Bible thumpers? You come back with stories about being beaten up by a fucking priest!"

"It wasn't the priest—"

The man's words were interrupted by a loud smack, and the biker stumbled backward, gaining control of himself only moments before tumbling on top of Greg.

Greg flinched instinctively, pulling his arm in closer to his body. The drums in his head protested by beating even louder.

"Not a priest," the biker mumbled. "But his, uh, his *friend.*"

"I don't care!" the Crab roared and moved forward again.

Greg pulled himself into a ball as the biker's thick boots came perilously close to his head.

"You are going to—ah, one of these churchgoers is waking up now. Why don't we hear what he has to say, what do you think?"

Greg closed his eyes tightly, but it was too late. The Crab had seen him, and he was coming for him. His first instinct wasn't to bound to his feet and fight or even run. His second instinct was to try and reach for Corina, to squeeze her arm as he had done before, but he hesitated when he saw that her hands had been bound behind her back. And this brief pause cost him the opportunity to react in any way.

He felt fingers in his hair, and he had no choice but to allow himself to be pulled to a sitting position.

He winced as he felt fresh blood leak from the cut in his scalp from whatever the biker had struck him with to knock him out.

"What happened in the church, you—?"

Greg opened his eyes and the man that had been holding him by the hair immediately let go and stumbled backward.

"Donald?"

34.

"GO ON, TELL THE sheriff what you told me."

The man in the jean vest looked at Deputy Williams, then turned to face the sheriff.

"My name is Dirk Kinkaid, and I used to work for Sabra."

The sheriff's mouth twisted at the sound of the man's name. Sabra was the faceless man behind the drug problem in Askergan and had been one of many problems that Sheriff Paul White had been unable to solve since taking office.

"Go on," he said, staring at the man sitting before him. It had been one of the worst days he had ever had, rivaling the day of the storm and the day of the invasion.

"Dirk here was speeding on Highway 2, when I—"

Paul's eyes shot up and he gave Deputy Williams a look. The man's square jaw clamped shut.

"Go help Reggie outside. Keep the townsfolk at bay."

The deputy looked as if he were going to add something else, but decided against it.

"Go!"

Before the door closed behind Williams, he hollered after him.

"Any word from Coggins?"

The man offered a confused look.

"No. Still nothing. You think he's still local? I mean—"

The Sheriff shook his head in frustration.

"I dunno! *I dunno!* Just keep fucking trying!"

The deputy nodded and quickly left the room. Sheriff White waited for the door to close completely before turning back to Dirk. Even then, he didn't speak right away, choosing instead to take a few deep breaths, trying his best to regain control. His heart rate slowed, but the frown remained etched on his face.

"What are you doing here, then?"

Dirk took a deep breath and stared the sheriff directly in the eyes.

"I'm gonna lay it to you straight, because whatever you and your men have been through over the past few days ain't nothing compared to what's going to happen next."

The sheriff's eyes narrowed. Sabra was bad, but he was just a drug dealer. The man was notorious for his obscene and obscure torture methods, but these only usually affected other dealers or junkies that failed to pay up. He thought back to the men that he had fought at the bar when he had retrieved Coggins the first time, how they had made quick work of them.

The bikers that surrounded Sabra were bad, but they also had an agenda. And killing random people was not on the docket… it was just bad for business.

The sheriff wiped his sweaty forehead with the palm of his large hand.

If history was any indication, after what had happened over the past few days, there would be hundreds of Askergians seeking solace in either product or the church.

Paul wasn't sure which was worse.

"Go on, then," he said. "Tell it to me straight."

The man nodded, and for the briefest of moments, Paul thought he caught fear in the man's face. As quickly as it appeared, it was gone.

"I've seen some crazy shit in my day, but this takes the cake. A couple of days ago, a man came to see Sabra—a regular junkie, through and through. We had sent a couple of hitmen out to collect from him, but for some reason, this man came back alone. I picked him up outside Sabra's compound, and I brought him in to see the boss. This, in itself, was strange. I mean, the men we sent to collect were *pros*, man."

Dirk paused as he waited to see if Paul caught his meaning of the word 'collect'.

He did, and Dirk continued.

"But he came to us… and he was blabbering about something to do with his son—nonsense, really. At first, I thought he was high. High, but relatively harmless, you know? Especially considering the biker army that Sabra had built up around his compound—what's the worst he could do? But this man, this Walter, didn't at all seem afraid. It almost seemed like he wanted to be caught. He wasn't—"

"Wait, what did you say his name was?"

Dirk paused.

"Walter."

Paul swallowed hard.

"Black hair, white beard? Skinny little shit?"

Dirk nodded slowly.

"You know him?"

Where the fuck is my boy?

Paul thought back to when the man had blown through the doors at the station, and how he had nearly strangled the racist prick when he was behind bars. But then, during the cracker attack, the man had escaped.

"Walter?"

"Walter."

"And you say he was there at Sabra's? Why?"

"Man, this is only the beginning."

And then, while Paul listened, his eyes growing wider with every word, Dirk told his story about Walter, about the crackers that budded off him, about how he had exacted his revenge.

When he was finally done, both men stared with wide eyes and pale faces. Even though Dirk had experienced it, Paul could tell that he didn't quite believe his own tale. But like young Kent Griddle's story that had been spun in this same room mere days ago, the sheriff knew that Dirk was telling the truth.

Paul exhaled loudly. On any other day, at any other time, he would have told this biker to go fuck himself, to get out of the station with his ridiculous story before he looked up outstanding warrants and threw him in jail. But this wasn't *any other day*, and the stress and anxiety that he had gone through over the past three days rivaled even the cracker attack. The danger wasn't as potent, perhaps, but the pressure and tension of dealing with hundreds of townsfolk, their heads filled with nonsense uttered by the new preacher in town, was equally as palpable.

He wiped sweat from his brow and encouraged Dirk to continue.

"The men… the men I work with, they have seen and done things that would make you cringe, Sheriff."

He paused.

"Remember Mayberry Street?"

Paul nodded hesitantly.

Less than six months ago, the sheriff had been called out to a house on the border of Askergan and Pekinish. A neighbor had called in, said that the smell was so bad that people in the neighborhood were starting to get sick.

Inside, the sheriff witnessed a scene of pure horror. Seventeen people dead, seventeen people dismembered — junkies, all of them. In the basement, they had discovered a mishmash of materials used for making meth. But it was such a mess down there that the sheriff was surprised that they hadn't blown the whole block to smithereens. No ventilation, not even a cracked window, for Christ's sake. Still, amidst the horror, it was clear who was responsible.

It was Sabra sending a message, and the message itself was clear: if you're mixing on my ground, you will face my wrath.

"Well, the bikers did that. And yet what Walter did, that was worse. Some men turned and ran... but most were so frightened that they stayed. They call him the Crab now, and he is the worst thing that we have ever seen."

Sheriff White stared at Dirk. He couldn't quite comprehend the fact that the twitchy man that had been in the cell, shouting racist insults, was this man, this *Crab*, who incited such fear in hardened bikers.

"You need to call the FBI or something, Sheriff."

"I did—I called them right after all of this started happening. Do you know what they did?"

Dirk shrugged.

"They sent me a pathologist. Some doctor... Doctor Eliza Dex. Said they couldn't spare any real agents."

"Well then call them again. Call them again, now."

The sheriff rose to his feet, stretching out his sore legs. He had been on his feet all day, trying to keep whatever semblance of peace still existed in Askergan.

"Dirk, I appreciate you coming here today, and for what it's worth, I believe you. Problem is, I've got over a hundred bodies in the morgue, and hundreds more townsfolk that are losing their shit over dead relatives. I've also got a shooting out at the church—the county is on the verge of collapse. And this stuff about Walter, or the Crab, or whatever, has to wait."

Sheriff White thought about that for a moment. Sabra's lair, so to speak, wasn't even technically in Askergan, which made him wonder why Dirk had come to him.

"Why did you come here? What does this have to do with Askergan? I know we have a drug problem, but—"

"Because Sheriff—because the Crab's beef isn't with Askergan." The man took a deep breath and then exhaled through his nose. "It's with you. And he's coming."

35.

GREG COULDN'T BELIEVE HIS eyes. Walter stood before him, and even though he hadn't seen his brother in decades, even though he had jet-black hair and a long white beard, even though he was a grown man now, he knew it was *him*.

It was his face, his eyes, the fact that despite his shocked expression, the man still had a permanent, sly sort of grin.

The Griddle Grin, as Kent had dubbed it so very long ago. Only it wasn't a Griddle Grin; never had been. Greg was even beginning to doubt that there was such thing as a *Griddle,* even though he had lived with the alias for more than two decades now.

It was a *Wandry* Grin, through and through.

Greg shook his head.

No. It's not possible.

"Quick," the man instructed the biker that had bashed him in the head. "Help him onto a chair."

"Yes, Walter," he said.

Greg's head was spinning, and it was all he could to prevent himself from passing out again.

It can't be.

Squeezing his eyes tightly, he tried to clear his head, to dismiss what was clearly an illusion brought on by extreme stress and exhaustion. But when he opened his eyes again and stared into Walter's face, he knew unequivocally that it *was* his brother; no one endured what they had endured, what *he* had endured, and forgot the face of the person that had saved his life.

But it wasn't Walter and Greg who used to hide out in the old oak tree behind their farmhouse.

It was Walter and… Donnie.

Still groggy, Greg felt his body being lifted and carried before he was dropped onto a massive chair in front of an even larger desk.

"Walter?"

The man with the white beard smiled.

"Yes, it's me—they call me the Crab now."

Then he reached down and embraced Greg. Walter smelled foul, and he appeared to be wearing some sort of leather coat, a deeply tanned job that covered not only his chest, but his arms all the way to his wrists.

"It's me, brother, it's me."

Greg squeezed his eyes together tightly.

Will I ever see you again?

I don't know. Maybe. I hope so.

I hope so too.

But now, after ending up here, in this place, Greg wasn't so sure.

"I told you I would find you," Walter whispered.

Greg knew that he should respond, offer a kindness, a thank you, maybe, but he bit his tongue. Everything was so confusing that he was at odds with himself.

Walter disengaged from him and then took a step backward, both men taking the opportunity to inspect each other.

The irony that he, the one that his father had so ruthlessly abused for years, had until recently been a completely upstanding member of society and a good father, a family man, was not lost on Greg. Conversely, his brother had become… what? Greg didn't know for certain, but he had heard enough rumors—and his present appearance added credence to most of them—to conclude that his brother wasn't a lawyer or a doctor, or even a tax-paying citizen of Askergan, or wherever the biker had taken him.

At that very moment of extreme stress and emotional deluge, staring at his brother's face, Greg thought that he finally understood why his father had beaten him so and had left Walter pretty much alone.

It was because Walter was like *him*, and Greg wasn't.

Hadn't been.

Greg's mind churned, taking him back to the last time he had seen Walter.

I will find you.

Embracing beneath the tall oak, tears flowing down their faces, Greg had used all of his willpower to turn and run—to leave Walter behind. But once he had made that decision, he didn't stop; he ran and ran and ran, running from Walter, from his mother, his father, and most of all he ran from *himself.* For years he'd tried to build his alias—Greg Griddle— into a real person and, for a time, he'd succeeded.

But that was before the rumors, the tales that somehow reached Greg's ears even as far as Vermont. Even though he had become detached from his previous life, he still kept his ears to the ground, tried to keep abreast of Darborough and the surrounding counties' news. And before long, he started to hear the stories about a drug addict named Walter, perpetually in and out of prison for petty robbery, dealing drugs, assault. For the most part, he ignored these stories, trying not to let them affect his new life, but when he heard about Walter knocking up a teenager, he couldn't help but take notice.

When the claims of child abuse came next and Walter abruptly vanished, Greg was inclined to move closer to "home". He was in no way certain that the boy named Tyler that shared the last name given to him at birth was Walter's child, and by extension his nephew—hell, he doubted that the boy's mother was even sure who the father was—yet he felt a strange proclivity for the boy, and he took it upon himself to look after Tyler, even if his involvement was mostly at a distance.

Greg had never completely understood why he did this, but if he were to hazard a guess at this moment, he would have said that the guilt of leaving Walter behind played a role. Part of him also hoped that by being there, Walter might come back, and he would see him face to face again, have a heart to heart, convince him not to be like Dad... in short, to be together again.

Like in the oak tree behind the barn.

I'll find you.

Ironic that Walter would utter those words, as for the longest time, Greg had known exactly where his brother was.

But it was only now that they were once again united.

"What are you doing here?" Walter said at last.

Greg had been meaning to ask the same question, but now that it was posed to him, he had difficulty answering.

"I—I—"

And then it all came crashing down again, and Greg broke into tears.

The two other men in the room waited. When the emotions finally passed, Greg tried to answer the man's query. Except the only thing he could manage was mumbling about Kent.

"My son, he was killed—murdered. After—" His voice hitched and he looked away. "—after all I did to try and keep him safe, to treat him right, he was *murdered*."

Walter's voice was tight.

"Murdered?"

Greg wiped the tears away and his vision slowly began to clear.

He was in a large room, he saw, complete with an ornate fireplace off to his right, with a large flat screen above it. There was also a large chandelier above with at least a dozen light bulbs. But despite the number of bulbs, they were the retro yellow type that did little to illuminate the large space. There was also a tapestry of sorts, a mish-mash patchwork of different shades of beige on the wall, that looked as if they had been stitched together with long shoelaces.

"Murdered."

"Tyler, too," Walter whispered.

Greg continued to stare at his brother. It was the same man, that was certain, but he was different. He had heard stories, of course, about how his brother had become a junkie and had become entrenched with unsavory folk. But he had never imagined this.

After all, Greg had been the one to leave, to run away, and he had left Walter alone.

This guilt ate him up, even to this day.

Walter's face suddenly changed.

"We have lost, brother. We have lost, but we will seek revenge. We will exact our revenge. You left me once, but no longer. We are together, and we will stay that way until everyone in Askergan, starting with the sheriff, feels our wrath. They will learn that nobody fucks with the Wandry brothers."

Greg thought about the sheriff, about how the big man had dismissed him even as images of his son's dead face floated through his mind.

"We will get all of those responsible for our sons' murders."

Greg started seeing red again, and his anger built up inside him.

Evidently, he had a little of his father's rage in him after all.

The jacket on his brother's chest slipped a little, and he realized that it was stranger than he had first thought.

"What are you wearing?" he asked in a quiet voice.

Walter sneered.

"Sabra," he said simply.

The word meant nothing to Greg, but he was pretty sure it was a man's name—and it made no sense. How could he be wearing a man? A designer, maybe?

"Sorry to break up this family reunion, fellas, but what are we going to do with the priest and his man?"

Walter turned so swiftly that the jacket he was wearing nearly fell off completely; the back was completely open. And now, with Walter's back facing him, Greg could see the torn edges—of a man's chest. It wasn't a coat; it was a skin.

Greg felt as if he was going to be sick.

"Shut up!" Walter suddenly shouted.

The biker recoiled, his face contorting into a mask of fear and disgust. The entire time, the biker had been unable to stare directly at Walter, clearly sharing Greg's repulsion at the sight of the human skin.

And fear and repulsion were powerful emotions—it was becoming clear that all of this was a tactic that Walter was employing to keep the bikers around to do his bidding. Greg knew this to be true, even though he had been conscious for less than ten minutes.

It was in their faces, hidden deep within their cold, hard eyes.

Greg watched as Sabra's skin slipped off his brother's shoulders, revealing something that was arguably worse.

Walter's skin was covered with a network of thick blue veins that crisscrossed and intercalated with his spine that jutted from his pale skin.

"No!" the biker screamed. "Please, no!"

The man turned to run, but Walter just stood in place. A second passed, and then his entire body started shaking as if he were having a seizure.

"All of Askergan will feel our wrath!" Walter yelled, and then he groaned and a cracker burst from his back.

As the crackers sped across the wooden floor towards the biker, Greg was distracted by another sight: the girl on the floor beside him.

Corina Lawrence opened her eyes and tried to scramble to her feet.

Greg's vision turned red.

No more hiding… no more hiding what I really am.

There was no such thing as Greg Griddle. Greg Griddle was made up; a fictional character in the horror story that was his life.

There was only Donnie.

Donnie Wandry.

I am Donnie Wandry. And my father gave me more than just this grin; he also imbued me with his anger, his hatred, his propensity for violence.

Donnie reached over and grabbed Corina's ankle and squeezed.

They would pay. They would all pay for what they had done to their sons—for what they had done to the Wandry boys.

36.

Sheriff Paul White stared at Dirk in disbelief. Then he grabbed his phone and frantically began punching in numbers.

The phone rang once, twice, then a third time.

"Come on, Nancy! Pick up!"

It went to the machine and Paul hung up. Then he tried again. When he got the machine a second time, he slammed the phone down on the table.

Almost immediately, Deputy Williams rushed into the room, his gun drawn. He aimed the pistol at Dirk, but Sheriff White told him to stand down.

"What else did he say?"

Dirk swallowed.

"He said that Askergan would pay for its sins… that you would feel the loss that he felt."

"Fuck!"

"What's going on?" Williams asked. The man had lowered his gun, but he was reluctant to holster it.

The sheriff's eyes bounced from Williams to Dirk and back again. Then his thoughts turned to the newly deputized Reggie—he couldn't even remember his last name—who he had sent to check out the church shooting.

If what Dirk had said was true, they were going to need more men.

Lots more.

He turned back to Dirk, eyes narrowed.

"Can I trust you?"

The question seemed to catch the other man off guard, and he didn't answer right away.

"Can I trust you?"

Dirk nodded. It was a risk, but he was running out of options. Askergan was like a boiler plate ready to explode.

And he wasn't about to let that happen. He wasn't about to let Dana and Mrs. Drew and Nancy and Reggie and all of the other residents down.

He didn't possess the same intuition that Dana had, but staring at Dirk's eyes, he knew that there was something about this man.

He could trust him, he thought, which was enough.

It *had* to be enough.

"Williams, go get Dirk a uniform. Askergan has a new deputy."

Then he picked up the phone and tried Nancy again.

When he looked up and Williams was still standing in the room, a confused look on his face, he spoke again.

"Go! And can anyone find Coggins?"

He looked around at their blank faces, trying but failing to keep desperation from his own.

Please, someone find Coggins. Once again, Askergan needs you.

For what felt like the hundredth time over the course of the last week or so, a single phrase echoed in the sheriff's head.

Askergan needs the good boys again.

PART III - SETH

37.

SETH GRUDIN WIPED THE corners of his mouth as the man that stood before him hiked up his khakis and began doing up his belt. He started to stand, but the man ordered him to stay on his knees.

"Stay down." The voice was strong and powerful, commanding respect. And after what he had just done, Seth figured it was only fitting.

"What about my money?" he asked in a sheepish voice. "We agreed on twenty."

When there was no immediate answer, Seth glanced up. It was dark out, and even though it was a full moon, it was partially blocked by the corner of the dumpster he squatted beside and also by the man's looming head. Still, there was enough light for Seth to make out that he was sneering.

"Should have got the money first, faggot," the man said with a chortle.

Seth looked away and he started to scramble to his feet when the man surprised him by squatting down to his level. His face was wide, his impossibly white teeth seeming to glow in the darkness. A hand grabbed Seth by the cheeks, forcing his mouth open. He felt the calloused pads of the man's fingers biting into his narrow face. Seth tried to shake the man away, but he had an iron grip, and his fingers only dug deeper.

Still smiling, the man said, "You're lucky I don't cut you."

They stared at each other for what seemed like an eternity, Seth at the mercy of the man's grip, unable to even look away from his dark brown eyes.

This was intentional, of course, but it didn't make his threat any less true. Staring into those dark, empty pools, Seth knew that this man who had petitioned him inside the bar was dangerous.

Very dangerous.

He was getting sloppy, and as a result, he had gotten himself into another situation.

Just remain calm; don't say anything that might enrage him. Just—stay—calm.

Seth's resolve nearly broke when out of the corner of his eye he noticed the man's hand slipping behind him.

You're lucky I don't cut you.

But the man's hand dug into his pocket and Seth heard the sound of jangling change and not the sound of a switchblade.

Then the man laughed and shoved Seth's head back as he let go. Rising to his feet, he tossed a handful of change at Seth as he rubbed his cheeks with both hands. A quarter hit him square in the nose and he grimaced.

With that, the man turned and walked away. It even looked like he had acquired a swagger to his step that hadn't been evident in his waif-like behavior in the bar.

Seth continued to rub his face as he watched the man go. Despite the john's laughter, Seth knew that that had been a close one, and his heart raced in his chest.

He was terrified.

Only after the man's footsteps could no longer be heard did Seth dare pull himself to his feet.

He brushed dirt from the front of his shirt, knocking the spare change to the ground where it tinkled like shattered glass. Even if he had been able to see it in the dark, he wouldn't have picked it up.

Even he wasn't that desperate.

Eyes downcast, he made his way around the dumpster to the door to the club. Relief washed over him when he saw that the twig that he had wedged beneath the door keeping it open was still in place, saving him the walk around… and the need to pay cover again.

He grabbed the opening—the door was exit only and lacked a handle—and pulled it wide.

Loud dance music and the smell of cheap cologne immediately struck him. He didn't particularly care for either, but after what had happened in the alley, he breathed in deeply through his nose and tried to let the music flow through him.

The man had been telling the truth; he was lucky that he hadn't been sliced open, or worse. Prostitution was always a dangerous business, but the incidence of violence in male-to-male interactions always seemed much higher.

Seth let out a deep breath and tried to calm his pounding heart.

The altercation in the alley was the second time that he had been threatened, and although the first time he had ended up with a bloody nose and a black eye, this time had been worse.

The man would have cut him, *wanted* to cut him. In fact, he was unsure why he *hadn't*.

A shudder ran through him, and Seth continued down the hallway, his pace quickening.

The narrow hallway was illuminated by LED strips on the floor and ceiling, which changed color and intensity based on the beat of the music. Every few steps, a green laser whipped down the hallway before continuing on its path and exiting out of sight. He passed a dressing room, its open door offering a quick glance inside the well-lit space.

A man was sitting on his chair facing the open door, but he never saw Seth; he was too busy looking down at his bronzed skin, rubbing silver glitter on his pecs. He was wearing a silver G-string and fairy wings that looked comically small on his large back.

Storm, Seth thought. As if answering him, the loudspeaker suddenly erupted.

"And now, all you queers put your hands together for your final act of the night: *Storm!*"

A cheer broke out from the end of the hallway, but Seth kept his gaze in the dressing room. Storm stood and stared at himself in the mirror. As Seth watched, more curious than anything else, Storm made his pecs bounce, then reached down and grabbed his crotch with a hand, shifting things around, propping his equipment up. The man had a smirk on his face, but he suddenly caught Seth watching him through the mirror and his smile faded. Storm quickly made it to the door and stepped into the hallway, roughly pushing Seth back against the wall as he traipsed by.

"No free shows," he grumbled.

Seth waited in the dark until Storm, a smile slowly creeping back on his face, made it down the hallway. With two large steps, the man jumped up onto the stage, his silver wrestling boots landing so softly that they barely made a noise.

Only then did Seth slink out of the hallway, around the stage, and to his usual seat at the bar.

You're lucky I don't cut you.

Seth shuddered again and turned his eyes to the stage, if for nothing else but to distract himself—and to forget.

38.

"YOU ALL RIGHT, SETH?"

Seth didn't turn immediately. Even though the last show of the night had ended more than five minutes prior, his eyes remained locked on the stage, and his mind in thought.

When a hand gently rested on his arm, he nearly jumped.

"Sorry," the bartender offered, moving away.

Seth stared at the man. He was cute, and like all the men who worked at the Glittering Fairy, he was in great shape. And he also sported a set of ridiculous wings.

"Sorry, Tom," Seth said, shaking the rust from his head.

"Rough night?" Tom asked, going back to wiping down several of the newly washed glasses.

Seth nodded.

Tom nudged his chin toward Seth.

"That what happened to your face?"

Seth instinctively rubbed his cheeks, which were still aching.

"Yeah."

"Another rough john?"

Seth nodded again and averted his eyes.

"Didn't pay, either."

"Shitty. You need a drink? It's past last call, but there's no one else here."

Seth looked around and realized that although he had been staring at the stage for what felt like an eternity, he hadn't noticed that pervert's row had cleared out. He turned completely around and surveyed the entire club. He noticed two other patrons toward the back, both quickly trying to finish their beers with a large black bouncer hovered over them.

Although he hadn't seen people leave, he wasn't surprised that they were gone. No one stuck around too long after the last show of the night.

"It's okay, bouncer won't tell you to leave if I don't want him to. Let me get you a drink."

Seth turned back to Tom. Under other circumstances, he might have thought the man was hitting on him. But not Tom. He was just being friendly, which was something that Seth desperately needed right now. In fact, as strange as it was working here, Seth didn't even think the man was gay.

"Can't pay," he offered glumly. "John didn't pay."

Tom made him a drink anyway; his favorite, gin and tonic.

He slid the glass over and Seth grabbed it.

"Thank you," he said, taking a sip. It was strong and tart— just the way he liked it.

Tom said nothing and went back to cleaning the glasses. As Seth continued to drink, he noticed that the place consistently started to brighten, as if someone was very slowly raising the dimmer. Then the music cut out, although it took a few seconds to realize that the ringing in his ears was a side effect and lacked the bass thump of an actual tune.

Tom passed through the swinging doors behind the bar for a moment, presumably leading to the kitchen, leaving Seth alone with his thoughts.

You're lucky I don't cut you.

The thing that scared Seth most about the encounter wasn't so much the prospect of being stabbed or sliced open, although that in and of itself was indeed frightening. It was how he felt about it; somewhere, deep inside his soul, he felt that he deserved it.

That he deserved to be cut up, to be killed.

As if eavesdropping on his internal monologue, Tom suddenly reappeared and stopped right in front of Seth.

"You got anyone to talk to, Seth?"

Seth looked up at the man and saw genuine concern on his face.

"No," he responded simply.

And it was the truth; Seth hadn't had anyone to really talk to in a long, long time. Since before—

He banished the thought with another large sip of his gin and tonic. It was almost empty now.

"How long have you been coming here?"

Seth thought about the question for a moment.

"Five years?"

Yeah, that sounded about right.

Still, *five years*.

Saying the words out loud made them more real. And they were a shocking revelation.

Five years was a lifetime.

He finished his drink, and Tom immediately grabbed his glass even before he could put it down. His first thought was that the man would quickly clean it—it was the last one left, he saw—but instead, the man refilled it.

Maybe he is hitting on me, Seth thought. *But why?*

"Five years," Tom said with an air of incredulity. He turned and flicked on the TV above the bar. The sports highlights were on, but Tom quickly switched it to the news.

"You gotta to get out of here, Seth... move on," he said quietly, turning back to Seth.

Move on to what? To where? I have nothing—I deserve nothing.

He wanted to lament his woes, but that wasn't him. He got what he deserved, and what Tom didn't deserve was to hear about his problems.

Instead, Seth turned the question on his head.

"What about you? You were here five years ago, too—you were here before I got here."

Tom sighed and made a face, the meaning of which was clear.

Typical.

"I'm doing my thing... taking courses during the day. For me, this—" He spread his arms out in front of him. "This place is just temporary."

Then he paused, which said more than words to Seth. This pause meant, *But for you, I'm not so sure.*

And he was right, of course; *this* wasn't temporary for Seth. This, coming here or to any of the other gay bars in the clubs looking for men who would pay a few bucks to get their dicks sucked, was what his life was—probably what it would always be.

And even at that, it was more than he deserved, he knew. In an absurd way, he was grateful.

Tom turned his back again, and Seth raised his gaze to the TV, just in time for to see the words '*Askergan County*' pass from the ticker to off-screen.

His heart skipped a beat.

Tom grumbled something about not wanting to know about Hickville USA and raised the remote to change it.

"No! Don't change it!" Seth's words came out louder than he expected, but they worked. Tom lowered the remote and peered over his shoulder.

"What? You want to—"

"*Shhh!* Turn it up!"

Tom made a face, but he obliged.

There was a pretty blonde on screen, and she was speaking intently to a large black man in a sheriff's uniform.

"Now, Sheriff White, can you tell us a little more about what happened here? What happened in Askergan over the last forty-eight hours?"

But despite his demand to Tom, he realized that he didn't care about what they were saying. There was something else that had drawn and now kept his attention.

Behind the sheriff and the pretty reporter, a house was smoldering, reduced to mere rubble. Several firemen were still trying to put out the remaining small fires.

"What is this place?" he whispered.

There was something about it, something that made it impossible to turn away. Something *familiar* about it, even though he was certain that he hadn't ever been to the place. In fact, there was only one place in Askergan that he had been —

And then Seth saw *him*, and his thoughts melted away.

The camera focused on a man in the distance, moving away from the burning house. He was too far to make out anything distinct, other than the fact that he was covered in soot.

"This man giving you trouble, Tom?"

Seth didn't even acknowledge the bouncer that had come over, likely drawn by his shouts.

"No," Tom said hesitantly.

And then the man on camera turned his head and stared directly into the camera lens. The gaze only lasted a split second before he looked away and then hurried off-screen.

A second, but that was all Seth needed.

"No," Seth moaned. He slumped back in his seat, but it was a bar stool and he slipped off the back.

His body collapsed awkwardly to the dirty bar floor.

The man on the news report had a beard, and his face was streaked with dirt. But it was him, Seth was certain.

And it made his blood run cold.

"No," he moaned again.

The man on camera had been none other than Jared Lawrence, the man that he had been running from for all these years.

Come

39.

SHERIFF PAUL WHITE DROVE so fast that he nearly rammed into a parked firetruck on the corner of Main and Highway 2. He swerved to the right and then whipped the wheel back to the left to avoid an overturned car at the side of the road. He made a mental note to get Johnny and his tow truck out here to clear the road a little better as soon as possible. Still, despite his near accident, he was surprised that the firemen and volunteers had done such a good job at getting rid of the cracker debris, which he had stressed as a priority.

Paul tried to push these thoughts, his work, from his mind. *Nancy, it's about Nancy.*

He flicked the police lights on and pushed the gas pedal just a little bit harder.

Relief washed over him when less than fifteen minutes later he pulled up to his place and saw Nancy's car parked in the driveway. He slammed the cruiser into park and jumped out, hurrying up the small walk to the door. Despite the sun having already begun to nestle, it was hot out, and he felt his shirt cling to his sweaty chest.

And it was the stress; that too had made him sweat.

Paul was shouting even before he opened the door — which was unlocked.

"Nancy!" he yelled, stepping inside. A blast of cool air from the AC unit hit him. "Nancy! Are you home? *Nancy!*"

When there was no answer, the relief he felt after seeing her car quickly dissipated.

"*Nancy!*"

He took a break from shouting and listened, trying to make out any sounds from inside the house.

His ears perked, and he heard the distinct sound of water running upstairs.

The sheriff didn't even bother taking off his boots as he took the stairs two at a time. When he plowed into the bedroom, the water suddenly shut off, and then he heard the shower door open. A second later, Nancy, blonde hair still wet, stepped into the bedroom with a towel tucked up under her breasts.

She didn't see him at first.

"Nancy!"

Nancy yelped and jumped back.

"Jesus, Paul, you scared me!"

Paul didn't say anything else; instead, he stepped forward and leaned down. Grasping her still shocked face in his hands, he kissed her full on the lips. Startled, she tried to pull away, but he wasn't done yet. He extended the kiss a little longer, breathing in her fresh, clean scent—a complete one-eighty from earlier in the day.

But that was in the past, her bullying questions on air forgotten. She was with him now; she was safe.

And that was all that mattered.

Paul finally released her, and Nancy immediately stepped backward.

"What's gotten into you?" she asked, her eyebrows furrowing. Yet despite her expression, her tone was soft.

"I'm just—I'm just—"

The sheriff was at a loss for words; he had been so certain that something had happened to Nancy, that she wouldn't be there after what Dirk had told him, that he hadn't actually planned what he was going to say if she was there... which, of course, she was.

Should I tell her? Should I tell her about Dirk?

Paul let out a deep sigh and decided against it. He tried to convince himself that the only reason that he was keeping it from her was because he didn't want to worry her, but there was something else, too. He didn't want her spreading rumors about an evil, cartoon villain on television, putting the already confused Askergan citizens into a frenzy.

Exhaustion should take hold any moment now, he knew, based on the hell of a day he had been through. But something held it at bay for a little while longer.

Anxiety.

Despite finding Nancy safe and sound, he was still anxious about what had happened to Askergan, and about what was going to happen.

The crackers, however horrible, had only been the beginning, he knew.

The worst was yet to come.

"Paul?" Nancy had a concerned expression on her face.

Fuck it.

Sheriff White had once heard someone say that rage and ecstasy were very close on the emotional spectrum, even though their implications couldn't have been more different. At the time, he hadn't really understood what this meant, but he thought he did now.

He was anxious, he was tired, but he was also *alive*.

Instead of answering, Paul stepped forward and kissed Nancy again. As before, her first instinct was to pull away, but when his probing tongue found hers, she changed her mind and leaned into him. He felt her hands wrap around his waist, and when she moved her arms, her towel fell to the floor.

Feeling her bare skin against him only encouraged the sheriff further, and he moved his mouth off hers, kissing first her jaw, and then the nape of her neck when she leaned her head backward. When he kissed her clavicle, she let out a soft gasp.

He continued down her body, moving slowly, kissing her as he went. He kissed the top of her full breast, breathing in her fresh scent. Then he kissed all the way around her nipple, which stood at attention in the air-conditioned room. His tongue darted, flicking her nipple, and Nancy moaned. Her hands were on the back of his head now, forcing her breast into his mouth.

Paul worked his way back up to her mouth, leaving wet trails on her damp skin. This time when their lips met again, she kissed him back—and she was *hungry*. Nancy didn't even bother with his shirt; instead, she reached down and undid his belt with one hand. A second later, she was inside his pants, grabbing his manhood in her small hand. With her other hand on the small of his back, she guided both of their bodies backward until her bare ass hit the edge of the bed. She gasped and fell backward.

Paul stared at her for a moment, loving the way her face was twisted in a devious smirk. She was pretty, but she was also one to take charge, and he liked that. For a moment, everything—the crackers, the bikers, and now the Crab—was gone.

All that was left was him and her.

"What are you looking at?" she asked, the smile still on her face. "You've got to finish what you started."

And then Paul could not wait any longer. He lowered his buttocks, and with one thrust, he slid effortlessly inside her.

At last, the smile was off Nancy's face; now it was replaced by an expression of bliss. Her eyelids fluttered and he thrust again. And again. And again. With every thrust, Nancy's mouth opened a little more, her moans got a little louder. Just as she was nearing her climax, Paul was distracted by a sound off to his left.

"Don't stop! Don't stop!" Nancy begged, but Paul's eyes had honed in on the closet door, which was slightly ajar. It was one of those sliding mirror doors, and he could see his tired face in the reflection.

Tired, so damn tired-looking.

He felt a pain in his left buttock, as Nancy dug her nails in. He turned back to her and saw that her eyes were open, her thin blonde eyebrows knitted.

"Don't stop, I said."

He almost smiled.

"Okay, I—"

Then he heard the closet door slide all the way open, followed by a man's voice.

"Yeah, don't stop, big boy."

40.

SETH STUMBLED PAST THE bouncer that held the door wide, and he nearly fell into the alley.

Tears streaked his face, and his heart was beating so quickly that he thought that it might burst from his chest. It was as if a switch had been turned inside his head—after seeing the face of the man he had spent the last six years trying to wipe from his memory, everything came roaring back.

Jared Lawrence.

Because Jared Lawrence reminded him of the sweet little cherub, Henrietta Lawrence.

The one he had tried to suffocate.

To murder.

You ain't worth nothing, faggot. Just a queer, sucking dick like a woman. That's all you are—a queer. Ain't worth nothing.

And now the floodgates were open, and with these memories came something else.

The voice.

The same one that he had heard so long ago on the wind. Only now it was different. Now it wasn't simply uttering a single command, but a series of coherent instructions. The same ubiquitous *'come'* was there, of course, but now there was more.

Come.

Bring the girl.

Come.

Bring the girl, Seth. You have been chosen.

The words were so clear, so distinctly not his and yet happening inside his head, that it made him queasy.

"Get help, buddy," the bouncer said before slamming the door closed. Seth nearly fell as he scrambled toward the dumpster. His right hand slammed against the side hard enough to make it ring, and then he doubled over, retching, unable to even lean over the bin before nausea overcame him.

His eyes watered with every heave—it was the most violent vomiting he had ever experienced. Up came the two gin and tonics, and the mess that he had swallowed from the john.

He heaved and heaved until there was nothing left. When the sensation passed, he forced himself to try and puke again, aware that this time it wasn't designed to rid himself of some sort of poison, but to get the *voice* out.

Gasping, Seth wiped the drool from his mouth with the back of his hand. He waited to see if more would come, and although his stomach ached and his throat burned, the urge to vomit was gone.

A joke—it wasn't real. I didn't hear that.

But he had heard it.

Bring the girl. You have been chosen.

Seth pulled his hand off the dumpster and tried to straighten himself on wobbly legs.

His heart still raced in his chest, and he suddenly felt a strong desire for another drink.

Or twenty.

Everything he had done had been to forget. And he had been successful… kind of. But now, Jared's face had been a trigger, and the voice had returned.

Tears streamed from his eyes, and he collapsed to the ground, not caring that he landed in his own vomit. His body was racked with sobs.

The voice was back, and as before, it gripped him inside his mind.

Come? Come where?

Seth started to moan, and buried his head in his lap, pressing his hands against the sides of his head so hard that it hurt.

"Leave me alone!" he yelled between tears.

He tried with all his might not to answer—he tried to ignore the voice inside his mind.

No—please, not again. Leave, like last time... like with Jared's family. Like after I... after the snow. When I turned and left and walked in the freezing cold until I couldn't walk anymore.

The voice had been inside his head then, and it was when he'd finally succumbed to answering that things had taken a turn for the worst.

Before he'd tried to smother Henrietta.

After Seth had wandered from Mama Lawrence's house, he had kept going; he'd kept walking long after he'd stopped hearing that harrowing voice. Eventually, he had hitched a ride and headed south all the way until he had hit Florida. Florida had been good for a while, and eventually, the hot sun had melted the ice that had wrapped his bones. And during this time, he had almost forgotten about the snow.

But then he had run out of money, and he hadn't been able to get any steady work. Slowly but surely, he had begun heading back north—in search of work.

At least that was what he had told himself all these years.

But maybe it wasn't coming back toward what he called home that drew him north; maybe it was something else.

Come.

Another wave of nausea hit him and he dry heaved.

The voice was there all right, and Seth began questioning whether it had ever left. Maybe the voice had always been there, just buried deep inside, and seeing Jared's face had simply made him aware of it.

It was all irrelevant now; what mattered was that it was there and it was stronger than before.

Come.

Bring the girl. You have been chosen.

Seth ground his teeth so hard that he felt tiny flecks of enamel pepper the back of his tongue.

No.

Come.

"Leave me alone!" he screamed into the warm night air. *"Leave me the fuck alone!"*

But the voice was inside his head again, and this time it wouldn't leave.

After his words stopped reverberating down the alleyway, and an all-encompassing silence overcame him.

He pulled his hands away from the sides of his head and cautiously lifted his gaze. When he still heard nothing, he opened his eyes.

Seth.

Seth moaned and his eyes rolled back.

It was as if he were asking himself a question inside his head using a different voice. Which was the definition of insane, wasn't it?

He remembered reading somewhere long ago that it wasn't crazy to ask yourself questions, it was only crazy if you answered them. Well, the next time the voice asked a question, he felt compelled to answer.

He simply could not resist the urge to respond.

Seth.

"Yes," he whispered, staring with blurred vision at the pavement that was only a few feet from his face.

Get the girl.

"Okay."

You have been chosen. Get the girl, Seth.

Come.

"Okay," he said again. His voice had obtained a strange monotone quality with which he was unfamiliar. Placing his palms on the damp pavement, he slowly pushed himself to his feet. "Yes, I'll get the girl. I have been chosen."

41.

SETH CARS. IT TOOK seven cars for Seth to find one that
had the keys inside. Well, technically not inside. He found the
keys in a small box under the driver's seat wheel well of a
blue Ford Focus. Which was great, because his elbow was raw
and bruised from smashing in car windows to search for keys.

It was harder than it looked, smashing car windows. For
one, you needed two or three good shots to send the small
cubes of shatterproof glass scattering. And even then, you had
to make sure you hit it right in the center to give yourself the
best chance. What made it more difficult was that after every
failed attempt, Seth's elbow became more numb, making it
difficult to muster up the same impact velocity.

But now, inside the Ford Focus, he felt good again. Great
even—better than he had in a long time.

Get the girl, you have been chosen.

It was as if this purpose, however bastardized and insane,
had re-energized him.

Get the girl, you have been chosen.

Seth revved the engine, put the car into drive, and sped
down the tarmac. He still felt lightheaded, and his throat was
raw from vomiting, but he also felt liberated.

Two hours to Askergan.

He would be there before sunup, all things being equal.
Which was good. After the storm all those years ago, he had
become a bit of a night owl, as his profession decreed, but at
heart, he was an early riser.

The streetlights blurred into a streak as he drove, the speedometer of the stolen car glued to 55 miles per hour.

It would serve him no good if he was pulled over in a stolen vehicle. No, he was the chosen one, and he had a mission now.

"Yes, get the girl," he said in a monotone voice. "Get the girl, you have been chosen."

His eyes were so dry from staring out the window that he was starting to see halos from passing cars.

He forced himself to blink.

"Get the girl, you have been chosen."

A green road sign whipped by him, and he caught a quick glimpse of three different locales listed on it.

Pekinish 78 miles.

Darborough 93 miles.

And there, beneath those two other counties that he had never even heard of, was the one that had meant so much to him then, and meant even more to him now.

Askergan 108 miles.

A smile crept onto Seth's face.

Get the girl. You have been chosen.

*   *   *

Construction and abandoned cars on the road slowed Seth down, delaying his arrival in Askergan until after six in the morning.

He didn't stop; not to eat, not to piss, not to even stretch his legs. He was determined now, and the voice in his head kept egging him on.

The rational part of his mind—what was left of it— demanded answers to burning questions.

What girl? Why was I chosen? For what? And who are you?

But whenever he attempted to pose these questions the same way he answered the voice in his head, they were met only with silence.

Empty, void space inside his head.

Like before—before seeing Jared's face. He was alone.

Twice Seth tried to stop the car, to pull over, to really think about what he was doing, but something—*come*—compelled him forward. Similarly, he found that thinking of exactly where he was going, specifics about directions, would cause him lock up. It was like trying to drive a car staring a few feet in front of the bumper; you were stuck making micro adjustments and the car jerked dangerously left and right. But when Seth just allowed his mind to be open, to let whatever or whoever was inside him of him do the guiding, the ride was smooth and uneventful.

So now, as he pulled up to a nondescript brown building that he had never seen before and put the stolen Ford into park, he wasn't overly surprised that he had found *the place*.

Still, although the rational part of his mind was buried for the time being, it was *there*, irritating him like a fresh mosquito bite with its nagging whisper, desperately trying to make him question what he was doing here. And when he stepped into the already warm sun and his eyes fell on the white letters on the side of the building that read Askergan Long-Term Care, his curiosity was only piqued.

Long-term care? What the hell?

Seth slammed the door closed and instinctively went to lock it, before realizing how ludicrous that was. After all, it was a car.

As he made his way up the long, wooden switchback path designed for wheelchairs that led to the front entrance, pesky

questions started needling him again—but when the answers
came, he was surprised that they were in his own voice.

Not his words, surely, but his *voice*.

Q: What am I doing here?

A: Get the girl.

Q: But who is she?

A: The girl.

Q: Why am I here?

A: You are chosen.

Seth swallowed hard and gave in, letting his feet instead of
his mind guide him forward. His movements were so unlike
him, so fluid without his typical angular gait, that he felt more
an observer than the conductor of his actions.

As he neared the door to the facility, another thought
occurred to him: *What if the place isn't even open?*

And then, another question quickly followed: *What am I
going to say? I can't rightly tell the clerk or nurse or whoever works
here that I am here for "the girl".*

He played the conversation over in his mind.

Hi, I'm here for the girl?

Excuse me?

Yeah, the girl. You know the one; I'm here for her.

Seth glanced up at the building before pulling the door
wide. The building was four stories high, and he counted at
least ten windows on this one side alone.

A minimum of forty rooms, but probably more.

He fell back into his fictional conversation.

*Sir? We have twenty females here at the Askergan County Long-
Term facility. Was there one particular girl that you are interested in
seeing?*

Just the girl.

Oh?

I've been chosen.

His fingers tightened on the door handle, and for the briefest of moments, he hoped that it was locked—that this would foil the plan, and vanquish the voice.

Send him back to Florida, back to reality.

Madness.

In the back of his mind—the last vestiges of the rational part of his brain, which was becoming buried beneath increasing more and more insulating layers of insanity—he realized that what he was doing, what he was *about* to do, was wrong.

He was a good person, despite his flaws.

This is not me, he thought, a single tear tracing a line down his pale cheek.

But then his thoughts turned to Henrietta's face as he lay the child on her back, bringing the pillow closer and closer to her cute nose and mouth...

No, it *wasn't* him; but he was doing it just the same.

When he offered the door a slight tug, it opened a little.

Turning his eyes skyward, he gazed into the bright sun until he saw spots.

Then he pulled the door wide and stepped inside, leaving any semblance of reality, of what remained of his rational mind, behind.

Seth, the voice instructed. *Go get the girl.*

42.

"**WHEN WAS YOUR LAST** confession?"

Father Carter Duke looked at the cigarette between his fingers as he rolled it back and forth and patiently waited for an answer.

Being a priest was harder than he'd thought, always waiting and watching, waiting and watching.

He just wanted to *do* something.

The man on the other side of the screen eventually cleared his throat and then spoke.

"Father, I have sinned."

Yeah, no shit. This is a confessional. And I asked you when your last confession was, not if you have sinned.

Carter took a drag from his smoke, enjoying the way it warmed his lungs and calmed his frustration.

"And what are your sins?"

The man hesitated again, and Carter heard the man sniff.

"Uh, excuse me, Father, but are you smoking in there?"

Carter, still staring at his cigarette, mulled his options.

Then he shrugged.

"Yep," he said simply.

He brought the smoke back to his lips and took another drag, turning slightly to ensure that the man on the other side would see the glowing cherry.

There was a pause as the other man clearly waited for more—for an explanation.

Carter sighed.

"What's your name, son?"

'*Son*'.

Just uttering the word gave him the creeps.

I bet Father Paul Stevens made the little boys call him daddy.

"Robert. Robert Cormath."

"Okay, Robert, I'm going to let you in on a little secret."

He exhaled a thin stream of smoke.

"I'm not like most priests, Robert. Like Askergan, I'm just a little bit different."

"Oh, okay," the man replied hesitantly.

Carter sighed again.

Buck up. Get into the game.

"I'm here for change, Robert. I'm not going to allow the Devil and his disease to infect Askergan any longer."

He turned toward the other man, spying him through the lattice.

"You were here when the bikers came. You saw what they wanted, and you saw how I dealt with it. Now, I'm not normally an advocate for violence, but you know what the Lord said..."

"Turn the other cheek?"

Carter couldn't help but smirk, even though he wasn't sure if Robert was being funny or serious. If he were to bet, he would say serious.

Robert didn't strike him as the sharpest card in the deck.

"Like I said, I'm here for change in the name of the Lord — an eye for an eye, *son*."

Carter put his elbows on his knees and took another drag. Then he waited.

He knew little of what it meant to be an actual man of God, of course, but he had very quickly learned that listening was a big part. Frustrating, sure, but also a little bit of a reprieve from his normal everyday banter, his constant thinking one step ahead, answering suspicious questions before they were even posed.

Eventually, the other man mustered the courage to speak again.

"Well," he said slowly. "Part of what I wanted to talk to you about was what happened earlier. About how I, you know, tackled that guy. And after your, uh, friend, took out the other guy, well, me and the others, we—we—"

Carter held up his hand.

"Robert. I'm going to be honest with you, sometimes there is a time and a place. And what you did—tackling the biker— you did it at the *right* time and the *right* place. The Lord thanks you. I thank you. That biker—both bikers—are bad men. And one got what he deserved."

Carter took a deep breath and paused to maximize the dramatic impact.

"And the other will get what's comin' to him, I assure you."

The priest suddenly clapped his hands together and smiled broadly. Robert jumped at the sound.

"Now, is that it, Robert? Is there something else?"

"Well, usually I'm given some Hail Marys or something?"

Carter shrugged, his suspicions about the other man's infantile intelligence confirmed.

"Seventeen."

"Huh?"

"Seventeen Hail Marys and you're all set. Ticket still punched."

"Ticket?"

"Never mind. Just do seventeen Hail Marys."

"Oh, okay. But there is one more thing, Father."

"Hmm?"

"I don't know if this counts as a sin, but I've been feeling pretty bad lately."

Carter waited. He fought the urge to roll his eyes when Robert continued to be tongue-tied.

"Listen, Robert. You're not the only one who has sinned in Askergan. In fact, I bet nearly everyone in the town comes to see me soon. So you gotta keep the words coming, my man."

"Sorry—I'm sorry, Father." The man cleared his throat and then set to talking again, this time speaking so quickly that Carter had to focus to make out the words. "So you know the house that burned? The one out by the water? *The* house?"

Carter said that he did.

The house.

Even before they had arrived at the church, he had commissioned Pike to do some research about Askergan. And amidst the tales that kept popping up, fantastical in ways that couldn't possibly be true, there was always one constant: *the* house. That phrase always referred to just one place in particular: *The Wharfburn Estate.*

Askergan certainly had its share of demons, including the creatures that had taken Father Stevens and were rumored to have come from the very house that Robert was alluding to. There were also other rumors, too, about a storm that had sent the county into the dark ages for more than a week. And then there was the tale of a serial killer sheriff that had skinned his victims.

Carter wasn't sure how much stock to put in these rumors, but if nothing else, seeing the late Father Paul Stevens being attacked by those strange crabs had opened his eyes. Didn't open them quite wide enough to put the fear of God into him, but the sight had at least instilled an inkling of the Devil.

"Well, that's my house."

Carter sat upright.

"What?"

"Uh-huh. Mrs. Wharfburn—the owner—was a great aunt of mine, apparently. And when she died, it came to me. But all this time, I did nothing with it. I mean, she even left some money behind, but I never touched that neither. There was this lawyer who told me some of the money would go to paying the taxes, but I never touched a dollar of it. It just seemed... it seemed like an evil place, you know what I mean? And besides, I already have a house. And I have a job out by the mill. I don't get paid much, but I don't need no more money. I gotta be honest with you, Father. I kinda even forgot about it. But now that the house burned down, and the rumors… I can't stop thinking about it. And I *still* don't know what to do with it."

For once, Carter was at a loss for words.

Is this a sin? Should I tack on an Our Father or two? What the hell is he getting at?

He reached down and picked at the peeling wood on the sorry excuse for a bench on which he sat.

Fuck, this church is stuck in the Stone Age. Modernization wouldn't be such a bad idea after all.

"Father?"

"Yeah?"

"What do I do with it?"

"Well, what do you want to do with it? Sell it?"

"That's the thing, I just don't want it. I got a job out at the mill. I don't need the money. And I know that the Lord says we should be grateful for the blessed gifts that thou receiveth, but I..." The man's words just trailed off.

Carter picked a foot-long splinter from the bench.

"Well, I think—"

But then a thought hit him like a shot and his eyes went wide. He tossed the splinter to the floor.

Modernization.

"Robert? What if I told you I had an idea of how you can get rid of the property and reduce your Hail Marys? A trade of sorts?"

"Father?"

"Yeah, a trade. Look around you; this church is falling apart. And besides, it's part of the *old* Askergan. I have plans for this county, Robert. A plan to modernize, to get the drugs out of the county. And what better way to start than a completely new church?"

Robert cleared his throat.

"That—that sounds great. But what does it have to do with me?"

Carter smirked.

"What if you gave the property to me—uh, to the church, to the Lord: We could build a new church there, start over."

"Oh, geez, I dunno. I mean, it's not a good place. Bad things have happened there."

Carter shook his head.

"That's perfect. I can bless the property, splash some holy water about. You can be the hero that cleanses the property— cleanses the *evil*—and is part of Askergan's rebuild. What do you think?"

"I'm no hero, Father."

"Bullshit! You saved my life by tackling that biker."

Carter made a clicking sound with his tongue.

"The Lord has plans for you, son. Big plans. And they start here. They start by being at the *frontier* of a new county."

There was a pause, and Carter hoped that he hadn't laid it on too thick.

Out of practice, all this waiting and watching. I need to stay sharp, I need to do something.

At long last, Robert answered.

"I—I think that is a fine idea, Father."

Carter slammed both hands down on the bench and the other man jumped.

"Excellent!"

Then he stood and pushed the rotting wooden door to the confessional open with his foot.

"Pike! Pike, get over here! We have some business to attend to!"

The smirk on his face grew into a full-fledged smile.

This was perfect, better than he could have ever imagined.

Modern County. I will change this place; I will turn it into my own.

43.

"HI," SETH GRUDIN SAID.

The woman behind the desk spied him through a set of reading glasses that were perched halfway down her beak-like nose.

"Yes? Can I help you?"

He tried a smile, but it felt so fake that he immediately abandoned the effort. It was too late; the woman's white eyebrows traveled up her forehead suspiciously.

"I'm here to see someone," he offered quickly.

Get the girl.

The woman put her book down—a John Milton thriller, he saw—and stared, waiting for him to continue.

"I'm a, uh, a friend. Do you guys have, like, visiting hours?"

"Family only, unless you make an appointment."

Seth's expression lifted.

"Can I make an appointment, then?"

The woman shook her head.

"By phone only. Sorry."

"Phone only? But I'm right here."

The woman quickly averted her eyes, a clear indication that she was lying.

"Sorry, it's policy."

"Hmm."

When Seth didn't react and remained rooted in place, he slowly detected her temperament begin to change: her perfunctory, abrupt posture and tone were transitioning into tepidity.

She was nervous, made clear by the way her beady eyes glanced first at then behind him. She sensed that something was wrong, Seth knew it. But she was underestimating just how terribly wrong things were.

Because if she had known, the woman would have turned and ran.

"Phone only," she reiterated, her voice slightly higher-pitched than before, "and then we get security to take you to the room. Who is it specifically you are looking to visit?"

Now it was Seth's turn to look around.

Security? At a long-term care facility?

He smirked.

Not likely.

"Just a friend. So I can't make the appointment now? I mean, I'm here. I'm right here, standing in front of you."

The woman leaned farther away from the counter and shook her head.

"I'm sorry, it's nothing against you. It's just policy."

Seth smiled.

"Oh, okay then." He showed his palms. "No problem."

He noticed a pen on the counter, one of the old-fashioned ones like from the bank with a beaded chain keeping it attached to the countertop.

"Do you think it would be alright if a wrote a note at least? I mean, I drove a long way to get here."

The woman hesitated.

"Yeah, that sounds okay. Let me just get you a sheet of paper."

The woman turned and started flipping through a pad of doodles, and Seth picked up the pen. He gave the chain a slight tug. It was only about eighteen inches in length, but it didn't seem very stable. With one hard pull, he was positive it would come loose.

A moment later, the secretary placed a blank piece of note paper down in front of him.

"Here you go."

This time the woman was the one that offered the smile, and Seth wasn't sure which one was more fake, his or hers.

This was an observant woman, Seth realized. She had an inkling that something was wrong here, something that went beyond a strange visitor at six in the morning not entirely sure who he was here to see.

No, there was something *else* wrong here, something very wrong.

But it was too late for her now.

Seth nodded and offered a quick thank you. Then he put the pen to paper.

Alice Dehaust, he wrote.

A name. One that he had never heard before, but just knew that it was right.

His smile grew, and he lifted the pen.

"Get the girl, you have been chosen."

"Pardon?"

Seth chuckled.

"Nothing. It's just that my writing is so bad." He spun the paper around for her to see. "Can you read this?"

The woman leaned her head back and scrunched her nose, forcing her reading glasses upward. Then she tilted the paper up and began reading.

"Alice Dehaust," she said with a shrug. "I can read—"

With speed he didn't know that he possessed, Seth's left hand shot out and he grabbed a fistful of her tight gray hair.

She cried out and tried to pull back, but his grip was too strong. With his other hand, he drove the pen into the soft area of skin just beneath her chin, snapping the ball bearing chain that tethered it to the counter.

The woman's eyes went wide, and blood immediately shot forward, soaking Seth's hand and arm in a warm spray. Still gripping both her head and the pen, he tried to drag the latter across her neck, like one might with a knife—to open her throat. But the pen was too flimsy, and he felt the plastic bend instead of cut through her skin. He quickly abandoned this idea and instead rammed the pen deeper, twisting it back and forth as he pushed.

The woman gurgled as her blood continued to flow, soaking Seth's entire hand now, leaking heavy drops onto the piece of paper with Alice's name on it.

Blood also leaked from her mouth, and her eyes went wide.

The woman tried one last-ditch effort to push back from the desk by jamming her hands on the counter edge, but Seth leaned against her, holding the pen and her hair so tightly that his hands ached. She struggled for only a few more seconds before her eyes rolled back. Seth kept his position until the pumping of her blood had become but a slow trickle. Then he let go of her hair and the woman slumped forward, her body weight driving the pen even deeper. Seth counted to twenty and then slid the now red pen out of her neck.

The woman's head smacked on the counter, and blood immediately began to pool beneath her as the last of her life seeped out.

"Get the girl. I have been chosen," he whispered, the smile still plastered on his narrow face.

Alice Dehaust: the girl.

Seth Grudin: the chosen.

44.

"SO, DID YOU USED to be a criminal too, or is that just me?" Dirk Hannover asked.

The other deputy looked over at him.

"Huh?"

Dirk chuckled.

The two men were alone in the station, left to their own devices when the sheriff had taken off suddenly. Deputy Williams, the senior ranking officer in the sheriff's absence, was out on a drug-related call. For a time, Dirk had been completely alone, manning the station after being deputized for no more than a few hours. That was okay, though. So far the job had seemed simple enough: placate the populace. This wasn't much of a challenge, of course, as not only did he have very little knowledge about what had happened, but no one else seemed to know anything either. Or if they did, they weren't sharing. So it wasn't as if he had to lie.

Around dinnertime, the flow of citizens had slowed, just as Deputy Reggie returned from the church shooting.

"Nothing," Dirk said. "I guess we're both newbies here, aren't we?"

"Speak for yourself—I've been a deputy for a whole week."

Dirk laughed.

Yeah, both newbies, that's for sure.

He leaned forward in his chair.

"What's your connection here, man? You from Askergan?"

Reggie's face darkened, but only for a moment.

"No, not from here."

"Then what?"

Reggie hesitated. There was a connection, that much was certain, but it was obvious that the man was hesitant to share.

Dirk didn't blame him. As he waited for the man to reply, he smoothed his handlebar mustache, then tightened his ponytail.

"Look, I don't mean to be rude, but I don't know you. I don't even think the sheriff knows you. I think—I think we should keep this"—Reggie indicated the two of them—"professional."

Dirk shrugged. He caught the man's eyes fall on the missing first three fingers of his right hand.

Nope, definitely don't blame you for being apprehensive.

In fact, when the sheriff had asked him to be deputy, he'd thought it was a ridiculously impulsive move. After all, he had been a biker up until a few hours ago—part of the problem that the sheriff was hell-bent on eradicating from the county, the same group that had threatened his life and the lives of the ones closest to him.

The sheriff couldn't possibly know that this wasn't the first time that Dirk had worn this type of uniform.

He made a fist, hiding his missing fingers.

If only they knew.

"No hard feelings. But the sheriff left in one hell of a hurry, and I have no idea when either he or the other deputy is going to be back. We are going to be here for a while. Gonna be awfully quiet if we can't find *something* to talk about."

Reggie nodded and looked away.

The two newly deputized men sat in silence for a good five minutes before Reggie finally broke it.

"I'm not much of a religious man, and I don't have much experience with this, but there is something strange going on out by the church."

"Sure. But I wasn't much of an altar boy either, as you probably guessed."

"Yeah, well, there is something weird out there. I mean, I went out there, just as the sheriff ordered. After hearing of the shots fired, I thought there would be some extremely distraught people, you know?"

Dirk nodded. Although most people in rural America, for which Askergan County most definitely qualified, had at one point or another during their lives fired a gun, and more still had in the very least heard shots fired, he knew that context played a huge role in their subsequent reactions. A gun was a gun, and a bullet a bullet, but it made all the difference in which direction they were aimed.

"But nobody seemed to care about that. I mean, I'm going to be honest, most of the dozen or so people there actually seemed happy about it, as if it was a good thing." He lowered his voice. "I found blood, too. Lots of it in the church. But no body, and none of the people that I talked to could give me a straight answer as to what happened. Kept saying something about how Askergan was going to change, modernize or some shit. That a couple of bikers came in trying to either sell drugs or collect from the sale—this was hard to get a bead on, too— and that they had shot at them and then vanished."

Dirk mulled this over in his head.

"Yeah, I thought the same thing," Reggie continued, reading Dirk's expression. "Vanished? That's bullshit. Bikers don't 'vanish'. They are covering for something or someone. But what? I mean, I'm new at this shit, but it was just weird, you know?"

Dirk frowned, recalling what had happened at Sabra's.

"Yeah, I've been in Askergan for less than a day, and I already know that there is something strange going on here."

And now it was his turn to host a far-off expression on his face.

What he had seen at Sabra's had been more than weird—it had been fucking horrible. He still wasn't sure what he believed, even though he had seen what he had seen with his own eyes. Although he was one of the very few bikers that didn't even occasionally indulge in the drugs that they peddled, he had more than once considered that maybe there was just so much of it in the air in Sabra's office that he had gotten high by accident. At this point, there really was no way to know.

Regardless, he wasn't surprised that the people at the church were acting strangely; heck, if there was ever a time to seek salvation, the time was nigh.

But that wasn't for him. Not for Dirk Hannover. What mattered to him was finding the one that had crippled his hand and stolen his family.

"But that wasn't the weirdest thing. The weirdest thing was the priest. He was—how should I put this?—*smooth*."

Dirk stopped tracing lines on the wooden desk with the two good fingers on his right hand and looked up.

He raised an eyebrow.

"Like James Brown smooth?"

Reggie shook his head.

"Like a used car salesman smooth, you know? Just less sleazy." He brought his hands together in mock prayer. "Father Carter Duke—saying all the right things, all the while keeping a smirk on his bearded face."

Dirk's breath caught in his throat. The deputy kept talking, but he wasn't hearing any of the words—he was preoccupied with the man's name: *Carter Duke.*

Clive Dirkson.

Chris fucking Donovan.

CD; always the initials CD.

For nearly two years he had been ensconced in the Skull Crushers, using their influence and connections to help him find the man that had become more and more elusive, his extortion, not to mention his reputation, shrinking in both magnitude and exposure.

And then about a month ago he hit the jackpot. A rumor about a pedophile priest, and pictures stolen by someone described as a stone-faced man dressed in a tuxedo, had spread through the biker ranks, and when it had reached Dirk's ears, he knew that he was close.

But not in a million years did he think that he was *this* close.

Dirk swallowed hard.

"What did he look like?"

"Huh? Who?"

"The priest."

"Oh, I dunno. Regular-looking guy. Medium height, medium build. Thick black beard."

Dirk could barely get a new breath in, and his heart had started to race. He unfurled his fist and stared at the nubs on his right hand.

"Hey, man, you okay? You look like you've seen a ghost."

Father Carter Duke.

Dirk got to his feet, ignoring the other deputy.

I've found you, CD. I finally fucking found you.

45.

"TAKE WHATEVER YOU WANT," Sheriff Paul White said. When the man that stepped out of the closet raised an eyebrow, the sheriff clarified his statement. "Take me. Just leave her out of this."

He was standing by the side of the bed, wearing nothing but his police shirt. Nancy wasn't so lucky: she was completely naked.

Naked and trembling.

The man with the gun had a shaved head, and it was covered in tattoos. Like all of Sabra's old crew, he was wearing a cut-off jean jacket.

"Well, here's the thing," the man said, wagging the silver pistol back and forth. His voice had an obnoxious nasal quality to it. "The Crab gave me some very specific instructions. And, unfortunately for you, it involves her."

Nancy moaned.

"Please," the sheriff pleaded. "It's me he wants. Take me."

The man shook his head.

"No can do."

The sheriff's eyes glanced to the middle of the floor where he had carelessly dropped his pants... and his gun.

"Don't move," the man warned.

It was an incredibly disarming thing, standing there nearly naked in front of a man with a gun. But there was no time to be bashful. He had read in a book once that the hardest thing for a man to do was to fight naked. At the time, he had scoffed at the idea, but now it dawned on him that if that was indeed the case, he was in for one hell of a night.

"Take me," he hissed through clenched teeth.

Nancy glanced over at him, and he saw fear plastered on her pretty face. Even when they had battled the crackers together, she hadn't shown this much emotion.

This was different; this danger was human—it was something that they both understood.

"Please," he begged, but when the man just smiled, he knew that all was lost.

It ends here. One way or another, it ends here.

"Get over here," the man ordered, indicating Nancy with a nudge of the pistol.

The woman stood firm, and he leveled the gun at the sheriff's head.

"Now."

Nancy again looked to Paul for something, anything, a *hint* at a plan, but the big man was at a loss.

The biker rolled his eyes.

"I'm going to ask you one more time, and then I start shooting. Get. Over. Here. Now."

And then, to Paul's disbelief, the naked woman took a small step forward.

I'm sorry, she mouthed, and took another step.

This can't be happening, this can't be happening.

It ends now.

When Nancy took a second step, Paul suddenly sprung into action. He reached out and shoved Nancy forward, confident that if shots were fired, they would be aimed at him and not at her.

Nancy stumbled forward and nearly fell flat on her face. Paul had hoped that she *would* fall, that she would land on the carpet and just lie on the ground. But she regained her balance just as Paul lunged for his gun belt.

It was a shitty plan, and the result was predictably poor. Even if Paul had made it to his gun, he would have never been able to unhook the clasp and actually draw the gun, let alone get a shot off.

But shots rang out nonetheless.

The first whizzed by the sheriff's arm, and Nancy screamed. When the second shot was fired, Paul wasn't so lucky. He felt a pressure in his left bicep, followed by a searing pain. He grunted and was reduced to crawling for his gun.

He almost made it. In spite of everything, he almost made it to his gun. But the biker was no stranger to this sort of thing, and he stepped forward and planted his own shove right between Nancy's breasts. This time she flew backward, and her head slammed against the wooden bed frame. Paul saw her eyes roll back as her body collapsed into a heap.

The biker took advantage of the distraction and jumped toward Paul, switching his grip on the gun to the barrel. Reaching down, he swung the butt in a wide arc, connecting with a solid *thunk* with the top of Paul's head. Stars erupted, turning the sight of his pants and gun belt into a galactic cornucopia. Still, despite his failing strength and equally tenuous consciousness, the sheriff continued to reach for his gun, knowing that if he could only grab it...

His vision started to tunnel, and the sheriff tried to shout out the word '*no*'.

Only garbled sounds came out of his mouth.

The last thing Paul saw before he lost consciousness was the biker's face as he squatted and leaned in close.

"The Crab has plans for you yet, Sheriff. This ain't over."

And then darkness came early.

46.

THERE WAS SO MUCH blood on Seth's hands that he couldn't see the pink color of his flesh peeking through. He tried his best to wipe the offending substance on his jeans, but it was no use.

There was just *too* much of it.

Once the name had come to him—Alice Dehaust—it had been easy to find out which room she was in. In fact, her file had oddly been on the desk, right beside the dead woman's John Milton novel.

Room 156.

Seth also found a letter opener beside Alice's file. Like the pen that he had used to kill the woman, the opener was old-fashioned, with a sort of embossed hilt, like a mini sword.

He slipped it into his pocket and quickly left the woman in a sticky pile of her own blood, making his way to Alice Dehaust in room 156.

Get the girl.

Seth wasn't sure if these were his words or those of the voice. Everything had melded together since he'd plunged the pen into the woman's soft neck.

The entire facility was deathly quiet, and all the doors were closed as if the tenants had somehow clued into what was going on and were tucked away safely in their beds.

The door to room 156 was also closed, and Seth stood outside for a moment, debating his options. Although the woman's name had finally come to him, whispered inside his head, he still wasn't sure what to expect when that door opened.

After thirty seconds of deliberation, he decided against knocking and instead tried the handle. It was unlocked, and Seth pushed the door open a crack, half expecting someone to shout at him.

But again, nothing happened.

Encouraged by the silence, he pushed the door open even farther.

And then he blew it wide.

Seth wasn't sure what to expect, but what he had in mind definitely wasn't the scene before him. The first thing that struck him was that there were *two* people in the room and not one. There was a woman on the bed, a pale-faced lady in her mid-thirties, Seth guessed — *the girl*. She was thin bordering on gaunt, with black hair pulled away from her face. There was a myriad of cables coming from beneath a thin blanket and hooked up to what various medical devices. An IV drip was connected to her arm.

Seth quickly glanced at the other person in the room. A man with a cropped red beard and slicked-back hair sat asleep in a chair, arms crossed over his chest. It took Seth a moment to see the slow rise and fall of his chest, to confirm that he was actually alive. The room smelled mildly of a campfire.

Never said anything about a man.

He stood in the doorway and again mulled his options.

Eventually, his hand found its way into his pocket and wrapped around the cold steel letter opener.

He tilted his head to the side, his eyes flicking from the girl to the man in the chair.

Get the girl.

The voice said nothing about the man.

He debated killing him, driving the letter opener into his throat, dragging it across, making a ragged, bloody smile in his neck.

But he wasn't a killer, despite what had happened at the front desk.

After all, that hadn't been him—that had been the voice.

Seth glanced at the girl. Like the man's breathing, hers too was deep and heavy. Something told him that with all of the wires coming out from under the blanket, she wasn't going to wake up anytime soon.

Making up his mind to avoid the man entirely—stealth was key—Seth let go of the letter opener and crept completely into the room, leaving the door open behind him. As he made his way over to the woman in the bed, he realized that all of the cords coming from her were going to pose a problem.

He had no idea how to remove them, or if removing them would cause the woman to wake up. And if his medical knowledge gleaned from television and movies was in any way accurate, he could expect a myriad of beeps and alarms to sound as soon as he pulled out the first cable. And unlike the woman, he doubted that the man would remain asleep.

Get the girl. You are chosen.

"Fuck," he whispered in frustration.

He was at the foot of her bed now, and his eyes glanced quickly from Alice's flaccid face to the man's. Indecision gripped him like the flu, and he stood, frozen, unable to act.

But then the man's face twitched and a sigh escaped his lips. This scared Seth, and he was finally forced to act. He withdrew the letter opener and took two aggressive steps to his left, toward the sleeping man.

Killer or not, he *had* to get the girl.

Get the girl get the GIRL GET THE GIRL.

Despite his previous apprehension, he intended to slam the blade into the man's neck, just below his beard line. But just as he thrust his arm forward, the man's eyes snapped open. Seth wasn't sure if the man moved—unlikely, given the shock on his face—or if Seth was so taken aback by his sudden awakening that his arm altered course.

Regardless, instead of driving the blade into the man's throat, he missed and the three-inch blade landed itself a little to the right, tearing through the man's t-shirt and embedding itself in a spot just above his collarbone.

The man cried out, but before Seth could withdraw the blade, the man's leg swung out and swept him off his feet.

Seth crashed hard to the ground, landing on his elbow and hip at the same time.

The air was forced out of him and he made an *oomph* sound. Even as he struggled to fill his lungs with a fresh breath, he was scrambling to his feet.

Get the girl.

You are chosen.

Seth had only made it to all fours when the man's foot shot out again. Instead of a sweeping gesture, however, this one came directly at him.

The rubber sole of the man's running shoe struck Seth directly in his right eye.

"Fuck!" he screamed, stars clouding his vision. He heard a cracking sound, and his eye felt as if it had been driven backward in his skull.

He instinctively reached for the leg that had struck him, but with his vision blurred in his right eye, he misjudged the distance and his hand fell short. The man's foot retracted, but this time when he fired a kick, Seth was ready for it and somehow rolled to one side.

The third kick missed its mark.

Seth sprung awkwardly to his feet, wobbling as dizziness took hold. The man was momentarily distracted as he tried to remove the letter opener from his shoulder, and Seth lunged with hands and fingers outstretched.

Voice or not, Seth had never been much of a fighter; he was too small, too frail. Weak bones, his mother had repeatedly told him. So his instinct to grab the man's throat—for what? To throttle him?—probably wasn't the best idea. Indeed, the man, even though he was preoccupied with the shiny metal letter opener protruding from his chest, had more than enough time to swivel his hips to one side as Seth came at him. Although he remained sitting, Seth still somehow managed to miss his neck—miss all of him, really—and instead careened into the now empty side of the chair. The man continued to roll out of the way, shoving Seth's face farther into the chair.

And now Seth was facing the wrong way in a teal-colored vinyl chair, the man that he had tried to kill standing behind him.

He heard something metal fall to the ground, and Seth knew that the man had tossed the letter opener aside.

"Who the fuck are you?" he shouted.

Seth swiveled to stare at the man. He was standing with his feet spread, his arms at his sides, fists and jaw clenched. A dark stain was spreading on his shirt, starting at his collarbone but soon extending across his chest.

He had been stuck good, but it didn't seem to bother him. The man had an insane look on his face, one that rivaled Seth's when he had stabbed the receptionist with the pen.

Seth's eye was still messed up, and the vision there had degenerated into a thin peephole of light surrounded by darkness. He found he could see better by simply closing his right eye.

"Who are you?" the man demanded again.

Seth said what came into his mind first.

"I am chosen."

The man's face twisted into a sneer.

Wrong answer.

Then it was his turn to lunge, but he didn't come at Seth with his hands outstretched like some demented poltergeist coming from a television screen. No, he came at Seth like a fighter.

The man's fist struck Seth on the bridge of the nose before he could even get his hands up to defend himself. There was an audible crunch and he howled in pain.

Hot liquid immediately leaked out of both nostrils and spilled into his mouth.

"I am chosen," Seth repeated, blood spraying from his lips.

"Yep, you sure are," the man said, and then delivered another punch directly to the same spot as the previous one.

Seth's nose was reduced to mush, and this time the sound that exited his mouth was a wet, bubbling noise.

He fell from the chair and slid to the ground, turning so that he landed on his back. Staring up at the man with the red beard with his one good eye, Seth could feel blood trickle down the back of his throat. His breathing had become labored, and with his nose spread across his face like pale peanut butter, he had to resort to gasping with his mouth. But each time he opened it, blood spilled into his throat and he gagged and coughed. In order to prevent from choking, Seth turned his head to one side and spat a wad of blood onto the clean white floor.

"I'm going to ask you one more time, you little fucker. Who are you, and what the fuck do you want with Alice? Are you one of the bikers from the bar?"

"I am cho—"

This time he didn't even get the entire sentence out before a swift kick was delivered to his ribs. He heard multiple cracks this time, and the air was forced out of him like a balloon being popped. Seth curled onto his side and gasped, trying desperately to breathe.

Get the girl, you are chosen, the voice in his head repeated, and if Seth had had any air left in him at that moment, he would have screamed.

How the fuck am I supposed to do that? How?

He spat more blood.

Blinking hard, he tried to clear the stars from his good eye.

Then he saw it, gleaming like a beacon on the floor: just beyond his arm was the letter opener. Another kick collided with his spine this time, and although pain shot down both of his legs, it also served to push his fallen body toward the weapon. Still unable to draw a full breath, he somehow managed to muster the strength to reach out and grab it, wrapping his hand tightly around the handle and pulling it into his body.

If the man saw, he didn't react.

"If you say that one more—"

Seth spun onto his back, swinging the knife in a wide arc. His only hope was that the man was close enough to make contact—somewhere, anywhere.

He got lucky.

For once in his life, Seth got lucky.

His looping arc not only caught the man by surprise, but Seth didn't even need to alter the trajectory when he flipped

over. The blade slid right into the sole of the man's foot. The
man screamed and hunched over.

At long last, Seth let out a moan and his diaphragm
relaxed, flooding his body with oxygen. Imbued with renewed
strength, Seth tried to leap to his feet.

Unfortunately, his cracked ribs prevented him from doing
any sort of *'leaping'*, and he instead only managed a half
crouched, half crawling position. But it didn't matter; he was
now at even height with the other man bent over, pulling the
blade from his foot. Seth hurled his body forward, his
shoulder connecting with the top of the man's head. Together
they spilled forward, and by some miracle, Seth, who still
couldn't quite straighten his body out, ended out on top.

At some point during their struggle, they had become
tangled in one of the cables from the woman on the bed. As
predicted, the machine, a square blue thing about the size of a
toaster, started emitting an obnoxious beeping sound.

The man grunted and went to throw Seth off of him, but
his arms were wrapped up in the tubing and when he
extended his hand, it only stretched a few inches before
snagging. The toaster thing came crashing down and landed
with a hard *thunk* on Seth's already bruised back and ribs.

He arched his back and cried out, causing the toaster-thing
to fall off him and finally stop beeping.

The man beneath him bucked, trying to flip Seth off, while
at the same time he tried to free his arms. It would be only
moments before the man recovered, Seth knew, and he had
very little time to think, let alone act.

He tried to locate the letter opener, but it was either still
way down below in the man's foot, or he had pitched it
somewhere as he had done before. What his reaching hand
did find, however, was the blue medical device.

Seth's finger grasped a handle of sorts and he swung it down on the man's unsuspecting head. The man grunted and thrust his hips again, but Seth used this movement to bring himself into a sitting position and swung again, this time by launching the toaster with two hands.

The man went limp and Seth tossed the machine aside. Still trying to get a full breath, he rolled off him and onto his back. For a good minute, he stayed nearly as still as the unconscious man and woman in the room with him.

The only sound was his noisy breathing through his mouth.

Staring at the ceiling with his one good eye, he finally broke the near silence.

"I am chosen." The words came out in an incomprehensible wet garble. A pang of intense pain radiated from his broken ribs and he clenched his teeth. "And now I'll get the girl."

47.

JARED LAWRENCE'S EYES SNAPPED open, and memories of what had happened in the church immediately came flooding back.

Corina! his mind screamed, and he tried to pull himself to his feet.

Only he couldn't do either: he couldn't scream, and he couldn't rise from a lying position.

Wide-eyed, he scanned his surroundings. There was something in his mouth, something like a tough jerky, hard and salty, which not only prevented him from screaming, but also somehow affixed his head to the table. The lights shining into his eyes were bright, and all he could make out was the shadow of a man hovering over him.

"Hurry," he heard a somewhat recognizable voice say. "He's waking."

There was an affirmative grunt and he felt an uncomfortable pressure on his thigh.

Did they take me? Did the man who grabbed Corina's arm take me? Her and me?

But before he could think these questions through, he felt more pressure on his leg, only this time it was deep and painful.

"Arggh," he sputtered, his tongue traveling up and down the length of whatever was in his mouth like a horse bit.

He closed his eyes against the pain and only opened them again when a few seconds later the pain and pressure subsided.

The lights dimmed, and the face over him slowly came into focus.

What he now saw was a belt was pulled from his mouth, and Jared licked at his dry and cracked lips.

"You're back," the man said, a friendly smile creeping from beneath his beard.

This too incited questions in Jared's mind—*back? From where?*—but like the other queries, he had no time to consider them.

"Where am I?" he asked. His throat was dry, parched. "Where is Corina?"

Confusion passed over the man's face, but this expression faded so quickly, Jared wasn't sure it had actually been there.

He tried to sit up, but the man gently rested his palm on his forehead.

"Best stay down for a bit longer—let the drugs kick in."

Jared squeezed his eyes shut again.

Drugs?

For a brief moment, he almost receded back into the oblivion that which he had just crawled out of.

It was all too much.

"He's good," he heard another voice say. "Got the bullet out, stitched him up—should be good to go."

The hand on his forehead gently caressed his head, sweeping his greasy hair from his face. This simple act felt good; after all this time and after all that had happened, it felt good to be looked after, even if he'd had to be shot to receive the treatment.

But then there was Corina...

"Corina?" he croaked again.

There was a silent pause, and this time Jared opened his eyes.

"We're looking for her," the man that still hovered over him said.

As Jared's eyes continued to adjust to the lighting, he realized that he recognized the man.

It was the priest—Father Carter, or something like that. The man's smile grew.

"My name is Father Carter Duke," he said, reading his thoughts. Then he waved a hand to the other man, the one who had been fixing his leg but who was now standing beside the priest. "And this is my friend Pike."

Jared didn't know what to say—what was an appropriate greeting for a time like this? *Nice to meet you? Thanks for saving my life?*

Neither of these two options felt right, so instead, he said what was most pressing. "I need to find Corina."

This time when he went to sit up, Father Carter didn't hold him down. The smile on his face, however, faded. A bout of dizziness hit Jared as he struggled to bring himself to a seated position. Once again, the father's hands steadied him.

"Jared," he said slowly. "We will find Corina, I can promise you that."

Jared, eyes closed again, couldn't help but guffaw at the words—after all, that was all they were: words. What could this priest possibly do to find Corina that he couldn't?

Faith wasn't one of his strong suits, and if it hadn't been for Corina wanting for some bizarre reason to stick around in Askergan after being pulled from the basement, he wouldn't have even been at the church. Still, he was a man searching answers, and after all this time when even the internet continued to draw blanks, there were only so many places that someone as desperate as he could go.

"I'm not a normal priest, Jared."

The man's eyes were serious, and for some reason, Jared had an inclination to believe him. After all, before he had been shot, the sermon that Father Carter had delivered had been anything *but* normal.

"And my friend here?" he continued, drawing Jared's eyes to the other man, the man with the stern expression and the strange name. "He's no normal altar boy. He can... he can find people, amongst his many talents."

Jared's mind flashed to the way Pike had so easily dispatched the biker in the church.

Many talents.

"Stick with us, Jared. And we'll find Corina. I promise."

Jared realized that the priest was holding out his hand.

His eyes darted from Pike to Carter and back again.

No, these were definitely not normal church people, and this place was no normal church.

Without thinking, Jared reached out and grasped Father Carter Duke's hand.

Only finding Corina mattered now; his only link to the past, his family. And if these men could help, then he would forge any deal he had to in order to find her.

Still, when the smile returned to Father's face, Jared instinctively wondered what sort of agreement he just bound himself to.

48.

THE SHERIFF AWOKE WITH a splitting headache. At first, he didn't remember what had happened, let alone where he was, and he just lay on the ground, staring at a bath towel.

A towel. Nancy's towel.

It all came flooding back and Paul tried to jump to his feet. But when he placed his arm on the floor, a searing pain shot from his right shoulder all the way to his fingertips.

"Shit," he swore, recalling that he had been shot. He glanced down at his arm and was relieved to find that the bullet had only grazed him, creating a flesh wound that had only bled a little. Some minor prodding with his other hand suggested that the bleeding had even stopped for now.

Nancy.

He used his other arm to push himself to his feet. For a second, his entire world spun and he thought he would come crashing down again. But squeezing his eyes shut somehow forced his equilibrium back to true, and the sensation passed.

Standing now, he probed his head next and found a nasty lump on his forehead right above his left eye. With a grimace, he quickly searched the rest of his body, from his chest to his naked legs, for any signs of injury.

Nothing seemed out of place.

Yet he couldn't help but think that he shouldn't be alive.

But he was, and so was Nancy, at least for now... or at least that was what his intuition told him.

Sheriff White quickly grabbed his pants and pulled them on; they seemed lighter than usual, and it took a moment to realize that his gun was no longer in the holster.

Fuck. The biker must have taken it.

How could I have been so careless? How could I have let the man sneak up on us?

But that wasn't quite fair, and he knew it. After all, the man had been camped out in the closet for... well, for God only knows how long. And the fucking creep had just been sitting in there, waiting and watching... the fucking guy had watched them have sex.

Still, he should have been more prepared; after what Dirk had told him, he should have been ready for *anything*.

Paul swallowed hard.

The Crab has plans for you yet.

He did up his fly and buttoned his pants.

"Yeah, I've got plans for you, too, bud. You and your biker crew."

Head still pounding, the sheriff fled his and Nancy's house, not bothering to lock the door behind him. He surveyed the road, squinting into the dusk.

I must have been out for a good few hours, he thought.

There were no cars on the street, and he didn't know if that was a good or a bad thing. He supposed if there had been some motorcycles there, it would definitely have been a bad thing. A thing that would have prevented him from getting to the station and rounding up his hodgepodge team of civilians and criminals to go get Nancy back.

After all they had been through, after all of the unbelievable things they had seen over the past week, the last thing that he would let happen was to let a group of drug-dealing bikers fuck up his life—their lives—or Askergan.

Nancy's face flashed in front of his eyes, her pretty face still damp from the shower, her hair wet and stringy.

I'm sorry, she had mouthed.

Paul wondered for what. After all, this wasn't her fault— none of it was *her* fault. This was his fault.

How had he let things go so far south since Sheriff Dana Drew had passed? How had he not been able to rein things in? Even before the crackers had invaded, there had been signs of the town going to shit, that drugs had started to infiltrate everything from the church to the schools.

And not just the high schools, but the fucking middle schools.

"I'm sorry, Dana," he said to the empty air.

Askergan County's sheriff pulled his cruiser door open and he stepped inside. It was like an oven in there, having baked in the sun all day, but he didn't bother turning on the AC or rolling down the window. With gritted teeth, he backed out of his driveway and tore back down the street. The irony of retracing his steps, of racing out here to make sure that Nancy was okay, only to lose her and then race back, was not beyond him.

But that was beyond his control.

He couldn't control the townsfolk, who were spiraling into a deep, dark hole; he couldn't control the bikers that had stolen Nancy from him, and he questioned whether he could control even his newly appointed deputies.

The one thing he could control, however, was himself. And he just prayed that it was enough. Enough to save Nancy, and enough to save the godforsaken county.

"Stay alive, Nancy. Keep it together. I've got some crab hunting to do."

49.

"JESUS FUCK."

Seth was staring at his ruined face in the mirror.

His nose was a mess, the usually straight and narrow reflection a flat mush on his face. He tried to wipe the blood away from beneath his nostrils, but it was quickly replaced by fresh liquid. But while his nose was bad, his eye was probably worse. It was pushed back from his face, a little farther than the other one. The pupil was wide, and the upper eyelid sagged over top of the sunken globe. A dark purple and red bruise was already starting to form on nearly the entire half of his face.

"Fuck."

Seth looked away; staring at himself would only serve to either make him sick or make him question what he was doing.

Neither would do, not now.

Probably not ever.

Get the girl.

Seth went to the bed, his gait awkward as he bent to his left, trying to insulate what he was certain was at least two, maybe even three broken ribs.

He was convinced that if the girl on the bed — *the girl* — hadn't awoken during their struggle, that there was a close to zero chance that picking her up would wake her.

Grinding his teeth against the pain, he reached down and threw the blanket off the girl. To his surprise, she was dressed in a pale blue dress that went to just below her knees.

He hadn't been expecting that; he had been expecting a hospital gown, or maybe scrubs... not a neat blue dress. His eyes flicked to the man that lay unconscious on the ground, a small trickle of blood leaking from a cut on his forehead.

He must have put that on her... *What is he? Her boyfriend?*

A cursory glance revealed no rings. Not married.

And what is so special about this girl?

She didn't look like anything special, what with her thin, pale face and black hair swirling about on the pillow beneath her head. He surmised that she might have once been pretty, but now she was just skin and bones.

Get the girl.

The voice was loud now, and Seth immediately snapped out of his stupor.

First, he yanked out the remaining cords and tubes that still hung from the woman and then, in one sweeping motion, he leaned down and draped the woman's thin arm behind his neck. Wheezing through the pain, he readied himself. Then, with a cry, he hoisted her body over his shoulder and across the back of his neck, like a fireman carry.

She was lighter than he'd thought, and he found that when he straightened out, the pain in his side became a dull grind.

He slid his right foot forward, wondering if, as light as she was, he would be able to support his weight and hers.

His ribs flared, but relief washed over him when he thought he could manage. He tried another step and was met with success. With a grunt, he took another two steps. Before he knew it, he was walking by the woman at the front desk who lay face down in a pool of her own coagulated blood.

Got the girl, he thought. *But why was she chosen?*

He spat a glob of blood.

Why was I chosen?

50.

"SO THAT'S IT? YOU'RE just going to leave, then?"

"Yup."

Reggie threw his arms up.

"And what am I supposed to do here all by myself? What if your biker buddies come around?"

Dirk scowled, and he pointed a nub at the much bigger man's chest.

"First of all, they aren't my buddies. They're—they're—" He thought about it for a moment.

What the hell are they to me?

"They're a means to an end, I guess. And now, thanks to you and whatever this place is, I've found my end."

Reggie grunted.

"What, the priest?"

"Oh, he's more than a priest," Dirk said with a sneer. He turned his hand to show the other deputy his missing fingers. "He took these from me, and that was only the beginning."

Reggie pushed his lips together, but he stepped away from the saloon-style doors separating their desks from the general lobby area of the station.

"We've all lost something in this battle... everyone in Askergan has lost something. And you're a deputy, for Christ's sake."

If he was trying to guilt him into staying, it wasn't going to work.

"I'm not from Askergan, fella. And a deputy?" he laughed. "For a minute. You too, by the way."

"A minute or an hour. Either way, you accepted the responsibility."

Dirk shrugged.

"Why are *you* sticking around?"

The man got a far-off look in his eyes.

"Doesn't matter. I'm here, I agreed to serve, and I'm staying."

There was a story there, but Dirk figured it unlikely that he would be able to extract it from the man this night. Besides, he had heard enough stories for one day.

He shook his head.

"Look, I get it. And I'm not trying to be a dick, but you don't understand how long I have been chasing this guy."

"The priest—Father Carter Duke?"

"Carter Duke, Chris Donovan, whatever his name, if he is as smooth a talker as you say, it can only be the one guy. I'm sorry. Really, I am." He reconsidered his previous words. "This *is* a dick move, no doubt about it. But I have no choice."

Dirk unclipped the deputy star from his shirt and placed it down on the desk.

"What about the uniform? The gun?" Reggie asked, indicating the pistol still on Dirk's hip.

"The uniform I'll dry clean and ship back to you, what do you think? But the gun, I think I'll keep that." He tapped the butt of the gun with the flat of his hand. It was on the wrong hip, he realized; with only two fingers on his right hand, not only would holding the gun pose a problem, but shooting it would be next to impossible.

He made a mental note to switch the holster over as soon as he left the station. Dirk slid past the other man, making sure to keep his eyes on him as he continued to back toward the door.

He didn't much like the way the man's arms, after he had put them down, had started to creep toward his own gun.

If the man drew now, he would have no choice but to surrender his weapon.

And he needed that gun. He needed it for Father Carter Duke.

"Look—" he began, but the door behind him suddenly opened, and if it weren't for the large body that burst through, he might have fallen out. Dirk went to turn, but he felt one large hand grab his shoulder, while the other grasped his gun. In one fluid movement, the gun was unclasped and it was removed from the holster.

Evidently, whoever had just entered the station had no problem with their right hand.

"You can leave if you want," a voice he recognized said in his ear. "But you can't take this with you."

51.

AFTER SETH HAD STARTED his legs moving, carrying Alice to the car was the easy part. It was lowering her into the back seat of the stolen car that was difficult.

His ribs were definitely broken, and his nose was a mess. But it was the sharp pain in his side, behind his broken ribs, that was the most worrisome. It felt as if someone was poking him in the lungs from the inside. He knew very little about medicine, but he knew enough that this was bad. And if it got any worse, he would be at risk of puncturing a lung.

Still, he was the chosen, and she was the girl.

With this in mind, he bore down against the pain and bent over. Seth cried out as he flipped the girl from his shoulders and onto the backseat. Breathing quickly through his mouth, on the verge of hyperventilating, he stood up straight, stretching his back to ease the pressure on his side.

He took one hitching breath, and then bent over again and quickly shoved her entire body inside, not caring when she only slid forward a few feet before her legs simply folded inside the vehicle.

"Arghh!" he shouted as a sharp pain ripped through his side.

He slammed the car door closed, but this time when he went to stand up straight, he felt something pop in his side, and then it was as if someone had driven a branding iron right through his body. Sweat broke out on his forehead, and it was all he could do to keep from collapsing in a heap.

Grunting and gasping, he managed to slither into the driver seat without changing his posture all that much. And then, like before, he was off, not questioning where he was going, only allowing himself to be led.

Less than an hour later, the stolen Ford careened onto the curb in front of two parked motorcycles. The vision in his one remaining eye had gradually dissipated to nothingness, and it had been many miles since he had seen the road clearly. Twice he had struck something, once hard enough to send the girl in the backseat airborne. Somehow he managed to put the car in park, and the engine hissed in the hot sun.

Seth closed his eye and lay with his head against the headrest, his hair matted with sweat, his breathing still coming in bubbles. Even when someone opened his door, he didn't move. And when a voice spoke, he remained still.

"He looks dead."

Warm fingers pressed against his neck.

"No, still alive. Barely."

"Can you move him? Put him in the passenger seat?"

There was a pause, punctuated by one of Seth's moans.

"Dunno. Don't think so. Looks pretty beat up."

"I'll call in a tow, then."

Seth heard the crackle of a radio, and a message was relayed to another man with a gruff-sounding voice.

"There's a girl in the backseat."

"Yep, I see that."

There was some sort of silent exchange, then Seth felt someone pat him on the shoulder. The sensation was nondescript, like a generalized pressure on his numb body that he could barely locate.

"Hang in there. The Crab has been expecting you."

And then everything faded to black.

52.

DIRK RAISED HIS ARMS and turned to face the man who had just pulled the gun from his holster.

Sheriff Paul White stared back, his expression grim. For a second, none of the three men in the room spoke—or even moved. It was as if they were all expecting something to happen, an act of God, a giant hand sweeping down, perhaps, one that would pick them all up and scoop them out of the hell that was Askergan and drop them down in a unicorn-and-rainbow-fueled utopia.

And then, unbelievably, something *did* happen. But while the intrusion was highly unexpected, it wasn't the act of a savior.

The door to the police station was thrown open, and a man with a red beard that Dirk had never seen before stepped inside.

His face was bruised and battered, and he was accompanied by the smell of blood.

"They took her!" the man gasped. "They took Alice!"

And then he collapsed, and the sheriff barely reacted in time to prevent him from falling to the floor.

53.

DONNIE WANDRY WATCHED AS the unconscious man with the battered face was carried into the room, his frail body laid across one of the biker's arms.

"He's here," the biker announced, and the Crab turned, a smile growing on his face.

The man had only recently removed the skin suit that he had been wearing—Sabra's skin, Donnie had learned—but he wasn't sure that what was beneath was any less disgusting.

The man's bare upper body was a mess, his chest streaked with hideously thick blue and red vessels of a nature that Donnie had never seen.

And then there were the white spots, the spots of 'healed' skin where the tiny white crackers had erupted. Six times Donnie had seen those crackers come forth, and six times he had seen the bikers consumed by them, devoured, before their chests had literally exploded.

There was also the other cracker, the one embedded in Walter's shoulder, that seemed to thrive on the man's excessive drug use.

"What should I do with him?" the biker asked.

The Crab indicated the large desk.

"Put him there," he said through his brown and yellow teeth.

The man nodded and walked over to the desk, laying the man down gently on top of it.

Another man entered the room next, and for an instant, Donnie thought he was experiencing some sort of bastardized déjà vu.

This biker also had a frail body laid across his arms, and the scene was eerily similar. The only difference that Donnie could discern was that this body was that of a woman.

Walter's smile grew.

"What should I do with this one?"

"Give her to Donnie; have him string her up with the others."

At the mention of 'the others', Donnie turned back to the task at hand. He gripped the heavy chain in both hands and pulled. With a grunt, the chain moved a couple of feet and then looped it around the hoop in the floor to make sure he didn't lose the slack. He pulled twice more and then wrapped the chain around the metal stake that he had driven into the solid oak floor.

He realized that the biker was beside him now, and was awaiting further instruction.

"Just put her down, I'll deal with her," he instructed, his voice oddly monotone.

The biker did as he was told, and Donnie turned to examine his handiwork.

Two women were strung up by their hands, their naked bodies hanging limply from the heavy chain that he had removed from the chandelier and affixed to the ceiling. Both of them, like the girl on the floor beside him, were unconscious, their hair dangling in front of their faces.

Two women, hanging, bruised, like Askergan itself, no idea about the fate that was about to befall them.

Two women, and soon to be a third.

For a brief moment, Greg Griddle tried to creep back into him, but he forced him away with thoughts of Kent lying on the gurney, his face purple.

Greg was gone—Greg died with Kent. And in his place was Donnie, the boy that was beaten and battered. The one that had his father's anger buried deep inside. The one that his father had mistakenly thought wasn't like him, that he was different, kind, compassionate.

But his father was wrong. Donnie *was* like him. Donnie was like him *and* Walter.

He was a Wandry through and through.

Running away hadn't changed that, neither had adopted a new name.

For a time Kent *had* changed him.

But now Kent was dead.

They will pay for what they did to Kent. All of Askergan will pay.

Donnie wasn't sure if he had said the thought out loud, but when the Crab spoke next, he was sure that he must have, because the words that exited the man's mangled mouth echoed those thoughts.

"Askergan will pay. Tonight they shall taste fear more potent than anything they have felt before."

Donnie nodded and felt a smile creep onto his own face.

And then he set about stringing up the third woman beside the others.

54.

"YOU CAN STAY, OR you can leave. No one is going to force you to hang around."

Sheriff Paul White scanned his men's faces.

There were four of them, aside from himself. Reggie, Deputy Williams, the biker Dirk Hannover, and of course Bradley Coggins.

Their faces were all traced with streaks of dirt, sweat, and blood, and it was clear that their sleepless tanks were running on fumes. They should retire for the night, get some sleep before making any rash decisions.

But there was no time for that.

They have Nancy.

They have Alice.

They have Askergan, for Christ's sake.

The sheriff cleared his throat.

"That goes for all of you. There is something brewing in Askergan, and what you have all experienced was only the beginning. There is a war coming." He paused and wiped the sweat from his brow. "And, to be honest, I don't know how we can possibly win."

Deputy Williams's eyes dropped to the floor.

"I know what you all must be thinking, because I have thought the same thing. 'Why fight? Why fight a battle that is futile, that we simply cannot win?'"

There was something akin to relief that washed over everyone's faces—everyone except for Coggins.

"There is a moment, a moment in every person's life where they have to stand up against impossible odds. Sheriff Dana Drew did it, as did his wife. And we did it—we did it when the crackers came, and we won... we suffered incredible losses, but we still won. And I know that it is incomprehensible to ask you to do it again, but I am. I'm asking you to do it, to sign on now, to hop aboard. To risk your lives for one of the few things worth saving in this world: a county. A county that has been pretty much ignored, but one that has such passion, that once held so much promise. So, please, it is unfair, unjust, and simply immoral, but before I ask you, please, ask *yourself* if you want to stand up."

A silence washed over them, and for a brief moment, the sheriff felt his heart sink.

They are going to leave; they are going to take off their uniforms, lay down their paltry supply of weapons, and go far, far away from here.

Part of him didn't blame them; part of him wanted to do the same.

But part of him also thought about Nancy, about how her pretty lips had formed those fateful words: *I'm sorry.*

He, for one, would not be laying down his arms tonight, and probably not ever.

He was in this for Askergan. He was in this for the long haul.

No matter what.

Coggins spoke first, and when he did, his cheeks were pinched in anger.

"I won't let them have her. They can have me, but they can't have her."

Good, that's two.

Williams was next.

There was another long pause, during which the sheriff kept his eyes trained on Williams, who chewed the inside of his cheek.

"I'm in," he whispered at last.

Reggie nodded next, and then the man surprised the sheriff by turning to Dirk.

"You know them best; we need you."

Dirk shook his head almost forlornly.

"You guys—I commend you guys. But I don't think you understand... Sabra had an army of bikers, a network whose arms reach far greater than Askergan. And these are bad men. I commend you for what you are trying to do here, to stand up to them, I really do, but it is as your sheriff said. It's futile."

The sheriff grimaced, and then something in Williams's face changed, as if Dirk bowing out was giving him permission to do the same.

They all needed to be in, he realized, even if *all* included a biker who he had just met, a muscular man who was probably just a general contractor or a union man by trade, a deputy whose resolve he had more than once questioned, and a troubled man who had lost everything and then some.

Thinking about the last man, about Coggins, gave him pause. Even though Paul had wanted Coggins to come back around, to rejoin the Department as a Deputy, an equally large part of him also never wanted to see his friend again.

Because not seeing Bradley Coggins again, never again hearing his stupid NHL trivia, would mean that the man had gotten out.

If there was anything that Paul had learned during his tenure as the Sheriff of Askergan, it was that this was no normal County. It had started with the blizzard, or maybe it even predated that, but regardless, once it started, the horrors that befell them all had snowballed and hadn't stopped. First, the shit that happened with Dana, then the drugs, slowly disseminating throughout the entire County, and then the crackers. It was as if every poison or plague imaginable had been unleashed on this corner of the northeastern United States, the once idyllic and beautiful County bereft of any crime greater than a stolen pack of bubble gum was suddenly awash with terror of the like that was better set in a horror film.

It had all gone to shit—and it had gone to shit on his watch.

Yeah, a big part of him wished that Coggins had gotten out. But another thing he had slowly come to realize about Askergan was that it had an uncanny way of drawing you back in, whether or not you wanted to be here...

This is only the beginning, he thought suddenly. *More people are going to die here before the County is rid of the poison that has infected everything.*

He swallowed hard.

If—if he could rid the County of the Crab and whatever other fucked up plagues haunted this place.

The sheriff turned back to the men before him.

There weren't enough of them; four or even five men weren't enough to take on an army.

He swallowed hard and opened his mouth to say something, to obey his initial instinct to tell them all to go home to sleep on it, when there was a commotion outside the door.

He raised his gaze, and through the window that wasn't boarded up he caught sight of dozens of small lights. It took him a moment to realize that they were either torches or flashlights.

"What's going on?" Coggins asked quietly.

The sheriff pulled away from the group and moved toward the door.

When he opened it, his breath caught in his throat.

There were more than two dozen people standing on the lawn, their faces identical masks of anger and disdain. He recognized a handful of them as citizens that had been part of the crowd in the station earlier in the day, yelling at him to do something. But while then they had been angry and frustrated, they were different now; not just angry, but *angry*.

And in the center of the crowd was a man with a medium build and a thick, dark beard wearing a priest's collar.

The man was a priest.

Beside him was another man, one with a polar opposite expression to the man with the beard and the smirk, a man wearing a three-piece suit of all things.

And then there was a third man, the only one of the three that the sheriff recognized. Although his face was drawn, his eyes downcast, it was none other than Jared Lawrence standing beside the two others.

Sheriff Paul White wasn't sure if this was a good or bad sign.

"Gentlemen," the priest began, raising his voice for everyone to hear. "It appears as if you are short on manpower, and by the looks of it, firepower."

With the word firepower, the men with the flashlights flashed the guns—a mishmash of pistols and what looked like hunting rifles—in their other hands.

"Let me introduce myself. My name is Father Carter Duke. I am here to offer my services. I am here to help you guys."

There was a small uproar as the men on the station lawn shouted their approval.

"I am here for Askergan."

The affirmative shouts increased in fervor, and something in the sheriff lifted.

He turned back to his men, who had joined him just outside the station doors.

Their spirits too seemed to have lifted. All except for Dirk, whose eyes were burning holes in the priest's Godly fabric.

But that didn't matter now; what mattered now was that the sheriff thought that they might just have the men that they needed to at least put up a fight.

Sheriff Paul White turned back to the priest.

"Father Duke, welcome to Askergan. And yes, we could very much use your help."

The night air unexpectedly filled with the sound of motorcycle throttles. Everyone turned to face the two bikes that made their way slowly down Main Street. They were going too slow to portray any sign of aggression, and the sheriff immediately put his hands out at his sides, indicating for his men to stand down.

He spied Father Duke looking at him, a sly smile on his face, and the parishioners, if that's what they were, followed *his* orders.

The way that they had obeyed the priest's order, and had completely ignored his gesture, gave him pause; his relationship with the strange, smooth-talking priest was going to be a complicated one, he knew, but what choice did he have but to accept his aid?

After all, without him, they were four, maybe five men against… what? A dozen? Fifty? It was hard to know how many of the bikers had stuck around following Sabra's demise. Clearly, if Dirk's story had any truth in it, many would have fled. But some would have stayed.

Some *definitely* would have stayed.

Problem was, even when Sabra was alive he had been an enigma to the Sheriff, and now that he was gone it was impossible to even guess how many men he had at his disposal.

What was clear, however, was that without the priest, they had no chance. But with him? With him, they *might* have a fighting chance.

A slim fighting chance, but still a chance.

"What do they want?" Reggie asked out of the corner of his mouth, and the sheriff just shook his head.

He had no idea what they wanted. Instead of answering, he said, "Be ready. Don't fire first, but be ready for anything."

In the end, despite Sheriff White's appeals, they were not ready for what happened next.

The two bikers turned and stopped, their bikes idling on the opposite side of Main Street. When they shut off their lights, all the sheriff could make out were the burning cherries of their cigarettes.

He stepped forward, coming up beside the priest.

"What do you want?" he shouted, his voice cutting through the warm air.

For a moment, no one answered.

"Someone put a goddamn flashlight on them," Paul grumbled, and several men obliged, bathing the men that were stationed forty or fifty feet away in a dull yellow glow.

It was clear by their shocked expressions that these men had not expected to see so many outside the station. They too, it appeared, were oblivious to the reach of the strange, new priest in town. This shock faded quickly, however, and their lined faces soon hardened.

One of the bikers slowly reached behind him, and the sheriff heard the men around him take a collective intake of breath.

"Stand down," he said. "Stand down!"

With a flick of his wrist, the biker launched something into the air, some sort of plastic bag.

Several of the priest's men scattered, and others still raised their weapons as if they were prepared to shoot the thing out of the air like a demented clay pigeon. But when they saw that it was only a bag, a large plastic bag, they thankfully refrained from shooting.

The bag was filled with a solid object that landed on the sidewalk in front of both the sheriff and the priest. As they watched, it proceeded to roll clumsily a few feet before coming to a complete stop.

"A gift," the man who had thrown the basketball-sized object shouted. "An offering from the Crab—just to show he cares."

The Sheriff didn't immediately turn to the object. Instead, he held his ground.

"What does he want?" he hollered back.

The man laughed, then indicated the sheriff with an open palm.

"You," he said with a chuckle. Then he turned to the priest, a sneer forming on his face. "Him. All of you."

The other biker chimed in next.

"The Crab wants all of Askergan. The Wandry brothers will rule this town!"

The sheriff made a face.

Wandry brothers? What the hell?

He knew of Walter Wandry, of course, but *brothers*? What were these bikers talking about?

"What—"

But Paul never got a chance to finish his sentence. The two bikers jammed their feet down in odd synchronicity and their bikes roared to life.

As they turned and sped off, the sheriff stood in silent confusion for a moment. He realized that at some point during the standoff, Coggins had made his way to his side, while the priest had taken a few steps backward. Together Paul White and his longtime friend moved toward the bag.

"What is it?" Coggins asked, his voice laden with fear.

A horrible feeling started to brew in the sheriff's guts. For the second time today, he had a sinking suspicion that Coggins would be better off elsewhere—that his friend would have been better off not seeing him today.

Or ever.

"What is it?" Coggins repeated, but the sheriff again abstained from answering.

Instead, he kept walking, crouching down when he eventually came level with the bag. It was filled with something dark, he saw, something that was hard to make out in the dim light offered by the men's flashlights.

He took the pen out of the front pocket of his shirt and tried to flip the bag over. It was heavier than he might have thought, and his pen bent as he pushed against the spherical object.

Eventually, it flopped awkwardly onto the other side.

"No," Coggins gasped as he caught sight of the contents. "No!"

The sheriff, fearing that he might be sick, turned away.

"No!" Coggins yelled again. He turned toward the dual taillights of the two bikes that receded down Main Street.

When Coggins pulled his gun, Sheriff White tried to reach out and grab his arm, to keep him at bay.

But he missed, and before he knew it, Coggins was walking down the sidewalk, screaming 'no' and emptying his clip at the fading motorbikes.

Sheriff felt tears spill from his eyes and pat softly on the plastic bag.

A part of him didn't want to get a better look; a part of him didn't want to know exactly what was in there, what Coggins had so quickly determined, but he had to.

He just had to know.

With his pen, he pushed the bag to one side again, revealing two wide eyes and an open mouth.

He was staring directly into a woman's face, her decapitated head stuffed into a plastic bag that was bound with several rubber bands.

And then it was him pulling his gun from his holster shouting 'no' into the night.

EPILOGUE

The knife easily cut through the skin on the back of her arms, drawing a razor-thin line of blood. After that, it was only a matter of teasing the blade beneath the skin, slowly cutting away the thin layer of fat from the muscle and sinew and bone beneath.

Walter's tongue poked out of the side of his mouth as he worked, and perspiration beaded on his brow.

He couldn't remember feeling this alive.

As if to affirm this feeling, the cracker in his shoulder tensed.

"Already?" he grumbled, intent on removing the last little bit of tissue that connected the woman's skin to her body before he acquiesced to the cracker's needs.

The cracker squeezed again, and he picked up his pace, knowing that he needed another hit to satiate the creature; there was no way he wanted to piss the thing off again.

Once since it had crawled up his arm and nestled beneath his shoulder—what seemed like an eternity ago now—he'd tried to resist the urge to use. And what had happened was a feeling he didn't want to experience again. A vice-like grip that had kept increasing in pressure until he'd been reduced to a ball of flesh curled in a fetal position. He wasn't sure what would have happened had Donnie not brought him a line of coke.

Thoughts of his brother reminded him that he was somewhere in the room with him.

"Brother," he said, his mouth dry. "I need you."

He heard shuffling behind him, and when he cut away the final connections of the woman's skin, Donnie appeared at his side, holding the silver mirror out to him.

Walter didn't even bother putting down the bloody knife; he simply leaned over and buried his head in the mound of coke, breathing in deeply with both nostrils.

He closed his eyes, waiting for it. Even though he knew that the hit to his brainstem, the sudden rush, wasn't coming, he still waited for it.

He yearned for it.

But the only thing that happened was that the pressure in his shoulder relaxed, and the thick vessels on his chest stopped pulsating.

There, he thought, *you happy now?*

And indeed the cracker was happy, at least for now.

He turned to his brother next and was struck by how tired the man looked. Dark circles clung desperately to the thin skin beneath his eyes. His brother's arrival, unlike Seth's, had been a surprise, and a welcome one at that.

And the girl, this Corina? That had been a wonderful addition.

"What should I do with her, Walt?" Donnie asked, clearly referring to the freshly skinned corpse on the floor before them.

Walt. Only Donnie called him that; the other bikers, the ones that hadn't fled or that he hadn't punished, called him the Crab. Which was fine, provided they obeyed him—he didn't give two shits about what they called him, to his face or behind his back.

"The girl?" Donnie asked again, and Walter realized that he had been staring. He looked away, turning his attention back to the body that he had just skinned.

Her chest was a mess, of course, having exploded after the cracker that had budded from his mottled flesh had infiltrated and then nested inside her body. Moments later, the other crackers, the tiny white ones, had first bubbled under her skin as if it were a piece of cellophane over a colony of maggots.

And then they had burst forth in all of their frothing ecstasy.

Again his thoughts turned to his son, to Tyler, and he wondered, not for the first time, if the boy had suffered a similar fate.

He shook the image from his thoughts.

It didn't matter now. He was dead, but Askergan was still very much alive.

For now.

Walter's eyes drifted back to the woman's corpse, traveling up past the hole in her chest and abdomen and stopping at the ragged stump of a neck.

He had cut her head off with a steak knife. He didn't think she was alive at the time, but he hadn't bothered to check.

"Walt?"

"Burn her."

Donnie nodded, and when he bent down to take the woman's skin, Walter grabbed his arm.

"No, not that. Leave the skin; I'm going to add it to the others."

Donnie nodded again, and instead grabbed the woman by a wet red ankle. Walter watched her being dragged away, leaving behind a bloody streak on the hardwood. He would get one of the bikers to clean that later.

Someone moaned, and Walter's eyes snapped up.

There were only two women chained up by their hands now, and one of them seemed to be waking. But this didn't interest Walter so much, and when the smile crossed his thin lips, its origins were rooted in his own handiwork.

Behind the two chained women was what looked like a series of quilts, all attached with thick thread reminiscent of shoelaces. Like a macabre tapestry, the skins of his other victims hung from the ceiling, all eighteen of them, starting with Sabra.

The edges of their flesh had started to curl, he saw, the dim lights in the room causing them to darken and dry.

His smile grew.

Askergan was going to pay.

END

Author's note

Many people perceive writing a book as a solitary experience, and in a way, it is. I zone out, fall into a Zen-like state of concentration, and hammer the keys (which most people find obnoxious, by the way—I really *pound* my keyboard). As pretentious as it sounds, however, this is honestly the easiest part of my job. After writing, the real work starts. There is the cover, for whom I have Dane and his team at ebooklaunch.com to thank. Then there is the editing, for which I have Tom Shutt to thank. There is also the marketing, which is a labyrinth that I am constantly battling to understand. It really is a team effort to bring a finished product to market.

I like to think that even with no readers, I would still write the books, but thankfully, this is one hypothesis that I don't have to test. Every review that you guys write, and the emails and messages I get from you stating that you enjoyed one of my books, puts a smile on my bearded face. I'm no altruist, but with the shit going on in the real world recently—including, but of course not limited to, the horrific events in Orlando—that has a tendency to sour one's outlook, I really do enjoy the fact that I have transported you, the reader, out of reality, if only for a few hours.

From the bottom of the four-chambered muscle that pumps blood to my body, I thank you, reader, for affording me this honor.

Special thanks goes to my beautiful, adoring, and patient wife who reads my books even though the horror/thriller genre is definitely not her cup of David's Tea. Even when she was in labor with our recent family addition, I was typing away, putting the finishing touches on the very book that you just finished reading. Without her, Coggins, Paul White, and the Lawrence clan would definitely not exist.

Thanks again for reading, and if you enjoyed this book I hope you are struck with the inspiration to leave a review where you bought it.

Best,

Patrick
Montreal, 2016

Made in the USA
Coppell, TX
25 May 2020